THE IFs

COLLEEN WEEMS

Copyright © 2017 by Colleen Weems

First edition: September 2017

Cover Design: Carloline Teagle Johnson
Cover Image: © Alexey Kuzma/Stocksy
Author Photo: © Jenny Shepherd

ISBN: 978-0-9992906-0-6 (print)
ISBN: 978-09992906-1-3 (ebook)

CHAPTER ONE

Flossie

Scurvy hadn't taken me yet, nor had the vapors, nor had anaphylactic shock brought on by an undiagnosed allergy to my own hair. It was, however, only a matter of time until a blood clot did the job. Blood clots were all the rage for newly dormant people like me; not for jerks in bicycling, hiking, jogging, or kayaking pods. People wrapped in cozy cardigans and organic cotton throws were expiring while music from their college days played softly in the background. Otherwise very comfortable corpses were going undiscovered for days and weeks, creating vacancies in highly desirable grocery and takeout delivery zones.

I didn't want to die wrapped in cashmere, face down in a bowl of pho. Not yet. I had just moved into a great apartment, and hated the idea of some heartless San Francisco real estate opportunist benefitting from my demise, so I went to a spin class at a new gym in my Noe Valley neighborhood. A few miles of going absolutely nowhere as fast as I could pump, might keep the Reaper away for a bit longer.

The Tuesday night drop-in Spinster class sounded perfect for a single girl looking to connect and exercise with like-minded women in a supportive, uplifting atmosphere. I arrived to class late enough to be stuck with Bike 19, which was wedged awkwardly behind a pole. I couldn't see the reaction of Bike 5's spinster when her raffle number was drawn and she was awarded with a yoga mat. I couldn't observe and learn from the perfect form of Bike 11's rider. The birthday girl on Bike 9, would never know I smiled affectionately in her general direction. I couldn't see them, which also meant they could not see how hard I was breathing, or that my out-of-shape heart was pounding too hard for a very basic amount of exercise, and nobody on Bikes 1-18 knew how close I came to dying on Bike 19. Bike 20's occupant might have been alerted to my distress, unless the pole between us absorbed the jarring sound of my grunting and wheezing. Had I died on Bike 19, as opposed to succumbing to a blood clot or scurvy in the comfort of my own home, at least my body would have been discovered by the latecomer in the next class. The chirpy girls in my session were not the open-hearted Spinsters I had looked forward to cycling to nowhere with; they could easily depart rosy-cheeked into the night, without noticing my sweaty body slumped over an uneven set of handlebars.

That night—the night I almost died on Bike 19—was the night I could finally identify what it was that I had been feeling, and why I had been storyboarding so many different and increasingly pathetic ways I could meet my demise.

I wasn't just busy. I wasn't preoccupied or shy. Even with all of the scenarios I considered for my premature and solitary death, I wouldn't call myself macabre. I wasn't introspective, deep, or thoughtful, even on foggy evenings when I sat on my couch with the sole purpose of being introspective, deep, and thoughtful.

I was lonely.

Lonely. Lonely. Lonely. Lonely.

I said the awful word over and over as I pedaled, hoping with each pump, I could make the feeling and the word and the humiliation leave my body and land on somebody else like the horrible spin instructor who was emerging as the suspect who most wanted me to die. I squeezed my eyes shut and tried to negotiate with whatever being was out there cataloging my thoughts; if I couldn't smite the spin instructor, then could my loneliness please leave me and sprinkle down on everybody else in the room, so each perky bike rider could sacrificially feel a tiny bit worse, so I could feel hugely better? When the music stopped and the lights came on, I knew my wish had not come true. I peeked around my pole to see the glowing, smiling girls drink from their cute water bottles, thank the complicit instructor, wish Bike 9 a happy birthday and leave together as if it was the most natural thing in the world. They were probably going for drinks where they would make plans for a girls' trip to Las Vegas or Taos.

I went home alone, drank a bottle of rosé, researched crime rates for Las Vegas and Taos, and drafted my last will and testament, which didn't take as long as I'd hoped.

Following my revelation on Bike 19, I rose from my disheveled bed each morning, to gingerly sip piping hot tea and gaze out my window at Garbage Alley, or as I called it in the only French I knew, *Ruelle de Déchets*. I established a painful routine of scalding my tongue and throat while waiting in vain for the stagnant alley view to change, and trying to convince myself that I had simply mistaken my thoughtful nature for loneliness. I lurked in that window like a caffeinated specter who had been trapped in the realm of the living, waiting for a good-hearted medium to assure me it was safe to cross over, because I wasn't lonely after all! I had simply been the unfortunate victim of exercise-induced delirium one fateful night in spin class.

Without access to a good-hearted medium, it was my job to say, "Flossie, you are fine. You have plenty of people in your life. You have a career. You have an apartment with an urban view. You are doing great." I would repeat my new mantra, "You are fine," until I was physically capable of making the long journey from the window to my desk across the room where I could melt into work. Without fail, however, evening would arrive, and not even a freshly uncorked bottle of wine could stave off reality. In our collective quest for intimacy, I'd shuttered my social media accounts along with every other person under thirty. Oh, I had achieved intimacy alright; maximum intimacy. I missed social media, and its ability to completely occupy five hours of my life so I wouldn't have to do it myself. Instead of scrolling through political arguments between strangers, and photos of bare feet propped up in front of the pool, my new evening routine included contradicting hopeful Morning Me by muttering the phrase out loud, so I could hear a human voice, "I am lonely."

I soon grew so intimately familiar with "lonely," that I could easily identify all the gradations of loneliness. There was Sad Lonely and Festive Lonely. After battling a hangover, I decided maybe my wine was exacerbating my loneliness, so that night, I drank one tiny glass of wine and followed it with a generous mug of tea. Night tea, I decided as I padded off to bed, was Sad Lonely, and wine was Festive Lonely. Sixty hours spent toiling away in my home office was Productive Lonely. Going to a hole-in-the-wall taqueria outside of my neighborhood was Adventurous Lonely. Strolling through a museum while wearing a designer cape was Parisian Lonely. There was Urban Lonely, Fashionable Lonely, and Academic Lonely. I could experience Rom-Com Lonely, Intellectual Lonely, and Bitter Lonely all before lunch, which if I was out in public, was High School Cafeteria Lonely, though in high school, I never had to eat alone.

I wrote a letter to my mother, allowing my meandering thoughts on loneliness to unfurl on page after page of expensive stationery. Instead of mailing my tome back home to Chicago, I tucked it away in a desk drawer unsure my mother should be subjected to all of my Keeping-It-Real Lonely.

Before I moved to San Francisco, I never wanted for friends. Camila and I were inseparable all the way through high school. She left Chicago to go to college in Iowa. After she joined a sorority, I selflessly commented on almost every party photo she posted. At Northwestern, Ginny and I drank wine instead of beer, and we talked to anyone who would listen about whatever exhibition we had just visited at the Art Institute. Ginny was the one who introduced me to my college boyfriend, Charlie. After I arrived in San Francisco, I briefly lived with roommates I'd found online. I'd expected sorority house surroundings plump with shared happy hours, late night chats, and Bloody Mary-soaked Sunday brunches. Kira and Kelsey brunched, but I was never invited. Lola did not smile, let alone chat; the longest conversation she and I shared was when she asked me if the dirty dishes in the sink were mine. They were not. The daily human contact provided by that living arrangement did not outweigh how insufferable I found the whole thing. The day I moved to my adorable one-bedroom Noe Valley apartment with the view of the garbage alley, provided the greatest sense of relief I had experienced as an adult.

Camila didn't post photos anymore, and I wasn't even entirely sure where she lived. Ginny was always traveling for work, and the last photo on her profile was she and I in our graduation caps. I'd even scoured the internet for Charlie. All of his social accounts had disappeared, and his number belonged to some other person in Illinois. Charlie wasn't dead, though. I checked.

The butchers and baristas on my block were too busy to chat. The lady from our neighborhood paperie spent most of her time in animated conversations conducted entirely in French. I thought maybe getting out of my apartment and working in the main office around humans might help.

When I stepped into the tiny reception space of The Cerulean Group's office, Fiona asked if she could help me.

"It's me, Flossie . . . Flossie O'Brien? I talked to you twenty hours ago, Fiona."

"Oh, of course Flossie, I'm sorry I blanked for a second. You were out of context."

"Out of context? I work with you and we're at work. Anyway, I need a desk today."

"We're full, but lucky for you . . . you can head home and work in your comfy clothes. I'm jealous."

"Is everybody here all day? I can wait. Hey, we can even go grab some food. My treat." I immediately knew I sounded too eager . . . hopeful. I cleared my throat, and looked at my phone like I didn't care what her answer was going to be.

"Totally booked all day, but aren't you sweet?" she purred, "And I have lunch plans. There's a new impossible-to-get-in-to place that Bob's gotten us in to, of course. Have you heard of pigs in a blanket? Sounds sad and gross, but it's some vintage dish that's supposed to be the world's most perfectly delicious bite of food."

"My mom used to make me pigs in a blanket."

"That is too precious. I'll let you know how it is!" I knew I'd been dismissed, and I walked back out the door without a word.

I'd had my hair blown out and my nails done. I'd stopped at the most revered pour-over coffee purveyor just so I could be seen in the office with their cup. My new oxblood pumps had made contact with the sidewalk for the first time just that morning. They were not walking shoes; they made me feel like I was tip-toing around on beautifully sculpted ballerina legs. I realized that morning how lazy and spoiled my feet had become; there were almost no demands on them anymore other than from shearling slippers or the occasional athletic shoe. My feet had gone soft and needed a reminder of what life was really like for the feet of a young professional. I didn't mind the blisters so much. They were the product of the good hurt that comes from wearing beautiful shoes, like the hurt you get exercising or from finishing an entire cheesecake or bottle of champagne without any help. My satisfaction came not from how I looked, but from the fact I had a legitimate reason to put on those shoes at all.

With showpiece coffee in hand, and showpiece pumps on feet, I quickly fell in with the throng of pedestrians, careful not to let my disappointment peek out from behind my game face. Everybody seemed to be on their way to somewhere, and by being a part of this group, I felt that I too had purpose. It didn't make a difference to me that my sole purpose out on the street that morning was to feel purposeful. If you spotted me that morning, you would have assumed I was taking care of business, and on my way to somewhere, where people were anxiously awaiting my arrival. *Of course* someone was waiting to see me; in fact, someone had put their whole day on hold to take a meeting with me. I was important; so in-demand that I started to walk a little faster; I didn't have time to saunter and take in the sights and the sea air.

I walked briskly, brushing by tourists who were emerging from their hotels, looking for the cable car, bickering about what to eat for breakfast, and wondering if they should run back up to their rooms for forgotten wool scarves and hats. I sighed loudly whenever a group of these dough-faced, doe-eyed newbies blocked my path. I maneuvered dramatically around them, surely giving them a thrill from their encounter with a real city person—an up-and-coming visionary—who was, as far as they knew, on her way to do a deal, take something public, or basically change the world. I'd probably just made their day.

I wound my way through the entire financial district where investment bankers, commercial real estate people, and other analysts all absorbed me as one of their own. Together we rushed from one place to another. Maybe some of them were doing the exact same thing I was doing, aimlessly wandering, pretending and comforting themselves with internal platitudes about the journey being the destination and the journey of a thousand miles beginning with a single, stupid step.

The morning crowd turned into a lunch crowd. My coffee was long gone. I was winded, a little cold, and the good hurt from my shoes was feeling a lot less good than it had miles and miles before. I ducked into the first cafe I saw that appeared to be worthy of my morning's executive persona. I ordered an herbal tea and a fig and brie sandwich, then tried not to limp, but limped, to a table with a view of the counter.

A bicycle messenger bought two oatmeal raisin cookies, and stuffed a wad of ones in the tip jar. A lady with a young child ordered a milk and double espresso. A handsome older man in a three-piece suit ordered a caramel latte and paid in quarters, and the disheveled younger guy behind him ordered a black coffee and paid with a one hundred-dollar bill. The next customer to order was a tall woman, maybe a year or two older than me. The heels on her shoes were taller than the shoes I'd slyly slid off my feet, and she looked like she was in no pain at all. Whatever gorgeous designer dress she was surely wearing was covered by a form-fitting trench coat. Her olive skin glowed, her makeup was flawless, and her black hair reflected the overhead lights and the diamond studs in her ears. She looked so effortlessly put together, that I imagined her hair went straight from wet, messy shower hair to glossy, swingy locks without her having to lift a finger. I smoothed my limp blonde hair, and sat up straighter, trying to extend my 5'5" body into something a little more significant. She ordered an herbal tea, just like I had, threw what looked like a five-dollar bill in the tip jar, and smiled at everybody behind the counter. As she waited for the tea, the cashier and the barista chatted with her. It wasn't flirting. It was just, regular, casual . . . conversation. The woman didn't seem inconvenienced by exchanging mundane pleasantries, and instead, seemed to show a genuine interest in the barista's concerns about the weather threatening her evening plans. After retrieving her tea and telling the barista to take an umbrella and go out and have some fun, the woman turned to leave and caught me looking at her. I wasn't just looking, I was watching . . . staring, rapt, mouth probably open like an idiot. Even though she didn't know I wasn't a crazy person, she didn't frown like anybody else would have. She smiled at me, almost as widely as she had to the baristas. Nothing about our momentary interaction felt uncomfortable. She just smiled, like any person might; one person smiling at another for absolutely no reason at all. She held the door open for the lady with the child as they left, and then the woman disappeared back into the lunchtime crowd outside. I strained to hear if the baristas were talking about her. They had already moved on to the next orders, though the one barista was still quite undecided about the weather's impact on her social life.

I summoned a car from my table, and forced my swollen feet back into my shoes. I smiled wildly at the baristas as I left, even throwing a hearty "thanks!" in their direction, followed by, "have a great afternoon!" I was confident they would have responded if I hadn't caught them in the middle of a hectic lunch hour.

When I finally returned to my shearling slippers, and my regular attire of yoga pants and a Northwestern sweatshirt, I sat down to work, only to find that absolutely nobody had needed me for the last few hours, nor had they noticed I was gone. I had a long list of deliverables, but none felt as urgent as my need to set up camp on my couch, drape myself in my cashmere blanket and stare at the wall.

It wasn't a dream, and it wasn't magic. It wasn't delusion, or a manifestation of a long-dormant mental illness, though who doesn't have something that's buried deep down there, waiting to spring out any moment? It was instead a decision I made while staring at the wall. I didn't feel like writing a letter to my mom or begging someone from my not-so-distant past to remember me and invite me back into their lives. I wanted to talk to somebody. And so I made a friend.

There she was, on my beautiful slipper chair that had never hosted a visitor. She looked uncomfortable though, so I moved her to the other end of my couch and provided her with a cashmere lap blanket. She was wearing a college sweatshirt too. Harvard? Princeton? No, what would we talk about? Stanford? No, she would have a ton of other friends in San Francisco if she'd gone to Stanford. She was probably a Midwestern girl like me. Michigan. There she was in a University of Michigan sweatshirt, and a cashmere blanket. She wasn't wearing the diamond earrings that she had on earlier in the day, and her glossy hair was pulled into a perfectly messy top knot.

I didn't know what to do next.

"I need a name," she said, reading my mind. Her friendly voice confirmed her Midwestern roots.

Right. A name. Nothing like Kelsey, or Kira. Half the girls in my third grade class were Grace, but no. Harper? That was popular.

"I think I look like an Olivia."

From the Diary of Jennifer Martin O'Brien
May 9, 2010

Flossie never fails to amuse me. It's more than amusement, though. It's delight. It's fascination. I'm enthralled. She's a whisper that gives you goose bumps. She's a child through and through, but I see my daughter first as a person. Her preferences. Her curiosity. Her vocabulary. Everything about her reads "fully formed human being" and not "freckly fourth grader." And in those moments when she doesn't strike me first as a small adult, I see a flower.

The spring warmth makes her bloom, and it makes me bloom too. We're both so happy when the sun comes out. She's started to dig up the treasures she buried in the fall, each item meticulously labeled for posterity. There was the Popsicle stick, "Fourth of July, cherry flavor, 31st Street Beach. Good but sticky—Flossie O'Brien." An abandoned snail's shell, "Found, front walk, August, nearly stepped on—Flossie O'Brien." She stashed away a dollar, the treasure with the highest street value at exactly one dollar, and wrote "Change from the Navy Pier Ferris Wheel, August, very high, was a little dizzy—Flossie O'Brien." Sadly, the tattered receipt that had served as her bookmark when she read my childhood copy of "Tales of a Fourth Grade Nothing," did not survive months underground.

Our little Y2K babies turn ten this year. Flossie and her friends are so smart and funny, and a million years ahead of where I was at when I was that age, and trying to be Madonna, and wholly convinced Emilio Estevez was out there waiting to meet me.

I hope she always unearths her treasures. She paints and draws, reads and creates, but she doesn't pretend anymore . . . Just last year, she fawned over her dolls, named them, re-named them, fed their plastic mouths with plastic spoonfuls of delicious air, changed their clothes, and read them books. Her bouts of motherhood fervor would only last however, until she ran out of interesting baby names and wanted to play something else. She would then carefully pile her babies behind the couch to nap, forgetting about them for days until I would gather my plastic grandchildren and return them to her room. I wish I had spent more time encouraging her imaginative play, instead of imagining what a wonderful grandmother I'll be someday.

CHAPTER TWO

I was twenty-two when I flew from Chicago to San Francisco with two huge suitcases, one newly obtained undergraduate degree from Northwestern University, one very boring haircut, zero boy-friends, and one entry-level job offer from The Cerulean Group, a consulting firm that sounded exotic to me, and like a mafia front to my father. Had I departed two weeks earlier, my packing list would have included one boyfriend named Charlie. The one boyfriend had abruptly decided that his future greatness depended on him living in Cambridge, Massachusetts, and his future happiness was not at all dependent on my presence.

My dad Tom was simultaneously relieved that Charlie was no longer part of my San Francisco plan, and dismayed that Charlie's absence had not stopped me from moving thousands of miles away for a job that neither he nor I fully understood. Throughout my college years, dear Tom often wondered aloud if the ultimate goal of a Comparative Literature major was to be Senior Vice President of Literature Comparing at a top liter-ature firm. I would then wonder aloud if I should forfeit my scholarship, so he could pay for business school. Then he would hug me and tell me I'd made both he and my mom proud since the June day I was born. He called me Professor Flossie for a while, then "The Prof," which soon devolved into "Proffy Flossie." As medium-hard as he tried to be supportive, Dad was not a fan of California, unlike my mother Jen, who had genetically predisposed me to harboring her same dream of not only living in California, but standing on the beach and throwing our winter boots into the conspiratorial Pacific. The boots took up too much space in my suitcase, and I hated litter, so I left them behind in my childhood bedroom, to be disposed of at a future time in an equally dramatic, yet more environmentally friendly way.

"We have vague, entry-level jobs in Chicago, Flossie. And what about your literature? Have you even tried to find a literature job in Chicago? How about the Midwest? If you're getting a job based on stuff you can't touch, you may as well go for literature."

"Dad, the Midwest literature jobs are all full. I looked into it."

Cerulean's office was housed in an old brick building on the edge of San Francisco's Financial District. I was assigned a small workspace that must have displaced a vending machine. Two or three times a day, someone arrived at my desk, dollars or a credit card in hand, only to say "Oh!" then walk away, looking disappointed and hungry. I spent those early days calendaring and coordinating conference calls, face-to-face meetings, company-wide meetings, training sessions, and communications schedules. I knew that a human being was not necessary to do my job. Had I pointed that out to anybody, mine might not have been one of the jobs that remained after Cerulean's right-sizing. I had been at my job for four months, and had found a comfortable albeit solitary rhythm in my work. One Friday afternoon, I sensed an unusual amount of activity behind me, and I turned around to see a variety of tearful and angry people packing their things and disappearing down the staircase. I had not been asked to coordinate or schedule any layoffs. The people I barely knew whispered to each other and exchanged knowing looks. I wasn't on the receiving end of any whispers or knowing looks, and I hadn't been anybody's future ex-co-worker long enough to earn a goodbye.

My boss, Dave, who had to be at least forty, was the closest thing I had to a work friend. Technically, Dave was my boss's boss. My immediate supervisor was my age, barely acknowledged my existence, and also did not say anything to me as she left with her fern and Matcha bowl and whisk.

I slipped out the door for home as soon as I could that evening, so as not to alert them to my presence in case they had simply forgotten I worked there. I heard nothing over the weekend. Then, first thing Monday morning, Dave called me into his office for what I assumed was a good old-fashioned firing. "Listen Flossie, you do good work. You're efficient, no-drama, and professional. We're restructuring Cerulean, shifting our focus, re-tooling, and repurposing. We're poised to do some cool things, but we need to streamline. I know you haven't been here very long, and we think you'll be a good fit for the new Cerulean, if you're ready for a challenge. Are you ready for a challenge, Flossie?

"Yes, wow, thank you."

"I'm sure it will be tough for a bit, you know, missing your Cerulean friends who were . . . freed up to explore other opportunities."

"I'll be okay. 'Friends' might be a stretch."

"That's good to hear, Flossie. That kind of attitude will serve you well here. We don't have the capacity for nonsense right now."

What Dave did not know was that compared to my other capacities, my capacity for nonsense was near limitless.

I'd been plucked from obscurity, so that I could be sent back to my desk to carry on with exactly what I had already been doing, and it was thrilling. I felt guilty for celebrating my own accidental cunning and ambition, while far more qualified people were . . . freed up to explore other opportunities. I would soon forget those people existed, while they would continue to not know my name nor that I'd stumbled right over them to get ahead in corporate America.

Cerulean's restructuring happened very quickly; Dave gave me a raise and changed my title from "Administrative Specialist" to "Associate," and then again to "Analyst." We moved to an office half the size of our old one. And in what felt like a potential professional pinnacle for me, I finally received invitations to the meetings I scheduled. My first would be in the presence of Bob Winn and Frank Drexler, of Bob and Frank fame. The salaries of my former co-workers went to keep the pair on retainer. I'd read their bios a million times. As Princeton roommates, they'd made themselves famous in corporate circles by accurately predicting every consumer trend, from the widespread rejection of the banana, pencils, and the color blue, to the resurgence of bananas, pencils, and blue. Frank was from Seattle where his parents were professors at the University of Washington; he was Korean, Swedish, and French and dabbled in fashion design and apiary science. Bob was from New Hampshire, a towheaded product of boarding schools and snarky vlogs. His specific shade of startlingly blonde hair had become such a popular source of "hair inspo," for young people in the know, the shade was eventually, unofficially named for him . . . Bob blonde.

Lori, a vice president the same age as my parents, held my laptop as I crawled over Dave's legs to my spot on the stool in the corner of Cerulean's supply closet-turned-conference room. Mike, a vice president who could have babysat my parents when they were children, held my coffee.

Frank and Bob appeared on our shared screen. Bob's voluminous turtleneck sweater looked like it was actively swallowing him whole, and Frank's thick dark hair was being held back by a headband. They sat in front of a large piece of abstract art.

"Where are you guys today?" Dave asked, squinting at the screen.

"L.A.," said Bob, already seemingly bored with the meeting.

"Fantastic," Dave said. "Let's get to it, shall we? I'd heard this was the direction things might go, but we wanted some on-the-ground feedback, not just analyst data. No offense Flossie."

I nodded in agreement about my irrelevance.

"It's true," said Frank, "We just thought you'd really want to focus on what's next, not what's dead."

"I'm sorry" I interjected, "what exactly is dead?"

"Social media," said Bob. He and Frank looked at each other and smirked, forgetting or not caring that I could see them.

"Come on, guys, It's not dead," Lori said as she leaned back in her chair, "Aren't we being a little melodramatic."

"I'm sure it's not dead to you and your peers," said Frank, "but it's definitely dead out here."

"How can it be dead? Literally everyone, and everything are on social media."

"Nope," said Bob, "What you're seeing when you log in to one of your feeds, are companies like yours advertising to each other, creating content for each other, disguising themselves behind shallow celebrity endorsements and artificially created tastemakers. Did anybody notice that the consumers— again, the consumers you care about—have vaporized?"

"Listen," Frank tilted his head, and spoke softly as if to console us. "Things die, it happens, and something else grows in its place. The world turns over and just constantly rearranges its drawers. It's not tragic, it's just life."

"We need to get ahead of this," said Dave.

"You're not really ahead," said Bob.

"Social media's our bread and butter," Mike finally chimed in after sitting back quietly with his brow furrowed in the general direction of Frank and Bob. "The very air we breathe is inner connectivity en masse. That's the future, and will continue to be.

You guys," he pointed to the screen, "don't have the benefit of experience. You get bored, and we pile in here so you can report from a rave that the sky is falling. Your little sisters aren't changing how the world works. This is a blip, we'll ride it out."

"What's going to happen to commerce?" said Lori, "The economy will collapse."

"The economy isn't going to collapse because our little sisters aren't posting selfies," said Frank, "and if the economy does collapse, then it needed to because it was artificially propped up, and should be re-built in a sustainable way."

Mike stood up calmly, and looked at Dave and Lori. "I don't need a lesson about the economy from a kid in a headband and yellow pants. I thought we hired these guys to tell us where people in their twenties like to go on vacation. Let me know when I can tell my clients what next year's hot new font will be." He scanned our small space, failing to find a route that would allow him to dramatically storm out of the room. Instead, he slammed his chair back into the wall so he could squeeze by me then step over Lori's legs.

Dave continued as if Mike had never been there at all, "Well, what is everybody—the everybody we care about—doing if they are not posting a poorly lit photo of their dinner?"

"I think you guys know it as 'going off the grid.'" Bob said, making air quotes with his hands, before pulling out notes on his ancient looking paper tablet. "We've heard, 'going feral,' 'introverting,' 'going anti-viral'—I like that one—and 'Thoreau-ing,' which I hate. The language is different; the parameters differ, but the movement has traction."

"So, it's a movement now?" Lori asked.

"Yes, an accidental one, centered on intentionality. At its core, the movement is about losing the superficiality of collecting fans and followers, and embracing the intimacy of a small group of people you connect with on a deep level. We're hearing 'pod' come up a lot, 'herd,' 'flock,' and 'pride' . . . we'll use 'pod' for our purposes here. A pod has somewhere between two and ten people, and the most intense ones communicate exclusively with letters."

"Letters? Handwritten?" Lori asked.

"And impeccable handwriting is of the utmost importance," answered Frank, "Proper handwriting was almost extinct, but it's back. Bob's been writing letters for months, and his calligraphy is insane, you should see it."

"Flossie, you're young. What's your experience been?" Dave looked to me.

"Well, I've had a few friends fall off the face of the planet; their profiles and accounts disappeared overnight, or haven't been touched forever. I assumed they died, but they hadn't, I checked. I didn't hear about them going into a herd or a pod or anything."

"Because they podded without you," said Bob. "With this unprecedented social segmentation, of course people are being left out."

"So," said Dave, saving me from having to acknowledge Bob's quick and astute assessment of my social situation, "what's our core message here?"

"Quality over quantity," Frank said. "Intimacy doesn't sink you into anonymity . . . it lifts you out of it. Scrambling for bandwidth, page views, followers, synthetically charmed lives, vanity . . . it all just reeks of sadness."

"Is this a rebellion against tech?" said Dave.

"No, and here's where it gets weird," said Bob.

"*Here's* where it gets weird?" interrupted Lori.

"A lot of the developers, programmers, coders—the purest technology types—started disappearing first, followed by people you guys called hipsters," said Bob.

"The Brooklyn guys," Dave nodded.

"Well, they're Newark guys now, but yes. Technology's a means to an end . . . a tool. People need to work, bank, watch movies, follow the news; but nobody wants to *live* online anymore. The coders are doing what they need to do so the world goes around, but even they are no longer virtual residents. Coders were going crazy . . . literally going crazy."

"So who's famous?" Lori's chin was in her hand.

"That's the thing," Bob said, "No more empty fame. No more internet celebrities. For years, people have falsely believed they can know someone by casually cyber-stalking them. That goes away, and you are gifted with the thrill of knowing *knowing* someone. We are also starting to see the potential for power groupings, with thought leaders and taste makers podding up. We've seen some extremists keeping it super tight with two or three-person groups."

"Make a note, Flossie." Dave said, pointing at my laptop. I

typed, "Power Pods. Extremists." I wasn't yet sure about what we were trying to do.

"This is an opportunity," Dave said, staring at me. I quickly typed out, "this is an opportunity."

Dave tried to pace the room's few feet of available space while he talked, but the area was so small it looked like he was just spinning in place. "We need to put together messages for our clients, identify new business targets who we can help thrive in this new landscape. We need to be on this now, not scrambling later. This will require everybody's best work, but let's work quietly for now . . . discreetly. Keep this under wraps." I wrote, "under wraps." Dave scrunched his body against the wall so he could open the conference room door all the way, then step out in to the very weird future.

Later, when I was home alone, and free from the judging eyes of Frank and Bob, I scrolled through my social accounts with purpose and professional curiosity rather than my usual boredom and liquor-laden isolation. Everything online seemed relatively normal; my feeds didn't seem as barren as Frank and Bob had suggested. When I looked closely though, two, ten, twenty clicks deep, I found that every article, photo, recipe, or meandering thought about Halloween, margaritas, or snow boots came from a company just like Cerulean.

Cerulean was ahead of the Introverting of America; that's what the headlines screamed. The young people were leading the charge, bucking the values of their boisterous, vapid, duck-lipped narcissist predecessors and leading an introspective, serious, but not too serious, revolt against superficiality. The visionaries at Cerulean had figured out how to monetize the very thing that wasn't supposed to be monetized in this revolution—genuine human connection. We re-tooled our clients for a social shift, then made damn sure everybody shifted. Dave was interviewed by cynical purists and giddy fanboys for business, pop culture, medical, and religious articles. He was a talking head on cable news, and spent his evenings writing his first book and handwriting letters to Frank and Bob. Dave's jealous competitors accused him of insider trading, though there turned out to be nothing illegal about capitalizing on a widespread change in how people use their time. All the while Mike fumed, and reminded me whenever we crossed paths, that this was just a blip and a fad, and we'd all see.

The Cerulean Group, and our tiny physical footprint was on the map, and a once-static industry that didn't even know they were static, took notice, including the fine folks of mega firm, Gamboge Consulting. Gamboge purchased Cerulean, making us The Cerulean Group of Gamboge Consulting. I suggested the acquisition might better lend itself to a new name like Verdigris or Cyan, but nobody thought that was funny.

Dave was an executive vice president, and Frank and Bob were recruited into Gamboge as Senior Vice Presidents of Forecasting and Thought Leadership. Frank sent me assignments and data via handwritten letters. Damn it if his handwriting wasn't exquisite, and damn it if I didn't save those stupid letters.

Gamboge labeled us "visionaries," and gave us room to do

whatever was needed not just to stay relevant and revolutionary. Cerulean moved again, this time near the docks, in an office park comprised entirely of rehabbed shipping containers. We were the new edgy San Francisco cousins in a network of less glamorous counterparts housed across the country in wasteful, bland, sprawling office parks using dated business strategies.

"We're leading the charge on going bigger by going smaller. Smaller is Bigger." Dave moved his hands so I could imagine his business brilliance displayed on the most boring marquee ever.

"So big is small?" I asked.

"Not exactly, Flossie."

"But, you just. . . ."

"Don't worry about it. Just know, we'll be very eco-forward."

"We're the most eco-forward office I've ever seen. The toilet paper is the worst and it's so hard to find a piece of paper, I sometimes have to write on my hand if I need to take a note. And then, our eco ink bleeds the second I start to sweat. And what if our office accidentally gets shipped out to Japan?"

"Don't worry Flossie, and I was waiting to tell you this, but congratulations, you'll be working from home, you won't have to worry about bad toilet paper, and your home office will never be accidentally shipped to Japan."

I moved into my Noe Valley apartment/office, leaving my disinterested roommates behind. It had only taken Kira and Kelsey a few minutes to recruit my replacement, and nobody was home when I left them with nary a note or a goodbye.

My new neighbors included a charcuterie shop a few doors down from my apartment, a juicery across the street, and a paperie on the corner. In the spirit of our block, I named my new home The Flosserie.

There was another apartment door across from the Flosserie, and I knocked on it every day for a week, without anybody answering. I didn't even hear any movement or signs of life when I covertly pressed my ear to the wood below the peephole. There was no stray mail lying around that offered a clue as to who might live there. A piece of tape had been haphazardly slapped on the apartment's outside buzzer, with the letters "T.B." scribbled in permanent marker. I considered for a moment, that this might be a medical warning, instead of initials, but I knocked again anyway.

I carefully arranged my office area, and identified the perfect place to drink my tea and take in the view of the *Ruelle de Déchets*. It was a busy neighborhood with constant foot traffic, and car traffic, and notoriously bad parking. It only took two days of working exclusively within my tastefully adorned walls to realize that even though my new neighborhood was teeming with other humans who were actively sharing my same sliver of the world, they all may as well have been running their errands on the moon. While I worked, they continued to pod up without me.

At Dave's urging, I'd shut down my social accounts, and was joining the ranks of the anti-social, social elite, "practicing what we preach, leading from within." Mike called it "pooping where we eat." He actually called it something else, but Bob was adamant that swearing was for old people desperate for attention.

Dave shut down his social accounts too, but I think it was harder for him, especially because it would have been the perfect and most efficient way to share his meteoric rise in the business world with his jealous high school classmates. He had podded up with a few executives, other people who'd spent time in the limelight for their visionary leadership. That's how Dave described it to me . . . "visionary leadership." I was developing a love-hate relationship with the word "visionary." Dave and his pod spent weekends sipping wine in Napa, hiking in the headlands, reading draft chapters of Mike's book, and massaging each other's egos while having actual massages.

One afternoon, after hours of staring at my computer, I went to my mirror and I stared at my face instead. My face was basically the same as it had always been. My eyes were puffy, and my freckles had faded. I hadn't been to a pool, or seen a pool, or much of the sun. When I was home for thirty-six hours at Christmas, my dad said he had more color from windburn than I did from living in beautiful, sunny California. I lied and told him I was coming down with something, and that I usually looked great. I hydrated and moisturized, but I looked tired, and like I needed to eat an orange. Did I have scurvy? Was I looking at the first signs of scurvy?

I was working more than ever, but in a vacuum. As I looked into the mirror, I wondered if I had the focus to actually work in a vacuum, like a vacuum designed to suck crumbs from the floor.

I thought I probably could. Did I look like a person who should have a cat? But having a cat meant vacuuming up fur balls all the time, and the cat, frightened by the vacuum, would scratch me, and I wouldn't go to the doctor, and I would get cat scratch fever, which when mixed with modern day scurvy, would kill me and nobody would discover my body until the autopay on my rent stopped working. Thanks a lot, vacuum.

I returned to my computer to take one more spin around the internet to find Charlie, when I heard a bump outside my front door, followed by a rattle. I tiptoed to the peephole and for the first time, saw someone using keys at the door across the hall; a guy whose features were distorted by the blurry glass of the peephole.

I flung the door open.

"Hi."

He jumped and dropped the bag he was carrying.

"You scared me." He frowned at the dropped cloth bag that exposed a small and expensive wheel of cheese from the shop down the street. He looked up and continued to frown in my direction.

I remembered I had makeup-free scurvy face and was wearing yoga clothes. At least I wasn't sweaty. Not doing yoga helped with that.

"Sorry to scare you. I can't believe we haven't met. I'm Flossie, your new neighbor."

"I gathered that. I'm Ty. I've been traveling and just got home yesterday. Welcome to the building." He was really committed to that frown.

"Again, I'm sorry about your cheese. I just thought I should say hi."

"No, no, it's fine. I was just surprised, that's all. The person who lived in your apartment before you hardly ever came out of there, especially if she saw me in the hall. I could see the shadow of her feet in the doorway, and feel her spying on me through the peephole before hearing her slippers shuffle away."

Ty was only slightly taller than me, and had flaming red hair. His face was round, and seemed capable of only conveying the very specific emotion of "You surprised me, and now I'm annoyed, and also tired, but mostly annoyed." He was dressed like Frank and Bob. A tight t-shirt peeked out from the neck of his bulky cardigan, topping off bright orange chinos and worn-in work boots.

"Ok, well, I should get this cheese inside, but it was nice to meet you Flossie."

"You too. But, wait . . . Ty?"

"Yeah?"

"Have we met? You look super familiar? Do you know girls named Kira and Kelsey?"

"I know a thousand girls named Kira and Kelsey, but I don't think we've met. People think all red-heads look alike."

The same day my delivery of vitamin-packed oranges arrived at my doorstep, I received word that our little group of Cerulean visionaries would act as honorary ambassadors at Gamboge's upcoming annual conference in San Francisco.

Dave, Frank, and Bob were the conference's keynote speakers.

I spent weeks planning my outfits and grooming. I visited no-nonsense professionals to tailor new designer clothes to fit my 5'5 frame, coax my strawberry blonde hair into being both strawberrier and blonder, and to buff and brighten my sun-deprived skin and faded freckles.

As I wandered the hallways of the convention center, fellow conference attendees, upon spotting my Cerulean badge, stopped me to offer congratulations or to compliment me on my beautiful city. I could only imagine what Dave, Frank, and Bob were experiencing.

I was sitting in a crowded workshop, "Tomorrow's Analyst Today," listening to the analyst panelists talking over each other about distribution channels, when the woman next to me leaned over and whispered, "You should be an analyst panelist. You're Cerulean, right?"

"I am," I whispered back, "but honestly, I would be a terrible analyst panelist. I have nothing interesting to say about distribution channels."

"No way, this is so basic. A better title for this seminar would be, "Yesterday's Analyst, The Day Before Yesterday.""

"I still have a lot to learn."

"I'm sure that's not true. I'm Etta, a Gamboge junior analyst, Denver." She looked to be about my same age. Her brown curly hair hung over her eyes, and her loose-fitting khakis were wrinkled.

"I'm Flossie," I said, pretending not to notice the khakis.

Etta and I ate turkey sandwiches together on a plaza bench

after the workshop. She'd worked for Gamboge just a few months, after her uncle got her the job, and she was still adjusting to being in an office all day. Before Gamboge, she'd worked as a ski instructor and a hiking guide. She said she wanted to pick my brain about work, but mostly she just asked about San Francisco, and how I went from studying literature in Chicago to analyzing things in San Francisco.

When we reluctantly parted ways that afternoon, Etta to the "Canary in a Data Mine" workshop in the Yosemite Ballroom and me to "Punk Rock Brand," in Sequoyah Room B, I asked Etta for her mailing address, and I gave her mine.

"Pen Pals. Nice," she said as she departed.

I forced myself to wait a week before I wrote to her. The void left by my departure from social media, was not as easily filled by written correspondence as one might expect. I tracked down Camila in Miami and wrote to her three times. She didn't reply by letter, but she did text, "got your note, sweetie, thx!"

I wrote to Lola, Kira and Kelsey, and immediately regretted wasting the stationery. I pictured them opening my letter, Kira reminding Kelsey who I was by pointing out the room I used to sleep in, then becoming bored by the second sentence, and throwing the letter away before she got to the third.

It was easiest to write to my mother. For anybody else, those letters were probably a torturous read, bloated with tedious detail. I pondered the energy of the city, the busyness of my days, the books I hoped to read, and my underlying anxieties surrounding a pending commitment to a new dentist.

My letter to Etta recycled my thoughts on my busyness, the energy of the city, the books I wanted to read, and my dental concerns, but I was confident that my mother and Etta would not compare their content. I made notes of ideas for future content: thoughts on farmers' markets (favorable), Donna Tartt books (favorable), wind (unfavorable), with a special section for food and drink: walnuts (allergic), pour-over coffee (fine, but was it necessary?), fried chicken (delicious, but very difficult to make at home) and finally, artisan cheese and California wine (what else do we live for?).

When I was feeling particularly Invisible Lonely, I received a letter back from Etta, and then proceeded to read it thirty times. Her attempt at calligraphy was admirable; the letter began, "Dear Flassie." She wrote about the weather, and a movie she'd seen, and her trip to the dentist, which was perfectly fine, beginner-level letter stuff. She found her stride when she started talking about the banality of our work and pondering what professions might not be saddled with redundant and excessive analysis; maybe bakers, babysitters, hair stylists, house painters, and amusement park ride operators. I didn't know if any of that is true—there could be inordinate amounts of necessary analysis for those careers—but I appreciated her reasoning that some lucky professionals are specifically tasked with the unquantifiable job of making people happy. Etta had also made so much turkey chili that her freezer was full of it, and she wished I was closer, so I could take some of it off her hands. Her neighbors were vegetarians and very judgmental about her willingness to kill a majestic bird for chili.

I wrote back, confessing that I too, wished I could be there to eat the chili, and that my neighbor also seemed judgmental, and was not a fan of being startled in the hallway.

Etta wrote again, this time mystified by how difficult it was to find things to do. She never used to have these problems. I was lucky, she wrote. Cerulean probably filled whatever voids I had—all of that energy, all of that excitement. She'd gone to a self-improvement seminar, hoping to unveil her passion. She dreamed that when her burning desires were finally revealed, she would realize her deepest passion was for analysis, solitude, and one day reaching the professional pinnacle of mid-level management. Unfortunately, her passion was for the very useless travel and adventure. She never wrote the word lonely in her letters, nor did I in my letters to her, though of course I desperately wanted to. My loneliness remained my little secret.

As I read Etta's letters, noting her improving penmanship, I sat on the couch and wrapped myself in the cashmere blanket. When pulled from the intentionally jaunty place of honor on the back of my couch, the blanket made me feel as if I were a wealthy socialite exhausted from parties and philanthropy and finally indulging in a little well-deserved me time. I wrapped it just-so, and lay there for a moment in my catalog perfect living room, a staged prop, so lovely in repose. Catalog shoppers could flip to my page and imagine themselves exactly where I was, glamorously comfortable and fully satisfied with their lot in life. Catalogs, however usually do not show the room's occupant thirty minutes later, wrapped in the cashmere blanket drinking pinot noir straight from the bottle while crying.

I was at the mailbox on the corner, depositing a return letter to Etta, when I heard Ty's voice behind me.

"Nice calligraphy."

It was my turn to be startled, and I slammed the mailbox door shut on my own finger.

"Hi. Thanks, I'm still learning. S's are hard."

"S's ARE hard," he nodded, thoughtfully.

"Wait, I know where I saw you," I said stopping him from walking away. "You were on the news."

"When?"

"A few weeks ago, for the pet thing . . . animal companions versus allergy sufferers in the workplace."

"Oh, yeah, that."

"Did you not know you'd be in the news?"

"I knew, but I didn't know for which thing. I'm also fighting waterfront construction, library closures in Marin, tree removals in North Beach, and discriminatory text books in Sacramento."

"Oh, that's why you look familiar."

"You don't sound happy. Are you part of the small-minded, backwards text book faction?"

"Not anymore. How'd that one go?"

"Pretty amazing. I mean, how else are people going to learn about the evils of discrimination, if we're not out there, educating, disrupting, challenging the system and people's innermost thoughts and demons, you know?"

"Yes, I guess, I do know. So, you're a. . . ."

"Professional activist. And what do you do, neighbor?"

"I'm an analyst."

"Of course you are."

"What is that supposed to mean?

"Nothing bad. It's just that . . . everybody's an analyst, but it's cool. What kind of analyst? Technology? Biomedical? Government? Public Affairs? Education?"

"Marketing, branding, and communications."

"Of course you are . . . nah, I'm kidding, that's cool."

"I know it's cool." I also knew that not one red hair on his weirdly shaped body thought what I did was cool.

"It is, it is. Alright neighbor, see you around. I'm late for a meeting. What's your name again?"

"Flossie."

"Of course it is. Good luck with your s's Flossie. You'll need it with that name!" And with that final insult he left, taking with him what I'm sure he perceived to be all of the social capital from our now-weird neighbor dynamic. Maybe it was better that we were not going to be friends. I was liberated from having to feel bad about showing up late for his birthday party, or obliged to bring in his mail, or trapped in a cycle of monthly game nights and happy hours.

From the Diary of Jennifer Martin O'Brien
August 2, 2013

We've just returned from the San Diego-to-San Francisco O'Brien Family Odyssey. It was worth all the money we saved to make the trip happen . . . it was worth not buying wrapping paper for the school fundraiser, and cutting my coffee budget down to nothing.

On day one of our trip, I could tell Tommy was worried Flossie was already heeding California's call. He pulled her aside and said something like, "Do you know how many people visit Chicago every year, Flossie? Thousands of people; millions, even! People think New York is the center of the universe, but it's Chicago. Busiest airport on the planet; culture, restaurants, music, fancy shopping, theaters, the most important museums and the greatest teams in the history of sports. We're a sports town! We're an art town! We're a business town! We're a working man's town! We're a beer town! We're a champagne town!" On day two, another tourist mistook Tommy for a guy on that show he likes, NCIS, and he calmed down and enjoyed himself a little.

I kept Flossie off her phone, otherwise she would have missed the whole thing while she was crushing candy, or texting Camila pictures of herself making the same silly face over and over again. She would have missed everything.

We went to the beach and Disneyland. My own family made fun of me for wanting to see Melrose Place, the courthouse from the OJ Simpson trial and the spot in Hollywood where River Phoenix died. I loved him, you know.

In San Francisco, we ate noodles and dumplings in Chinatown, and watched workers in gloves fold fortune cookies. We ate clam chowder at the wharf, and rode a cable car up and down the picturesque hills. I thought Tommy might die, because he leaned so far from the cable car into traffic to snap what turned out to be very blurry photos of the city. We walked half-way over the Golden Gate Bridge before he said, "I get the idea!" and made us turn around and walk back.

I loved California, like I knew I would. Maybe it was the air. California air was warm, yet weightless, unlike the heavy air at home that makes me feel like I'm constantly breathing in Chicagoans' combined sweat and heavy breath. California air felt so light that people floated down the street instead of walking.

On a whim in Carmel, we stopped to look at real estate flyers and gawk at the prices of bungalows and shacks. I said we'd have to sell Flossie to live here, and then she said, "Flossie would sell Flossie to live here." She became very quiet, and I could see the wheels turning in her head . . . or maybe a movie playing in her head of future Flossie, making a go of it in California.

She stared at people in restaurants, eavesdropped on their conversations, and laughed at their private jokes. She stood on her tiptoes to look in people's windows. I suppose she does the same at home, craning her neck to see inside windows of the apartments we pass on the L train. She points them out to me sometimes. "Hey look, the people in Charlie Bucket's house are eating their cabbage water. The drug dealer has company. That woman's hiding from something bad she did. She'll get caught though."

CHAPTER THREE

"I think I look like an Olivia."

"You do," the sound of my own voice cutting the silence was jarring. It even cracked a little from lack of use.

"Now what?" It cracked again.

"You look stressed. Why don't you grab that bottle of sauvignon blanc you didn't finish last night?"

I left Olivia on the couch and fetched the bottle. I paused at the cabinet before retrieving two glasses. It was afternoon and I didn't want to drink alone.

I gulped one glass down in the kitchen, and poured another for myself before returning to the couch. She . . . Olivia, I guess . . . was still sitting there, flipping through a magazine from my coffee table, like she'd sat in that spot dozens of times. She smiled when she saw her wine glass on the table.

"Relax, this isn't a big deal. I'm your friend, Olivia. We met on a flight from Chicago to San Francisco. We both happened to be moving out here at the same time right out of college. We didn't know anybody else, and became fast friends. We hated your roommates, Kira and what's-her-face, and talked about them behind their backs. Then, I helped you find this place and helped you move in, waving traffic around your truck and flipping off that driver who almost hit you, remember? I have two roommates in a mini-loft south of Market. I'm here a lot, though. I think your neighbor's a tool, and am convinced he fell in love with you at first sight, but I think you are too good for him. We love brunch and happy hour. I'm a graphic designer, and am currently between boyfriends, of which there are many. However, I always have time for you, my very best friend. I appreciate that you always listen, and you're very funny. You appreciate that I give great advice and am honest to a fault. We watch movies in our pajamas, and my goal is to get you to go out more, cut loose, and meet a great guy. I'm the one who keeps you from drunk-stalking Charlie. That's it. Not so hard is it?"

"No, I guess not, I just ..."

"Well don't 'just.' Again, my being here is not a big deal, it was bound to happen. Better that I'm here now to keep you from going crazy rather than me showing up later after you've already gone crazy and don't know the difference."

"Fine."

"Excellent, so let's talk. Where do you want to start? Frank? Bob? Fiona? Pigs in a blanket? How much Dave has changed? That time he wore his bike shorts and those clip-on cycling shoes to the office, and you wanted to take a picture, because it was kind of awesome to see proof that mid-life crises are real?"

"This is crazy. I feel crazy."

"You're not crazy."

"I would feel better about that, if it was anybody other than the imaginary person in my living room who was trying to assure me I'm not in the middle of some kind of epic breakdown."

"Honestly, Floss, you might be. Breakdowns happen. They can happen to anybody. They happen every day to normal people, they can happen to anybody who's under a lot of stress. But if it is, and I'm not saying it is, but if it is, it's probably just temporary, and you need someone to see you through it. Should we call your family?"

"No."

"Fiona? Etta?"

"What? No."

"OK, well then you're stuck with me. I'm imaginary. I know that, you know that. That's the important part. You know I'm not real. You fully understand, in every cell of your wine-dependent body that I'm not here. We've established that, and I'm getting bored with this. Let's watch a movie. You don't have to talk. Get used to me, or don't. If this is truly too much for you, I'll leave, and you'll probably be fine, and you will laugh about it tomorrow . . . alone."

"Alright, sorry, fine. Let's watch a movie." It was one I'd seen before, a girl likes a guy, he doesn't notice her, then at the end, he does notice her.

"Groundbreaking stuff," Olivia said, about fifteen minutes in to the guy not noticing the girl. "How many times have you seen this?"

"I don't know." I knew. It was four times. She didn't say anything about my lie.

"My being here will help, but I'm afraid the part of your brain that holds culture, passion, romance, and gray area non-analytical thinking will atrophy. When's the last time you painted? Or set foot in a theater of any kind? When's the last time you saw a concert, went to a party, made out with some random guy, or read a book?"

"I read. Also, I'm not eighteen."

"You need literature. I think literature, ironically, is going to be the most real thing for your brain right now. You had a passion for it. I'm not real, your job, which is virtual, is basically theory, and kind of imaginary."

"I'm an analyst. A very real analyst."

"You're analyzing perceptions, theories, preferences, ideas, and even numbers which in all honesty, you can't touch or hold in your hands. Everything's so wispy. It's like you're in the middle of a hologram. I can see why letters are a thing."

I didn't say anything back.

"Okay, I'm not trying to start a fight, especially today. You know I love you, I just worry. Now, I know I'm the one who suggested a movie, but let's watch a real movie please. Preferably something independent or award-winning. It would be good if somebody's disabled or a prostitute."

"Or a disabled prostitute."

"Now you're getting it. You need to have a real emotion that's not just you being sad for yourself. If you're going to be sad, you should be sad for the disabled prostitute."

I fell asleep on my couch that night, having done zero work

the entire day. I did however finish off a second bottle of wine. The more I drank, the easier it was to make small talk with Olivia, which I found to be true when I was faced to talking with real people as well.

When I woke up the next morning on my couch and with a colossal headache, I forgot for a moment what I had done . . . that I had invented a person so that I could have a friend. I raised my head to inspect the other end of the couch to see if she was there. She wasn't, and I was disappointed.

I could either remain on the couch thinking about my headache and my descent into madness, or I could distract myself by thinking of something else. Remembering that I was still a little bit in control of something, Olivia walked out of the kitchen, wearing fresh clothes—ripped jeans and a little blazer—subtle makeup, and her hair loose and swinging as she moved.

"Good morning!" she said enthusiastically. She was genuinely happy to see me. "You're looking a little rough, sunshine. You still have coconut water in the fridge. Drink that, and then I'll go to my office."

I raced through my day, working as fast as I could to make up for the previous day's absence. Nobody had noticed that I missed the entire day. Had I been kidnapped while wandering the city, I could have easily been taken to Canada, assuming there was more than one kidnapper allowing them to sleep and drive in shifts. When I called in to the office, I asked Fiona how she liked her pigs in a blanket.

"They were divine," she cooed. There is no way she thought

pigs in a blanket were divine. I would for sure need to talk to Olivia about Fiona.

I logged out at 6 o'clock, just in time for Olivia to walk through the door.

"Hey, girl. How was your day? How's the headache? Did you stay hydrated? Are we cooking or going out? She went into the kitchen and hoisted herself up onto the counter to watch as I poured myself a glass of coconut water, opened a bottle of rosé, and pulled out the pots to make pasta. I chopped tomatoes, and herbs and boiled water as I listened to Olivia chatter about her day, and a new client, and a married co-worker who shamelessly flirted with her.

The details of Olivia's life came so easily to me. I could see her office as if I'd been there. It was an airy warehouse space with a huge footprint. It was full of desks, people, and activity, and Olivia was at the center of it all. She worked with the premier, high-profile clients, and they all loved her.

The next morning I woke up early and made two omelets and two cups of coffee. Olivia and I started reading the same book so we could talk about it. I found myself taking breaks from my computer, so I could gaze out at the *Ruelle de Déchets* and think about what kind of day Olivia might be having, as if I were watching her from afar. I could see her ordering a cappuccino and a croissant, then leaving a big tip, and chatting with the flower vendor as she picked up peonies for her desk. I could see her snapping a picture of a cute dog and texting it to me as a part of her ongoing campaign to get me to adopt a pet. "It's the best way to meet a guy in this city," she'd say.

She wore chic pants suits to meetings, and flirty dresses when the sun was out. She looked equally stylish in stilettos, bohemian sandals, and sneakers designed for teenagers. When we spent evenings eating red licorice dipped in rose, she wore her Michigan sweatshirt, with her hair thrown into her signature messy bun.

I toyed with the idea of her being fluent in Japanese, but abandoned the idea when I realized that since I knew not a word of Japanese, I couldn't even imagine what it might sound like coming out of her mouth. I settled instead on Italian, which I heard plenty of in Chicago. I pictured her at the artisan meat shop, ordering in Italian, and the cute guy behind the counter instantly falling in love with her. She was funny. She did an impression of Fiona that made me snort laugh.

We stayed in and cooked, drank wine, and binge-watched shows she picked out for us. I was settling in for another evening on the couch, when she turned to me, "Listen Flossie, I think we need to get out of here. All of this pasta, wine, and binge-watching . . . I love you, but I worry about your heart."

"You think I'm getting fat?"

"That's not what I'm saying. Embrace your body, whatever, but humans need to go outside. Humans need to move their bodies, and be around people, and you, Flossie, are a human. Let's go out."

"You know we can't do that."

"Sure we can. Let's go for a walk. I'll be right there."

"But I just got comfortable talking to you in here, I can't talk to you out there."

"That doesn't matter. You need to go for a walk, and I need to get out of here. Hey are you ever going to paint this place? Remember when you moved in you were going to do something with like, a yellow wall?"

"Yes, I'll get around to it. Okay, we'll go outside."

"Right now?" she looked hopeful.

"It's dark. It's cold. I'm not wearing a bra."

"Okay, grandma, we'll go tomorrow. We're going to walk the Embarcadero."

"No, that's where Cerulean's office is."

"Then we'll go down to Crissy Field. But you absolutely have to put on a bra, and you have to wear at least a little makeup. I'm not saying you need to go have your hair blown out, or overthink this. You just need to get used to going places, without it being such a huge deal that you have to prepare for a week, okay?"

"That's kind of mean."

"It's not mean; it's said out of love. Look cute, but not like you had to try too hard. Hey, I have an idea. Just set yourself up as if you're making a call, then when you want to talk to me, people will just think you're on the phone. I'm a genius."

The next day was beautiful, when I had hoped for rain or dangerous, movement-inhibiting, science-fiction-level fog. I wished for freak snow flurries, a typhoon warning, a tornado warning, or even just a broken ankle that would keep me inside. But as I stared out my window, lamenting the perfect weather and my healthy ankle, Olivia came bounding in to the apartment with her key, looking as if she was ready to lead a class of supermodels in some kind of yoga-lates-Lat-in-dance-weightlifting boot camp. Her designer athletic gear clung to her totally fit physique. I'd squeezed into the same athletic pants I used to wear around the house before devolving into generously cut pajamas.

She looked me up and down. "Do your hair a little bit, throw on some lip gloss, a little blush, grab your phone, and let's go. The day waits for nobody."

The walking trails were crowded for a weekday. I spotted pods of people out hiking, and sitting in the grass solving the world's problems. Tourists had their cameras aimed at the majestic Golden Gate Bridge. The occasional loner ran by, looking focused and unconcerned with their solitude. I had my phone out and poised for a "call," but for the first fifteen minutes, Olivia and I walked in silence. I didn't look at her, but out of the corner of my eye I could feel her looking at me.

She spoke first. "Alright, talk to me. You can do this." I looked at my phone and pretended to call her.

"Hey it's, me," I said for the benefit of the zero number of people who were paying attention. "I still don't know about this."

"What's to know? Is anybody looking at you?"

"No."

"Of course not. Let's pick up the pace a little, I don't want you to have to buy new pants. Can you walk and talk at the same time?"

"I don't remember."

"Let's find out. Tell me about work. What's your new project?"

I walked and talked like a pro, and Olivia listened. I had forgotten what my voice sounded like outside in the world. I remembered walking and talking with my parents during the summer. I thought back to gossiping with Camila in my back-yard, and strolling to get a pour-over coffee with Charlie and asking thoughtful follow-up questions about his coding stories. Nobody at Crissy Field gave me a second look as I walked along, yakking away. When handsome joggers passed by, Olivia would try to get me to turn and watch them. She pointed out cute dogs she thought might look good in my apartment, and marveled at a crane as it spread its enormous wings and took off from a dune, but mostly she just listened.

Though my feet were still recovering from my oxblood pumps, I felt like I could easily and happily walk ten miles without noticing. And unlike that day in the Financial District, I did not care who saw me or where anybody thought I might be going, or if they thought I had anywhere to go at all. Other than the good looking joggers and adorable dogs, I started to pass people without seeing them at all. I made dinner for Olivia and myself that night, sent her home, and went to bed without wine. I slept like a baby.

Olivia and I walked every day for a week, always with the headset, not always with the outfits of spin instructors. We strolled the neighborhood, window shopped Union Square and Fillmore, and bundled up to watch surfers navigate the waves of Ocean Beach.

I talked for hours and hours, which likely added up to days' and weeks' worth of talking. I told Olivia every detail of my every work day. I read her an an article on cotton candy. I told her how my mom had signed me up for martial arts when I was a kid, but I hurt myself immediately, and never went back.

I told her about the summer I turned sixteen, and got the world's worst haircut . . . as in the worst haircut to have ever been given and/or received since the first time one human took a sharp rock, or a dull machete, to another human's hair with the sole intention of making that human's hair shorter. It had been a terrible summer. When I wasn't hiding in my bed, or staring numbly into my phone to see what other people were doing with their long hot days, I worked at our neighborhood rec center. I held sticky hands and doled out cheese crackers, remembering who was nut-free, and who was gluten-free, and who was dairy-free. I refereed basketball games without fully understanding the rules, and I painted butterfly wings and tiger stripes onto sweaty, smelly, squirmy faces. I took all the money I saved, and I made an appointment at a fancy salon on Michigan Avenue, feeling mildly awful about cheating on Shannon, my childhood hairdresser from the mall. The new stylist didn't look at the picture I showed her, and chopped my hair into the shape of a Christmas tree. I was crushed, and in hiding, and I spent months studying and writing while my hair grew out, and boom, that hideous haircut got me a scholarship to Northwestern. Olivia asked if I had pictures of the haircut.

Helloooooo, Floss!

It's your dad. So this is how you want to communicate, huh? Not that I don't want to talk to you, or send you a text like a normal person, but you mentioned letters, so here's a letter, and if this is how everybody your age is communicating these days, here I am, writing a letter like I'm Abraham Lincoln. Speaking of Illinois, when are you coming home? It's been a long time. We'll do all your favorite stuff, eat at all the places you like. We'll get dogs, just the way you like them, no pickle, right?

Things are fine here. How are you? How's your job? How's California? How are you feeling about the Cubbies? Don't tell me you're a Giants fan now. You can tell me a lot of things, just not that. Or if you're a vegan. John—remember him, my buddy from down the street? Anyway, John said he heard that California was trying to pass a law that would make everybody vegetarian. It didn't sound true, but I guess you never know.

Listen, you can write back if you want, but I wouldn't be mad if you texted, or called or came home, whatever. Proud of you Flossie.

Love,

Your Dad

I couldn't go anywhere, let alone back to Chicago, until my kitchen was painted. Olivia and I were on the kitchen floor masking off the cupboards. I was happy for the task; I didn't have to look at her directly while I answered a barrage of uncomfortable questions.

"Flossie, seriously, Charlie's been your only boyfriend? Nobody in high school?"

"I guess you could say I had a boyfriend during my freshman year. We kissed a couple of times, went to a school dance, talked on the phone. But he wasn't that smart, and we weren't interested in any of the same things. But he told me I was pretty, and he was nice, and had really clear skin for a fourteen-year-old boy."

"But he was boring?"

"Yeah, I guess. Looking back though, I may have been the boring one. I eventually felt exhausted trying to come up with things to talk about."

"And our relationship now doesn't exhaust you?"

"You and me? No. Why?" That wasn't entirely true. The fact that she was of no help in painting the kitchen, was turning out to be physically exhausting.

"Lest you forget, you're really maintaining both sides of our conversations."

"That's different."

"How so?"

"Flossie, have you ever thought of really trying to meet someone new?"

"Like a guy?"

"Yeah, like a guy."

"I've looked around, I guess. I work a lot, and nobody's really trying to meet new friends these days."

"Of course they are. People are always seeking out other people, and yes, even new people . . . it's human nature. Maybe you should go out . . . like to a bar."

"I'm not going to a bar by myself."

"I'll go with you."

"I can't go to a bar, and then sit there, and talk to you on a fake phone call. Nobody does that. What could you even do to help me in a bar? Catch the eye of a guy, make conversation, and then talk me up and introduce me?"

"What if you just went to a bar, had a few drinks, and got up the courage to talk to someone—anyone—the bartender, even? The first guy that sits down, or looks your way? Just to remember how to talk to people out in the world."

"Not right now. Please don't push me."

I didn't like being pushed. And I didn't like the shade of yellow I had just rolled onto the wall. It looked like an envelope had been left in the sun too long . . . yellowed, not yellow. It was the perfect color if I was desiring the effects of decades of cigarette smoking in the kitchen without the inconvenience and expense of actually smoking. Maybe it would be better when it dried.

"Don't push you? You're not suffering from a traumatic brain injury. You've become introverted . . . nurture vs nature, and this upside down universe you've found yourself in means that nurture has successfully beaten the extravert out of you."

"I was probably always an introvert."

"Not like this, you weren't."

"Listen, I have another Gamboge conference coming, and I get to go. Dave promised, and I immediately non-refundably booked it. Etta wrote to tell me she's going to be there, and we even made plans to hang out every night, and not just hang out, but actually go out to places. Oh, and it's in Las Vegas." I surveyed my painting, letting the Vegas news sink in for Olivia. Maybe I should paint just one wall, and see how cigarette-teeth yellow looked in the light of day, but I'd already done all the masking.

"Vegas? I'm coming with you. You need me."

"You can't come," I said while still not looking at her. "It's for work, and it's just in Vegas; I'll be fine. I'm a grown up, I can handle myself just fine without being kidnapped or murdered."

"That's not what I'm worried about. I'm worried that you are going to *waste* Las Vegas. This is the opportunity I was literally just talking about. Finally, a chance for you to get out there. A conference means people from everywhere, descending on Las Vegas, ready to cut loose. People go *cah-razy* at conferences anywhere. But Las Vegas? Wow."

"Well, you are probably thinking of people who go to conferences in movies, and don't get your hopes up, nothing *cah-razy* is going to happen. These are the people I work with."

"But you don't work with them, really. They're people who are from New Orleans, and Orlando, and Minneapolis who just happen to kind of have the same job as you but you never see them, ever."

"I guess. It really is work, Olivia. At the last one, I mostly listened to a lot of analysts analyzing analysis."

"Hush. Tomorrow we shop. Tonight? Spin class."

Olivia

I can have opinions and thoughts that are different than Flossie's. That's healthy for any friendship. If she wanted a guardian angel, or a boring yes man, or a grandmother, she would have made me that, but she didn't. I am the way I am, because that's what she needs. I enjoy talking with her; I don't hang out with her out of obligation. We just happen to be in a particular stage of life, where she needs my help. There might come a stage in our friendship, where she will need me to need her. But until then, I'll look out for her best interests. Of course I could be out doing other things. One of my roommates manages a restaurant; not just any restaurant, but Potato Cellar. Just try to get a table there. I could get in, any night, any time. Yes, I'm pretty, but it's not enough, even for me. I'm nice, when I don't have to be. I'm down to earth. I'm brave. I'm fun. I'm smart. I'm interesting. I'm artsy, worldly, well-traveled, and stylish. I could probably hang out and be friends and pod up with absolutely anybody I wanted to. But I choose a friendship with Flossie over all of that. She is just that great, and I am just that outstanding of a friend.

CHAPTER FOUR

I'd been off the plane for about thirty seconds, when Olivia sidled up next to me. "Get out your phone, I want to talk to you. We didn't talk the whole flight."

Olivia pulled a scarf from her very expensive Italian leather weekend bag. Inside was just exactly what she needed, expertly curated, expertly folded. She would know just what to bring for a few days in Vegas, a month in New York, a weekend in the Hamptons, or an impromptu getaway to Cabo.

I leaned my own worn carry-on against an airport slot machine. I fake-dialed my phone, and to temper the fears of any potential observers wondering if I was making a real phone call, said "Hey, it's me, I just landed."

"Ok, Flossie, here's what's going to happen; we are going to the hotel, you are going to freshen up, put on an outfit of my choosing, and then we are hitting the hotel bar, hard."

"It's two in the afternoon. I'm technically working. You have a job, you should know this stuff."

"Fine. But you will need to freshen up. Redo your makeup, fluff up your hair, change your clothes. And you may not know this, but a good Vegas trip actually begins on the flight. People are starting to loosen up, so by the time the plane lands, they are already in pre-party mode. I don't know if they pump pheromones into the terminals here, or what, but people are already scoping out, you know, the situation. Put some lipstick on right now. Stand up straight, and start looking around and paying attention, but not in a desperate way, just in an 'open to the universe' kind of way."

"You're bossy." I said while digging through my bag for lipstick.

"No, I'm demonstrating decisive leadership skills and I'm acting in your best interest."

"Don't forget, I'm going to the analyst meet-and-greet this evening, and I'm catching up with Etta."

"Fine. But make sure you meet and greet more than Etta. Do you think she's going to help you or hold you back? We can't have a hanger-on impeding your progress."

"She's cool Olivia, and nice. You might even like her."

"We'll see. Now let's go."

I was ready. I stood up straight, threw back my shoulders to announce I was open to the universe, and walked confidently toward the exit with Olivia.

It was harder to maintain my open-to-the-universe outlook on life with Olivia coaching me through the getting-ready process. For someone who was lounging on the bed, in Las Vegas, she was very intense.

"I am not going to a club. I am going to work," I finally had to tell her during our showdown about whether or not I could pull off a late-afternoon smoky eye.

"This is the closest that work comes to going to a club unless you actually work in a club. I already gave in and approved that boring dress."

"It's not boring. In fact, I think it might be a bit much." I looked down at my black sheath dress. It was belted, and fit well, and I felt a little bit pretty in it. I slipped into my oxblood pumps.

"It's a step up from your normal work outfit. Put on the little jacket. That will take you from middle-aged real estate agent— wait, real estate is too sexy middle-aged analyst to sophisticated, but not too sophisticated, young executive who's ready to talk multi-media, Turks and Caicos, and how much you love silk sheets."

"You've seen too many movies."

She stood next to me, immaculate in a black pantsuit and low-cut blouse. "I am going to be there, eyeing the room for prospects. If you need me, signal me or something. Take your phone. And a lipstick. And a pen. Do you have your room key? Did you drink any water? Grab a coconut water when you can, alright? Stay hydrated. You don't want to wear yourself out in the first few hours. Pace yourself."

"Got it."

"You look amazing Floss, don't be nervous. Just go do this."

Etta and I spotted each other right away, though we'd only arranged our meeting by letter, like our ancestors might have done had they wanted to meet up in Vegas. She and I had exchanged close to two dozen letters in the year since we'd met, but we had never actually spoken since the last conference. I had forgotten what her voice sounded like.

"Flossie, you look great. I'm underdressed," she said as she attempted to smooth and straighten the oxford shirt that was tucked into her dark jeans. "Of course, I should have called you to find out what Cerulean people were wearing to this thing."

"Stop. Actually, I feel really weird in this. I'll go change."

"Very funny, Flossie," she laughed, and hugged me. "I can't believe I'm seeing you again. My pen pal!"

It was my first hug in months, and the first hug from a human I wasn't related to since I graduated from college. Earlier in the day, I'd brushed hands with the flight attendant as I accepted a drink, and touched shoulders with my seatmate on the flight, a banner day for my human contact metrics. I counted Etta as my closest friend outside Mom, Olivia, Fiona, and the clerks at the artisan meat shop; oh and Camila and Ginny, I guess, but I hadn't spoken to either of them in the last year, but if I got married today, in Vegas, that's what my wedding party would look like.

Etta was coming to the conference with a brand new promotion. I congratulated her, and she rolled her eyes. "It still hasn't made me fall in love with being an analyst, but it's better than getting fired. My life is totally boring, as I'm sure you figured out from my equally boring letters. I want to hear about every single thing you are doing, even if it is work stuff. I'm sure whatever is happening at Cerulean is a million times better than what I'm doing. I heard about your new office. It's a phone booth or something, right? What's that like?" Olivia was standing a few feet away sipping a complicated looking cocktail. She frowned, and mouthed, "Let's go!"

I put my attention back to Etta, who hadn't finished her list of questions. "Are Frank and Bob here? What are they working on? Are you allowed to say?"

Olivia was trying to catch my eye. I looked at her, and this time, she waved an arm around the room pointing at all of the people I was not talking to, then mouthed again, "Let's go!"

I shook my head slightly, and mouthed, "No." That's all it took. Etta stopped mid-sentence, and looked over her shoulder to see who'd caught my attention.

"Is everything okay?" she asked.

"Oh yeah, I saw someone from my office across the room, and they were waving me over, but I don't need to talk to them."

"Do you need to go?"

"No, it's fine, really. What were you saying?"

"No, let's go see your friend. Maybe you can introduce me?"

"They're gone now. You wouldn't want to meet them anyway. Seriously, please continue."

I was mortified, and stared directly into Etta's eyes so intensely as she talked, I'm sure I made it weird. I'd screwed up already. It was only a few minutes of mixing my own alternate world with the real world, and I couldn't do it. If we were the only people in the room, she would have already figured out there was something wrong with me.

We looked at our conference materials and mapped our schedules: welcome talk; company-wide mixer in the ballroom, then we'd stroll down the strip. We'd go to the same Accidental Analyst panel in the morning, then go our separate ways, so she could head to Manufacturing Yesterday, Today, and Tomorrow, and I would hit Online in an Offline World.

After a dry welcome from the Gamboge Managing Partner, a repetitive salute to the brilliance of Dave and the visionaries at Cerulean, too few canapes and too many drinks, Etta and I set off on our scheduled impromptu walk down the strip. I had counted on the cocktails to serve as the social lubricant I needed to be an interesting conversationalist. I'd practiced enough at home with couch rosé, couch sauvignon blanc and even couch merlot, but I couldn't focus. Looking at the curls of Etta's hair made me dizzy. My shoes felt like stilts. Someone within one hundred feet of me was eating an oyster, and the overwhelming smell of it propelled me out of the room, while clutching the sleeve of Etta's oxford shirt. I let her lead me on the maze toward the exit through the casino and out to the street. It took forever. The night air and lack of slot machine clatter should have brought some relief, but the lights and noises outside the casino were just as assaulting to the drunk senses, as the cacophony inside. People swirled all around me.

I made it twenty feet down the strip, before I told Etta I thought I might die from being outside, and needed to go back. She was on one side of me, and Olivia was on the other side of me, propping me up for the nine-mile walk back through the hotel casino and to the door of my room where I dug around for my room key, as the girls held me steady.

"Can I help you in there?" Etta asked with concern as I finally pushed the door open. "Are you going to be alright? Do you really think you are going to die? I can't leave you like this. Also I think there might be legal issues since you said 'die.'"

"Sorry I said that," I said, trying to pull myself together to sound as sober as possible. "I'm not going to die. The strip was freaking me out. All those lights, all those people with all of those giant test tubes full of what? Daiquiris?" I made a note to never drink a daiquiri. "We'll be fine. Thanks you guys."

"Flossie? You don't sound okay."

"Etta, tomorrow's early, I might have to catch up with you at lunch. Ugh, lunch. But we'll be fine, we've got this. You go get some sleep."

"You keep saying we. Do you have a roommate?"

"Oh, uh, you and me, like 'We've got this girrrrl, we've *got* this conference.'" Now, horrified and quickly sobering up, I tried to sound drunker than I was just to cover.

"Okay, well, for the record, I feel very uneasy leaving you like this."

"I'm going to drink water and then I'm going to bed. Seriously, go get some sleep. What is it, two in the morning? Three?"

"I'll be fine. It's ten thirty."

When Etta finally turned to go, I stumbled around the room until I had located one of the water bottles I had bragged about, and opened it, spilling only a quarter of it. Olivia was standing at the foot of the bed, smirking without any hint of the concern she had shown me just weeks ago.

"Well, that was smooth. I have to give it to you though, you really did try to party."

"Don't talk to me right now."

"Drink your water. I mean, the first night! The first night! You're that girl."

"What do you mean, 'that girl?'"

"The girl who shows up at college, and has never had any freedom, and goes wild the second her parents leave, and then pukes all over the place before people are even unpacked. Then, for the rest of the school year, she can never live down the first impression she set as 'that girl.'"

"Well, that was specific. You don't think anybody noticed, do you? I thought I was okay, I was just kind of wandering around with Etta, I didn't strip or dance on the table or anything. I think all of that wine I lonely-drink at home kept it from being worse than it could have been."

"Perhaps I shouldn't have encouraged you to hit the bar hard. Anyway, people probably noticed. Etta for sure noticed. And she definitely noticed how kind you were to keep including me in everything you were going to do . . . 'We'll be fine. We've got this.'"

"Do you think she thinks I'm crazy?" I was fumbling with the zipper on my dress, wishing I could ask Olivia for help.

"No, not yet." She sat and watched me fumble.

"What do you think of her?" I asked, pretending not to care.

I peeled off my shapewear and instantly felt better as the restrictions on my girdled body were mercifully loosened, allowing the alcohol more space to travel around and dissipate. That's what it felt like was happening in my body, anyway. I wished I knew more about science.

"She's cool, I guess. I mean she's very . . . earthy. She put up with all of your nonsense."

"She's a friend."

"I know, but she's obviously as lonely as you are too. Even though you were kind of an embarrassing mess, she still seemed thrilled to be out with you."

"She works a lot like I do. She doesn't have a pod. She's trying, you know? It's hard out there, Olivia."

"*You* feel better than you used to."

"I guess." I brushed a few of my teeth and splashed enough water on my face to effectively ruin a hotel washcloth with my faceful of makeup.

"Maybe she should make a friend of her own. A friend like me."

"Ha, right." I turned away from Olivia, who was now in her pajamas as well. I closed my eyes, but could still see ghost images of her spinning in the darkness.

"I'm serious. A new friend might take the edge off her isolation."

"I'm not talking about this right now, I need sleep."

"Okay, well drink your water and think about it."

"Think about what?"

"Telling her about me."

I sat up, just a little, "So you want me to tell one of the only human friends I have, that I have an imaginary friend? She won't be my friend for long."

"I don't get a judgmental vibe from her. I saw her outfit."

"Good night Olivia."

"Drink your water."

Olivia

I watched Flossie sleep. She hadn't eaten enough, and she certainly hadn't consumed enough water; she would feel terrible in the morning. She thought I was being unkind, but I really did worry about her. I'm strong and confident. I give great advice. I still haven't needed advice about anything, which is starting to get old. If we're being totally honest, which I always am, that evening, I started to feel a little one-note. I was ready to develop some depth, which I could only achieve with just the right amount of interesting vulnerabilities.

I had to half-carry Flossie back to the hotel room, sharing the weight with Etta, who couldn't even appreciate how much I was helping her. I'm the one who encouraged Flossie to hit the bar; which I did because I was supposed to, but I knew she was likely to make a mess of herself. For a second I thought she was serious when she said she might die on the sidewalk. I could picture her collapsing at the feet of an insurance salesman from Arizona. I've read about people like her withering away in their apartments and dying from blood clots. Essentially, they die because they have nowhere to go. I watch her when she falls asleep on the couch sometimes, wondering what would happen to me if she died?

Well, look at that . . . I am vulnerable. I'm totally independent, yet utterly dependent. Interesting.

CHAPTER FIVE

I found Etta in the back of the Accidental Analyst panel ball room. She had been looking at the door, and waved me over when I walked in.

"You made it! How are you feeling? I felt terrible leaving you like that. If you didn't show up, I was going to come check on you."

"I'm fine. Listen, I'm really sorry about last night. I hadn't been out in a while. I'm embarrassed."

"Don't be! I had a blast. I haven't been out either! Are you still up for going out tonight? Maybe now's not the time to ask. I'll wait until you've had coffee and eggs."

"Yeah, I'll go. I just thought you wouldn't want to after the idiotic way I acted last night. I promise, that won't happen again."

It happened again, kind of. Etta and I dressed up, and went to a steak house in the hotel. It was after two bottles of red wine, and insanely tiny portions of steak, and maybe one fingerling potato each when the crying started. But it was Etta crying, and I was thankful.

"God, Flossie, I'm losing my mind. I'm trying so hard, but I feel like I'm wasting away as a person. I don't connect with anyone at work. Getting a coffee is the highlight of my day. The baristas are always so nice, and they know my name. 'Hi Etta! The usual?' And I'm like, 'Hi Margaret, yes the usual.' And then I say, 'How's school Margaret? Are you ready for finals?' and then she says 'of course not,' and then I say, 'well, you'll be fine.' Then I go home and analyze that conversation for three hours."

"That's okay, Etta," I said, trying to sound reassuring. "I think what you are describing is called friendly conversation. That's not pathetic, it's polite, and normal, and part of the social contract."

"But then," she continued, still crying and seemingly un-affected by my wisdom and heartfelt assurance, "the next time I was in the coffee shop, which was like, later in the day, I said, 'Hi, William, I haven't seen you for a while, is everything okay?' and he said, 'Thanks for asking, I had to take some time off to go see my mom, she has cancer.' So what did I do? I come back the next afternoon and I'm like, 'Here's a card, William, and a muffin basket.' And I realized that in that moment, I'm a loser. I just gave a muffin basket to a guy who's surrounded by muffins all day. And he gives me a funny look, but says 'thank you.' I could have stopped there. But did I? Did I Flossie?"

People were starting to stare at us. Etta wiped her nose on her linen napkin.

"I'm guessing, no," I half-whispered.

"No! I didn't! Because the next week, I invited the baristas over for a dinner party. First they were quiet, I think trying to decide if I'm dangerous, or if I'm pathetic. And then William, realizing I'm just pathetic, says, 'Aw, that's so nice, but we're busy.' *We're* busy. He answered for everybody and they let him. They just nodded, and tilted their heads, and they all felt sorry for me. I had to start going to a cafe further away that serves terrible coffee. At the new place, I was worried that maybe I was on some kind of barista-stalker watch list, so I really tried to establish boundaries for myself. But the new baristas were so nice, too, Flossie. They started saying 'Hi Etta!' when I walked in, and my heart soared, and I'd get the butterflies. That is not an appropriate reason to get butterflies, I know that. I almost did it, again, Flossie. I almost invited that group of baristas out, too. I thought it would be fun to celebrate New Year's Eve with them. To stop myself, I went back to the first place, and all of my old non-friends had quit. I bounce around now, to be safe. I can't stay too long in any one place or it will get weird. Do you even still want to be sitting here with me right now? Maybe you shouldn't."

"The other day, I counted the neighborhood butchers on my very short list of friends. You're not weird, Etta."

"I am, Flossie." She took another gulp of wine before I could stop her. The more wine she drank the sadder she became. I would have to point out to Olivia, that at least I was a fun drunk. "You have it all together," Etta said, with wine dribbling down her chin. "I mean, you're smart, you're beautiful. You're sophisticated. If a person like you feels lonely, then what chance do I have?"

"I don't have it together. I don't. You saw me last night."

"You do."

"I don't." I took a huge gulp of wine, and leaned in. "I'm

lonely, too. So lonely."

"No. You're just being nice, and I appreciate it."

"Etta, I'm lonely. I'm desperate. I'm so desperate, I . . ."

"You're so desperate, you what?"

I leaned in. "I have an imaginary friend."

Etta stopped crying just a little bit and laughed. "You do not. Thanks though."

When I didn't laugh, she leaned in too. "Flossie, are you being serious right now?

"I am . . . I am being serious. I wish I wasn't. I can't believe I'm telling you this, I just . . . I thought you would understand. I was really lonely. I had to stop being so lonely."

"Was?"

"I mean, I am still . . . lonely I guess, but I feel better than I did."

"Wait, is everything okay? I mean, are you feeling alright?" She'd stopped crying. She wasn't amused, or relieved. She was concerned.

"Forget it, Etta, I've made a mistake. Please just forget it. Have some more wine."

"Wait, Flossie, I'm sorry, please tell me about it. I want to understand. I just had no idea you felt like I do. Please tell me. Please."

"You cannot tell anyone, Etta, I'm serious. I count you as a friend, and I hope you think of me as one too; enough of a friend, that you wouldn't tell anybody about this. Etta, please."

"God, no, Flossie, I won't tell.

"I do have an imaginary friend. I created her on purpose. I didn't have a breakdown. I mean, I had to have had some kind of breakdown, to have come to a decision like that, but I know she's imaginary. I don't feel like I'm by myself all the time. I can function. Being alone day after day with my thoughts was a nightmare."

Etta had stopped crying, and her mouth hung open. "Wow. Would you, uh, would you tell me about her? I mean, how does it work? Do you talk to her? Does she talk to you? Do you hear her and see her?" I hoped she wasn't mocking me.

"I talk to her, a lot. She's a good listener. But she talks too; she's smart, and she gives good advice."

"But the advice . . ."

"Yes, I know it's really advice from some part of me."

"Like the angel on your shoulder."

"I wouldn't necessarily call Olivia an angel."

"Olivia? Is she a devil?" Etta arched her eyebrows at me.

"No, not a devil either, just like a person. A friend . . . who listens."

"What does Olivia look like?"

"Well, I saw this woman at a cafe, on this weird low day I was having where I was really acutely aware of how alone I was, and how invisible I felt. Anyway, this woman—a real woman—walked in, and was so nice, and pretty, and put-together. She carried herself with such confidence, but not in a rude way. She seemed to know who she was, and then she looked at me and smiled . . . like a nice, friendly, not-weird-at-all, totally normal smile. But it was kind of a Namaste moment."

"The divine in me acknowledges the divine in you."

Etta listened carefully as I explained my arrangement with Olivia.

"That's brilliant."

"It's not brilliant, Etta, it's pathetic. I can't believe I'm telling you all of this. I really can't. You'll never want to talk to me again."

"That's not true at all, Flossie. I feel like you're the first person in this weird world that sees me and understands me. At this moment in time, drunk, and still starving after that $50 sliver of steak, I do not hate myself."

"I know what you mean," I said as thoughtfully and wisely as I could muster. "I don't hate myself either anymore, I guess."

"Since Olivia."

"Right."

"What about your family?"

I shook my head and gulped; I didn't feel like talking about my family.

Etta, perhaps sensing my discomfort, changed the subject to what should have been an even more uncomfortable topic. "Is Olivia here?"

"In this restaurant? Right now? No. She's in Las Vegas though."

"Um, Flossie, I don't know if you remember this but you kept saying 'we' last night. Was she your 'we'?"

I took a long sip of wine. "Yes, and I'm embarrassed about that. Olivia was actually the one who suggested I tell you about our little arrangement."

"Really?"

"She thought maybe . . . now please, I don't mean any offense, she thought maybe you could benefit from having a friend like her."

"Really?" Etta sat back in her chair, and quietly stared at the ceiling.

I hadn't thought this through. Etta had her own issues, she didn't need mine too. What was I doing? Trying to make her as weird as I was? She was impressionable and the only person with skin, and not related to me who had any interest in my life, and I was trying to ruin hers.

"Okay," she said, looking at me.

"Okay?"

"Yes, I'd like to try it. Why not?"

"Because it's weird, and there's a chance you could feel worse about yourself."

"I couldn't feel any worse about myself than I already do. Anyhow, you were just telling me how much it helped you. So, will you help me? You and Olivia? I've got to do something Flossie, or am I going to lose it. I'll try anything to stop feeling like this."

"I'll help you."

We brought cocktails from the bar to my room where we kicked off our shoes, and sat on the bed.

"Is she here?" Etta said, looking around as she sipped from her piña colada.

"Just a second, I don't know how this is going to work

exactly. She and I have never interacted with anyone else. So, let's see, Olivia?" Olivia sat in the chair across the room, sipping from a water bottle, wearing her Michigan sweatshirt and smirking. "Olivia's here. She's relaxing. She's wearing a University of Michigan sweatshirt—that's where she went to school, and her hair is piled on top of her head. It's dark hair, very shiny. She's tan, like all the time. Pretty much look at me, and then imagine someone the opposite of me."

"Alright. Um, hi Olivia."

"She says hi," I said with as much assurance as I could muster.

"Olivia, I'm Etta. Flossie has told me a little bit about you."

I translated, "Good things?"

"Yes, good things. I was hoping you and Flossie can help me. Flossie, am I doing this right? I do feel weird."

"That's because it is weird. Try this. Close your eyes, and picture someone you want to be friends with. Maybe a real person you used to know, maybe someone you just saw once, like me with Olivia, or maybe even a mix of people you know, or a movie star or something."

"Okay." She closed her eyes and leaned back on the headboard. Olivia watched her closely, more curious than amused.

A minute or so ticked by before Etta opened her eyes. "I don't know, Flossie, the only person popping into my mind is this awful cheerleader that went to my high school. I'm not very creative."

"Maybe try again. Perhaps the cheerleader is a good starting point . . . remember it's not actually her. Her personality is going to be whatever you want it to be."

Etta closed her eyes again and took a deep breath.

I waited before I asked, "Is it still that girl, Etta? The cheerleader?"

"Yes."

"What's her name?"

"Emma."

"Is that her real name? Do you want to give her a different name?"

"I'm good with Emma."

"Okay, Emma it is. Emma and Etta. Remember, she's your friend now. She's not mean to you. Maybe in high school, she always wanted to be your friend, but was intimidated by you."

"Ha! Intimidated by me?" Etta opened her eyes, and rolled them in my direction.

"Yes, because you're cool and smart. Seriously, stay with me here. Emma was just putting on a show for everybody in high school, pretending to be something she wasn't. But you guys met up again, at that coffee shop with the muffin guy, and instead of stalking the baristas, you and Emma ended up chatting, then you went shopping or something."

"Not shopping. I hate shopping. Hiking."

"Perfect. Hiking. And she's not superficial anymore, she's really cool. What does she do?"

"She teaches yoga."

"Yes, perfect! She teaches yoga. Is she here now? Can you see her?"

"I can!"

"What's she wearing?"

"She's wearing one of those little exercise tops, and yoga pants and her hair's all tied up, and she's just really peaceful and thoughtful." I was starting to see Emma take shape.

"OK, that's great. What did you talk about the day you went hiking?"

"She apologized for being mean in high school, and she told me that during college, she had to go to rehab, and she found herself and she was glad to see me so she could make amends. And she thinks running into me was a sign from the universe."

"What do you guys do when you hang out?"

"We do yoga. We hike. You would think she's a vegetarian, but she's not. She loves my chili. We ride bikes. She thinks maybe I should quit my job because sitting all day is terrible for me, and one day she'll start her own yoga studio, and I can run all of the business-end stuff."

"Etta, I love that, but make sure you don't quit your job to manage a yoga studio that does not exist."

Etta opened her eyes, and blushed. "I've gone too far, haven't I?"

"No, no, I'm sorry, I shouldn't have said that, but tell me something. How do you feel?"

"Weird. But, also, maybe . . . excited?"

It felt like I had been holding my breath since the moment I'd shared my secret with Etta. It was one thing to walk the line of my own sanity, but dragging someone else into my delusion felt like I was breaking a societal code that would land me in some kind of moral jail cell with a bunch of stage moms and people who protest affordable housing developments.

"Okay," I said, determined to be more of a life coach and less of a bad influence. "Let's try something. Emma's here, you should talk to her."

"What do I say?"

"What would you say to me? I can leave if you want."

"No, I want you to stay."

"But if it helps, Etta, I can see Emma based on what you've told me. And, Olivia's here too. I'll start. Hi Emma, I'm Flossie, and this is my friend Olivia. It's nice to meet you. Etta's told me a lot about you." I wasn't quite sure what to do next. Wait for Etta? I could see Emma, and I could see Olivia see Emma. I didn't get a warm fuzzy vibe from Olivia so I shot her a glance that begged her to please, please, please be nice.

I looked to Etta and nodded, encouraging her to lead the way.

"Um, she says hi. She wants to me to relax."

We continued our semi-awkward charade of a conversation for about an hour. Etta was more comfortable talking about Emma than talking to Emma. Emma's dad was a dentist, her mother a teacher. She was allergic to bell peppers, and had traveled through Southeast Asia and Australia. She was a dog companion and woke everyday before dawn. She felt passionately about helping people live their truth.

"What bugs you about Olivia?" Etta asked. She had started taking notes.

Olivia, who mostly sat quietly listening to Etta go on and on about Emma, sat up arched her eyebrows.

"Well . . ." I said, trying to look at Etta, and not to Olivia. "Not a lot. She's encouraged me to do things I wouldn't have otherwise done, for sure. I guess if I had to pick something, it would just be that I thought she would be sweeter, you know? She's kind of pushy. I guess it's good, because if she were too nice, we would only sit in the house eating ice cream and feeling sorry for ourselves . . . well, sorry for me."

"You could have called me, you know, when you were lonely," Etta said, reaching for my hand.

"I know, and thank you. If you lived closer, it would be different. Listen, we've got that Data Dump workshop in the morning. Go to your room, and talk to Emma without us sitting here staring at you. If you still want to be my friend in the morning, I would love that." The realization of what I had done came back over me, and I felt my chest tighten. I moved my arm from Etta's comforting grip. My breath was short, and I felt tears starting to form. "I will understand," I continued, "if you realize what a weirdo I am, and you bail. I will understand if you want to go back to the way things were and never speak of this night again. I can do that. I hope you don't hate me. I don't know what to say really, I'm just suddenly freaked out again, and I've done something terrible and irreversible, and I'm desperate for it to be okay. I don't know what a panic attack feels like, but I'm guessing it feels like what I'm feeling right now."

Etta grabbed my hand. "Flossie, breathe, it's okay. We're good.

I'm in this with you. I'm not going to tell anybody about tonight, or Olivia. I'm so thankful that you're trying to help me. Keep breathing, get some sleep. I'll see you at Data Dump, and I guess we'll know then if we ever talk about this again. Come on Emma, we gotta go." Etta winked at me, and disappeared through the door. I could see Emma follow her out.

I waited until I was sure they were out of earshot before I talked to Olivia. "So, what do you think?"

"Well, I find it interesting that you think I'm so pushy."

"You didn't hear the parts before that, where I credited you with saving me from oblivion?"

"Do you mean that?"

"I do, Olivia. I feel better since you came along, and I hope Etta can feel better too. I just hope I didn't screw it up with her . . . I kind of need her."

"You didn't screw it up, she's into it."

I waited anxiously at Data Dump the next morning, straightening my skirt and scanning the room, my thoughts undulating between worry and peace with what I'd done the night before. I'd left Olivia sleeping in the hotel room, anxious to see if Etta would show up, if she would show up with Emma, and whether or not she would talk to me.

People flowed into the conference room, eyeing each other as they do at the beginning of every workshop and panel. Some people are better than others at quickly scanning a nametag for the information they need, to make a quick decision as to whether the badge wearer is worthy of their time. My Cerulean badge didn't offer me the same congratulations and star status as it had the year before. Our counterparts relegated to normal size offices, doing their normal work, were probably sick of hearing about us. Not as many people wanted to sit next to me, or ask my advice, or introduce themselves. I pulled my jacket over my badge and focused on the door. The facilitator had stepped to the podium, and I had just about given up on Etta when I finally saw her jumble of fuzzy hair appear in the doorway. I smiled sheepishly and waved my hand just subtly enough that if she chose to ignore me, I could turn the wave into me shooing a bug. She smiled widely, and slid into the empty chair next to me. "Hey," she whispered with as much enthusiasm as a whisper could carry.

"I thought you weren't coming."

"I overslept. I stayed up most of the night, talking to Emma. I talked and talked and talked. I told her everything, like every single thing about me. Every secret. Every pathetic or depraved or whiny thing I've ever thought. I think I'm a little hoarse. Do I sound hoarse?"

"I can't tell, you're whispering."

"Listen to this, I got a letter from Etta today. Olivia came across the room to read over my shoulder.

> *Dear Flossie and Olivia,*
> *Let me just jump right into it, because I can't wait*
> *another second, and also I'm a little afraid I'll lose*
> *my nerve and not send this. Seeing you both in Las*
> *Vegas was the highlight of my year. I know it's only*

been about three weeks since the conference, but you bringing Emma into my life, has changed the content of every day since. I feel lighter, like a new person. Does that make sense? I didn't realize how far I'd let myself go down a hole of self pity and resentment. Sure, sometimes I feel weird, because I know she's not real, but at the same time, who cares? Emma is real to me. The happiness I feel is real. I don't feel alone. I was lonely, you guys . . . LONELY! I had never been a lonely person. I was always around other people. I had so many followers and friends online too, and I totally took it all for granted. I'm not taking anybody for granted anymore. So I wanted to let you know how much I appreciate you.

I'm doing yoga every day. Emma makes me, and next month I'm doing a cleanse—no meat, no sugar, no booze, which is probably what every month is like for most people in San Francisco. I'm going to teach her how to ski. She's never been. I use your phone trick, and we go places all the time. I feel totally free.

I talked to my brother. Did you know I have a brother? Robert. He's been off in his own world for so long. He's a sweet kid, a bit of a stoner, but he never really goes out of his way for anybody else. Anyway, when I talked to him, he said I sounded different . . . happy. He asked my secret, because he's going through a rough patch. His girlfriend broke up with him, and

all of his old friends are traveling or moving or get-
ting married and having babies, and he's an editor
who works from home. He's afraid he might need
to move in with our dad. Do you think I should tell
him? You know, TELL HIM? I won't mention you.
Anyway. Let me know what you think.
With love and so so so much gratitude,
Etta

"Well, look at us. And look at her handwriting, it's so much better." Olivia took a bite of an apple.

"She does sound happier. I'm so relieved, you don't even know."

"Do you think she's going to tell her brother? Do you care?"

"I guess I don't care."

"What if she tells somebody at work? What if she gets fired or ostracized, and then it comes back to you? What then?" Olivia asked through a mouthful of apple.

"She wouldn't throw me under the bus."

"She probably wouldn't intend to, but what if she does?"

"Oh no, do you think my all of my friends will turn against me?"

"Very funny, but the jerks you work for are all about image. They're all podded up and won't understand. You'd be gone in a hot minute."

"You don't know Etta, like I do."

"And how well is that really?"

"Well enough."

Flossie turned fourteen this month, and she starts high school in the fall. In four years, she'll be the same age I was when I met Tom. Because she's still so tiny, I think Tommy has a hard time accepting that she's a full-fledged teenager and we are becoming less interesting and less tolerable by the day. She's smart, but still very innocent, and if I'm being brutally honest with myself, I am also having a hard time with how fast time is going. I don't love that she's on her phone all the time. In fact, I kind of hate it. I was ok losing her to Harry Potter or to her own imagination, but I hate seeing her stare into the stupid thing for hours on end. Then I look around and everybody her age is doing the same thing, and I start to understand how Tom can get so snarly about kids these days.

Camila stayed over last weekend and I don't think the girls said ten words to each other. They watched different makeup tutorials on their phones for hours. I offered to help them do real makeup, and they said "no thanks" and kept watching their videos. Then when they ran out of tutorials they watched cat videos, which I admit, are really addicting. They tethered themselves to the wall with their phone chargers, and whenever I walked by one of them would kind of flop over knocking over the stray popcorn kernels that had collected in their hair and on their stomachs.

I look at my phone a lot, but it's for work, and that's how I get my news, and keep up with my friends, and find recipes. Looking at my college roommate's kids' graduation photos is totally different than hours of makeup tutorials.

CHAPTER SIX

I hadn't laid eyes on Bob or Frank in a month. Fiona was no longer the receptionist because she was made a vice president and sent to Southern California to plant the office of Cerulean LA. With Bob and Frank's help, she was looking for a tiny office with just the right vibe. They had narrowed the real estate choices down to a former operating room in a once-abandoned "hopefully haunted," hospital-turned-live/work space; a former guest room in a once-abandoned, *definitely* haunted, hotel-turned-live-work space; and a beach bungalow where Leonardo DiCaprio had reportedly once visited.

I was certain Dave had forgotten I existed, which is what made my promotion to senior analyst such a surprise. Olivia was certain that her obsession with my work-life balance, and the energy that came from leaving the house once in a while was what made my work shine enough to not be forgotten. She and I drove down the coast, we went back to the museums I frequented when I first moved to the city. We went out to movies and restaurants where we were regularly surrounded by other people. We went shopping every week, and to spin class, and across the bay to get sunshine when we needed it. She dragged me to a bar, where I met a guy. It was quickly obvious he and I didn't have anything in common, and he almost immediately excused himself to go the restroom, never to be seen again, but I did technically meet him.

"What are you doing?" Olivia shrieked as I made my way for the door of the bar, once it became clear that Logan had made a break for it. "He's coming back, Floss! He had to pee! It happens."

As much as I was I was getting outside, I insisted that Olivia and I celebrate my promotion at home, with a pitcher of sangria, and an unapologetic binge-watch of *Eleanor*—"the sexy, edgy dramatization of one of our feistiest first ladies." I needed a dose of salaciousness.

Sangria goes down easily, and Olivia and I were talking, loudly, and laughing hysterically over Eleanor—not at her, but with her.

And then, I heard, it . . . a knock at the door. It was too late for a delivery. I peered through the peephole to see Ty on the other side.

"Hey, there neighbor," he said cheerily when I pulled open the door.

"Flossie," I reminded him.

"I know that," he fibbed, fidgeting.

"I just heard you in here and realized we hadn't talked for a while, and so I thought I would say hi."

"Are we too loud?"

"I don't mean to interrupt since you have company." He

peered over my shoulder into my apartment.

"I was . . . I mean, my company's not here. I was talking to a friend . . . in Chicago."

"Oh, well, I just wanted to say hi. Sorry, I'll let you get back to it."

I looked over to Olivia, who pointed at her own glass of sangria.

"Ty, I made sangria and I'm watching *Eleanor.*"

"*Eleanor*? I love that show. What episode? What about your Chicago friend?"

"Episode two, and I hung up."

"Two? You are so behind!" and with that he was in my apartment. A human person was visiting me socially in my apartment.

"Don't tell me anything. I'm serious. No spoilers," I said shutting the door behind him.

"She's a historical figure, so I'm sure you have at least some idea of what happens."

He was headed to my kitchen. "You have a lot of glasses for just you and Eleanor."

"Yeah, well, I . . . I use a lot of glasses." I pulled a clean one from the cupboard, poured his sangria, and moved to the couch.

He took a seat a few feet away, and won at least a few points by going out of his way to reach for a coaster on the coffee table. "I like what you've done with your place, very cheery. Very feminine."

"Thanks."

"I guess mine kind of says, 'busy intellectual lumberjack.'"

"That's how you think of yourself? As a busy intellectual lumberjack?" I gulped my sangria.

"No! If you were to go into my apartment, that's who you would guess lived there. No, no, I think of myself as a sexy, intellectual lumberjack."

By the end of episode three, when Eleanor meets Lorena Hickok, I was dozing off, but Ty was loosened up, and not shy at all about providing a running commentary to the show.

My eyes snapped open, when I heard him say, "Well, you probably have an early day tomorrow." I sat up and checked to make sure I hadn't drooled. "Sorry, sangria makes me sleepy. Yeah, I guess it will be early, but I'm sure you have stuff to do also . . . though I haven't see your face in the news lately."

"Oh, I'm taking a break," he said as he stacked our plates and glasses. "I was just getting so burned out. All of my causes were running together, and if you do it long enough you can't take any client without there being a conflict of interest with another client. Every cause has a counter-cause, and I can't do it all. Having that much passion about everything takes a lot out of a person."

"I haven't done a lot of passion-mustering, myself. What are you doing with your time off from being passionate?"

"I was going to travel."

"Oh yeah, why didn't you?"

"I live in a major travel destination, so I'm just having my existential crisis right here, in beautiful San Francisco while exploring neighborhoods I've never been to before. I'm saving my money and Rio for when I don't hate myself so much."

"Hate yourself? Why do you hate yourself?"

"I don't, I'm amazing. It's just a saying."

"That's not a saying."

"If I did hate myself, I don't really, but if I did, you wouldn't understand anyway. You always have people over, and you have your sorority job. My career was all-consuming though, and ever since I took a break from work, I'm kind of useless and invisible. I haven't felt invisible since I was a kid. Before you say anything, yes I have considered the possibility that my sparkling personality has alienated people who think I shine too bright. But it feels like that list of people is long. Honestly, Flossie, I've been in my apartment for daaaaaaayyyyyys by myself. Going crazy. I don't know. You don't want to hear this. Why am I telling you this? I should go." He took the plates to the kitchen, and with a sudden and complete lack of braggadocio, he looked like a fourth grader waiting to be picked for dodgeball.

"Nope, Ty, I get it," I said as I blocked the door. Why did I say that? Could I not let even one person think I had it all?

"Right."

"You don't know me yet. I'm not a sorority girl type."

"Right."

"Listen, why don't you come over tomorrow night? We didn't finish *Eleanor* and it's getting good."

"That Eleanor, what a minx."

"I know, right? So will you come?"

"You know," he said rubbing his hand on his chin, like he was thinking in a cartoon, "After all that oversharing, I should say no; otherwise, I'm just over-eager, and not at all mysterious. But, fine, I'll come. I'll bring wine."

"Come for dinner, I'll make Chicago dogs. Bring your own pickles if you want them, though."

"Perfect. Hot dogs are so hot right now. And I heard there's an amazing, impossible-to-get into pigs-in-a-blanket place. What kind of wine goes with Chicago dogs?

"The liquid kind."

"Well that was weird," Olivia said from her spot across the room after Ty closed the door.

"I mean, sure, he's a little annoying," I whispered although I'd already heard his door shut, "but I felt really bad for him. It was kind of thrilling, though."

"It's thrilling to having a sad, asexual man in your apartment?"

"What? No. He is kind of asexual isn't he? He's vulnerable, but we shouldn't bring that up. No, it's weirdly thrilling to feel sorry for someone who's obviously worse off than me. You don't think he thinks I asked him on a date do you? I just felt sorry for him. Anyway, you're the one who suggested I invite him in."

"Yet another charity case for you to adopt. You're a loner magnet."

"You think so? You think I'm a magnet? I'm going to bed before you ruin my good mood."

The next evening, Ty greeted me by telling me my apartment smelled like an old man's car. I greeted him back by informing him that what he was smelling was the dinner I'd been preparing for him.

"Sorry. I don't know why I stay that stuff," he said, shaking his head. "I think nothing smells more appetizing than the inside of an old man's car. It was very nice of you to invite me over. Here I brought rosé . . . it felt like the most appropriate wine for this dinner since it's closest to hot dog color."

"That makes sense, thank you," I said taking the hot dog-colored bottle from him.

I didn't pour a glass for Olivia, and she frowned at me as she went to the freezer for the vodka.

"So, Ty, I don't think you've even told me where you're from." I handed him the hot dog I'd assembled.

"Because I don't tell anybody. I'm from Reno, but it doesn't really go with my personality. I just don't need people looking at me differently because of that. I really get, like, how people can feel they were born the wrong gender. I don't feel like I'm from Reno, you know? I should have been born here or LA, or New York."

"Yes, it sounds exactly the same thing as gender dysphoria. How have you lived with that all of your life? You are very brave."

He made a pinched face at my sarcasm. "Wow, you're sassier than I remember when we first met."

"You weren't very nice."

"Now I'm vulnerable and you're not very nice. This hot dog is amazing. I mean, I want to write a poem for this hot dog. Now come on, we need to see if Eleanor and that reporter lady fall in love."

"Déjà vu," I said as I lay back on the couch with the headache that you can only get from enjoying two glasses of rosé, and three hot dogs.

Two hours later, Ty turned off *Eleanor*, and looked at me.

"Are you leaving?" I asked.

"No, just chatting."

I sat in the silence, suddenly uncomfortable because we were doing exactly no chatting.

"See," he said, playfully shoving my shoulder, "this is what I imagined when I moved to the city. This experience. Right now."

"I'm not going to have sex with you," I said matter-of-factly.

"I hope not," he laughed.

"Oh, are you gay?" I know I sounded relieved.

"No, I don't know, but I just meant that this is the exact scenario I imagined for myself. Having a super casual weeknight hangout with my alcoholic, foul-mouthed, man-crazy neighbor, but with none of the sexual tension. And me not wanting to hook up with you, does not automatically make me gay. Hook-ups are a dime a dozen and honestly, so boring. You're much more interesting as a friend. Friends are more valuable anyway . . . rare, you know? Like when our moms all watched *Sex and the City* and they tried to decide who in their book club was the Charlotte, and who was the Samantha, and everybody secretly hoped their friends thought of them as the Carrie. Anyway, there were a million guys in and out of their lives—the *Sex and the City* girls, not our moms—but they always met for brunch no matter what. They knew it was their friendship that was important."

"First of all, I'm not foul-mouthed, and I'm not man-crazy, and I'm just gonna say it, I'm totally a Carrie. And we're friends? I mean, you'd like to be . . . friends?"

"Aren't we? I just kind of thought, like maybe we bonded over *Eleanor* and our living situation, and we're close enough in age, and two hangouts in a row? I just assumed. Also, the previous tenant was a million years old and didn't speak English and died in what I guess is your bedroom. We didn't really hang out. Is she haunting this place? It seemed like maybe she had unfinished business. But anyway, you're probably in a pride, or a pod, or clique or whatever they're calling them now."

"No."

"No? No you're not being haunted, or no you're not in a pod? Because since I've been around more, I hear you in here talking all the time. I haven't seen anybody come over. But it sounds like a party. I've been really jealous. See? We have to be friends because I keep telling the popular girl embarrassing stuff about me. I guess, going from feeling like I was the center of the universe to disappearing and nobody caring, just sucked the air out of me. I'm having a hard time adjusting. You wouldn't understand."

"Listen, I don't hate that you keep calling me the popular girl or the cheerleader or whatever. But, you should know, it's not true."

"You're just saying that to make me feel better."

"No, I'm alone too. I'm lonely too."

"Who are you always talking to in here? You *are* being haunted."

"Don't worry about it, trust me."

"Who are you talking to? Please tell me it's Mrs. Lee's ghost. Please tell me that. I want it to be that so badly."

"It's worse than a ghost."

"A demon? That's cooler, but you're right, it's worse."

"Worse."

"Worse than a demon? A poltergeist. Honestly, I'm not sure if that's worse or where it falls on the supernatural spectrum."

"I have an imaginary friend," I blurted it out to shut him up. He'd pestered my biggest secret out of me.

"You're messing with me."

I shook my head, feeling immediate, acute, profound regret. Maybe I could take it back and tell him I was messing with him about not messing with him.

"What? You can't be serious." He stared at me.

"I am ... serious. You believe ghost, demon and poltergeist— not necessarily in that order—but not imaginary friend? I was so desperately lonely, I needed someone to talk to, out loud. I hated myself too, Ty. I tried everything, well not really, but I tried a lot of things, mostly I tried work. Work didn't fix it. My voice box was about to atrophy. I was getting really bitter, like I'd been abandoned by my own generation. It just wasn't happening for me. Life wasn't what I thought it was going to be. I needed to take the edge off."

Words were spilling out of my face, and I couldn't stop them. It felt much different than telling Etta. I was in my own home, but I didn't feel any kind of home field advantage. I didn't really know Ty. And the blank look on his face didn't give me any clues about what he was thinking. The words came even faster, fueled by the discomfort that hung in the air. "My friend is Olivia, and she keeps me company, and she makes me feel better. There, I said it. Do you feel better now? Are you going to call the authorities and have me taken for my own good? Is this the big "gotcha" moment you've been waiting for? Two nights together of you telling me how vulnerable and lonely and pathetic you are and you get me to tell you the most embarrassing thing a supposedly sane person can admit. Now you know. Do you feel better now?"

When he started to laugh, I started to cry.

"Oh, Flossie. No, none of that. I'm sorry." He dropped to his knees in front of me, hesitating only for a second before pulling me into a hug where I snot-cried all over his super soft t-shirt. He squeezed tighter. I liked my Etta hug, but this, not-from-a-relative hug # 2 made me feel like an overstuffed tube of emotionally wrought toothpaste, being squeezed by a red-headed man-child.

When my sobs slowed, Ty patted my back and repeated, "It's okay. It's okay. It's okay." I broke from his hug when my neck started to cramp.

"I'm sorry," I muttered, looking at his soaking t-shirt.

"No, I'm sorry, I just didn't know what to say, and I get paid to always know what to say. You know, most people try pot, or cocaine, or skydiving, or sex when they need to take the edge off, but whatever. The people who pretend to have it altogether— they're the freakiest of them all."

I chuckled, and more snot came out. I attempted to even things out by using my own shirt to wipe my nose.

"Classy. What does your special friend think of that?"

"This is a nightmare. This is officially a nightmare."

"I'm sorry, I'll stop." He climbed from his spot in front me back to the couch. "You're obviously vulnerable, why don't you tell me what's going on? This is way more interesting than *Eleanor*."

And so I told him. I told my annoying neighbor about Charlie, and Kira and Kelsey, and Fiona and Etta and my walk through the Financial District, and about the woman who walked into the coffee shop that day. I even told Ty how for a little while, Olivia thought he actually liked me, but then we forgot about him because we didn't see him for so long.

"Wow, so, this is your lifestyle now."

"I didn't mean for it to be that way, but yes."

"The best things in life, aren't usually what you intend to happen. I respect your choices, Flossie."

He left me with a hug that night, and a promise he would drop by again. The next day, I sent Olivia to her office and I threw myself into my own work. I didn't want to think about what could happen now that I'd told multiple people about Olivia, and I certainly didn't need her hanging around, staring at me all day, shaking her head, and reminding me that I'd given my deepest secret to the mouthy weirdo across the hall. If I wasn't so full of worry about what he might do to torture me with this, I might have experienced relief, perhaps even more relief than when I'd told Etta. My entire imagined existence was now even more seeded in reality, and acknowledged by another living, breathing human being with skin I could touch.

Twenty-four hours after he came over with the hot dog wine, Ty knocked on my door.

I opened the door a crack and stared at a spot over his shoulder instead of looking into his eye, "Did we have plans? I'm in the middle of work."

"Can we talk for just a minute? Before I chicken out?"

"You did call the authorities after all, but you feel bad, so this is the warning to get myself together, or head for the hills before they come to take me away?"

"No, Flossie, can I come in?" His hands were shaking.

"Are you okay?" I forgot about my looming detainment.

"Yes," he said, taking a seat. "I've been thinking about what you told me . . . your lifestyle choices. And, I want in."

"You want in to what?"

"The lifestyle."

"Lonely spinster workaholic?"

"No, the imaginary friend thing. It needs a better name. You said you helped your friend create hers and they're happy as clams, right?"

"Yeah, what are you asking? You want me to help you create a friend?"

"Yes, I do. I have some ideas though."

"Are you serious, or are you messing with me?"

"I hate being alone Flossie. I'm terrible at it. I can't hang out here and watch you work every day. I can't go to a bar every day.

The people I know through my causes obviously don't need me. Anybody I ever saw socially have gotten into those stupid little pod things without me. Singles groups are the worst, and you never know what you are going to get. I miss social media so much, you don't even know. It will come back right? People can't keep up this fake interpersonal nonsense forever, can they? I mean, what have I got to lose?"

"I don't know if I can drag you into this. There's a very good chance you will feel worse about yourself and question all of your life choices. You might feel embarrassed all the time, even when you're at home by yourself."

"You don't feel like that.

"I did for a while."

"But it passed. And it passed for that other girl."

"It did for us, but there's no guarantee it would for you."

"I still want to do it. Help me."

"Fine, but I'm working right now."

"Work-life balance, girl. Put the work away. Is your friend here?"

"No she's working, too."

"You're no fun."

"Give me a minute to close out some stuff." When I returned to my couch, Ty stretched out on my couch with his eyes closed. "Are you sleeping?" I was annoyed that I'd put my work away for nothing.

"No, I'm preparing for visualization. Visualization is very powerful. I visualized myself getting out of Reno, and I did.

And then I visualized myself as a successful person, and I was. I mean, I am!" he corrected himself while thrusting a finger into the air for emphasis. "Now I'm visualizing next-level me, loved, beloved, happy, free, and unfettered by boring social constructs."

"And as a grown man with an imaginary friend."

"Yes, and not just any imaginary friend, but the best one. Let's get to it." He closed his eyes again.

"Alright," I said, trying to remember what I'd said to Etta in Las Vegas when we were conjuring up Emma. "Let's start with the easy stuff. What does this person look like? Who pops into your head? Who's going to chill with you and have a beer on a Thursday? Who are you going to look for at the bar, when it's super busy? Who's going to sit quietly and listen to you talk about your day? Who's going to sleep on your couch because you guys stayed up too late shame-watching every episode of *Sex and the City*? Who's going to give you really good advice? What's something you would do on a Wednesday?"

"Make homemade chowder."

"You are not marrying this person. You're just hanging out. You want to make homemade chowder with them?"

"Yes."

"Fine, homemade chowder. Who is it?"

"He's definitely black. I feel like my best friend would be a really cool black guy."

"What's his name?"

Ty lay with his eyes closed, lips pinched from the stress of the task at hand, and the physical demands of weighing his options. I retreated to the kitchen to pour myself a glass of wine while he thought.

"You know," I yelled from the kitchen, "people take less time to name their human babies!"

"This is huge, Flossie, his name is going to totally shape who he is. It can't be boring. I need to be able to extract a really organic nickname from it. But he's an entrepreneur, so it should have a mature, classic vibe, but nothing stuffy or uptight. He's a good person. He's really cool, and he's really funny, but with a dry, quiet sense of humor. And he makes fun of me a lot, but it's a sign of love and respect. Jason? I could call him Jay. Jordan? Will? Trey. That's it. Trey." Ty's eyes sprang open.

"Alright then, Trey it is."

"What's next?"

"What's he like? Where's he from? What are his hobbies? What's his favorite food? What does he drink?"

"Let's see, he's a DJ, obviously, and an entrepreneur, I'll have to think about what kind of an entrepreneur. He's from a swanky suburb, like Mill Valley, but he doesn't tell anybody that, like I don't tell anybody I'm from Reno. Oh, he speaks French and Japanese. He likes whiskey and lemonade. He's perfected paella, and that's how he closes the deal with his dates. But he's not a misogynist, or gross, more of a romantic. He reads a lot, and is a photographer, and is a really talented painter."

"He sounds like quite the Renaissance man. How did you meet? What's your backstory?"

"Hmmm," he said, sitting up and finally taking his feet off

my couch. "I was working on rescuing a little beat poetry place that he loved in North Beach, and we worked together, and ended up taking it back from the clutches of evil developers. And then he did a spoken word piece about it."

"Can you see him Ty? What's he wearing?"

"He's got red pants on. And a black sweatshirt, and basketball shoes."

"Cool, okay, well, let's say Trey is on the couch. What would you say?"

Ty swallowed hard and then just stared into the emptiness at the other end of the couch. I cleared my throat, and looking in the same direction said, "You know what? I'll start. Hi Trey, I'm Flossie. This is my place, I'm Ty's neighbor."

"Hey, man, thanks for coming over," Ty's voice cracked and his initial enthusiasm was nowhere to be found.

"This is the weirdest, hardest part, Ty . . . talking to them out loud for the first time. You feel stupid, right? Crazy?"

"A little bit."

"Look, it's normal to feel like that."

"Nothing about this feels normal."

"You'll get over it. Go home, hang out with Trey, see how it works for you."

"You won't try to eavesdrop on me making an idiot of myself, will you?"

"No, I don't want to know your innermost thoughts. You're Trey's problem now."

Dear Flossie,

Sorry it's been so long since I've written. I'm glad you told Ty. It's a hard thing to keep major parts of your life a secret. My brother and his new friend have hit it off quite well. They sit in the dark all day and play video games, but they seem really happy.

Emma and I are having a blast. The job is fine, and I'm so happy that it's the not first thing I think about when I wake up. For a while my brain was used mostly for work, or wondering what I did wrong in my life, or coming up with talking points I could use with the barista that day.

Emma and I are off to Hawaii! Can you believe it? I've never been. I'm excited to see the sun, and para-sail, and eat pineapple until I am disgusted by pineapple. We'll send you a card from there.

Please give our love to Olivia,

Etta and Emma

CHAPTER SEVEN

My June birthday had not felt the same since the heady, Great Gatsby-esque era of social media when our birthdays were trumpeted to the masses through our online profiles, and we were bathed in virtual balloons, confetti, shallow "HBD!"'s, and "happy b-day"'s, and it was revealed to the world who among our "friends" truly knew how to spell our names. But we felt loved, or at least liked and remembered. Once everybody became too busy keeping up with the Joneses by not keeping up with the Joneses, birthday fervor was lost to the generation ahead of us who had learned to write special days on calendars.

But when my big day rolled around again, my twenty-fifth, peonies arrived with a card signed "All my love to my precious girl, Mom." The delivery guy didn't say Happy Birthday and Ty wasn't even home to stick his head out of his doorway to see what had arrived, and then to ask what the flowers were for, and then to offer to buy me a pizza and a bottle of rosé to celebrate. I put the gorgeous and expensive pink peonies in the window, and as I adjusted them so they would be visible from the street below, I heard Ty's door open and close, and then a hardy laugh.

He and Trey had been somewhere, and they hadn't been over to see me in days. Inspired, but not proud, I knew Ty represented my best shot at not being completely pathetic on my birthday.

An hour later, I heard Ty's bell ring, and the ensuing discussion in his doorway. I smoothed my top and my hair, and waited for the knock at the door.

"These were delivered to me by mistake," said Ty, "they had my apartment number and everything, but they're yooooours! Happy Birthday!! I snooped. These are from your office, which is nice . . . you made it sound like the people there sometimes forget you exist. But shame on you, you didn't tell me it's your birthday! What are you doing tonight? Should we grab Trey and Olivia and leave this building for a change?"

"Well, I guess; but nothing fancy."

"I haven't worked in forever . . . it won't be fancy."

I wore a dress, and Ty smelled as if he had bathed since we had parted ways that afternoon. We shared a ride downtown, then crammed ourselves in the entrance of Herd, so we could then wait for an hour to feast on grass-fed buffalo burgers and rosemary beer. A casual observer might assume we were on a second date, maybe a third.

"For a newly introverted world, people still go out a lot," I said as I shifted yet another time so somebody else could squeeze into the waiting area.

"They're all connecting in person. I hate it. They're all so smug about it. Look at them, laughing and looking each other in the eyes, and being totally present. It's gross. It's unnatural."

"I know. Hey, how are things with Trey?"

"Good, he's got so much wisdom, you know? Like, street wisdom."

"He's from Marin County, and he went to Yale."

"Oh yeah, no I changed that part. He's from a really rough neighborhood in LA, but went to Yale. He's a totally inspirational success story. I'm glad we're out, yes to celebrate the glorious miracle that was your birth but also because I really want to talk to you about something."

"I'm intrigued. What is it?"

"Maybe not here exactly, there are a lot of people."

"Give me a hint. It's not about sex is it?"

"Seriously, what is wrong with you? Why do you always assume that's the next thing I'm going to say? I have never brought up sex in any of our conversations, ever. Can we please, going forward, just assume that whatever I'm about to tell you, or ask you, is not sexual, like, at all?"

"Fine."

"It's about our IFs."

"Our IFs? Is this a meta, existential discussion about our paths and callings and our human tendency to constantly question our place in the universe, and the seemingly infinite parallel realities we create with every decision we make?"

"What? I don't think any of the words you just said go together. No, our IFs, Trey and Olivia. Our Imag-"

"Got it, *I* dot *F* dot." I looked at Olivia, who, leaning on my version of Trey, seemed bored and tired from standing in her heels.

"Yes. I think you stumbled on to something pretty huge; you, mentally fragile, socially stunted birthday girl, you."

"Seriously, what are you talking about?"

"I think we shouldn't hoard our IFs."

"Hoard them?"

"When I'm out walking with Trey, I look around, and people are alone everywhere. Half of them give me this eye contact that says, 'talk to me please, I'm dying over here.'"

"And do you talk to them?"

"Ew! No! Tell me something. Of the people you know who have IFs, how many are happier now?"

"All of them. Although it sounds like Etta's brother has kind of a destructive relationship with his. Etta said that he and his IF haven't come out of the house in weeks. She's afraid he's going to have a stroke or something."

"But he's probably pretty happy in there?"

"I guess."

The harried hostess, called, "Tea! Tea!" and once we figured out it was Ty, led us to a tiny table tucked between two over-crowded boisterous groups of attractive, well-dressed people and their steins of lavender and rosemary beers. Olivia and Trey looked annoyed at the table for two we'd taken, and made their way to the bar.

"Okay, where were we? Oh yes, I've been journaling about my experience with Trey, and it's incredible how he's already changed my life."

"He and Olivia are at the bar by the way."

"Flossie, listen, this is important. I need you on board. Or at least I feel that I need your permission . . . I'm almost certain, you've started a revolution. Well, you're about to, with my help. Or I'm about to with your help."

"A revolution?"

"A social revolution. You're the mother of a new subculture, and I want to be the father. Oh Flossie, I've always wanted to create a subculture. This is it. This is our chance. It's perfect. It's weird. It's subversive. It's going to uproot social norms. It's kind of sexy and certainly not for everybody. It will be a little controversial, but it's about community, but also, the anti-community."

"Calm down, Ty. I still don't know what you're trying to ask me, or tell me, or what you want from me."

"I want to go public with the IFs, but in a really organic grassroots way. I want to find other people like us. Successful, attractive, otherwise perfectly normal people, who are basically social refugees now because of all these pretentious pod people. We'll find a few early adopters, and introduce them to the lifestyle. Trey and I are writing the first draft of an article about it, but we want you on board. I know some under-the-radar, but not too-under-the-radar outlets who would go crazy for a new subversive lifestyle to champion. This is your creation. You deserve to be there, you should get the credit, well at least a lot of the credit."

"You're kidding me," I growled, looking around to make sure our neighboring tables weren't paying attention to us. Of course they weren't. "You want to go public with this? I can't! I have a career, and family that needs to think that I am doing just fine."

"And that's it, Flossie. That's the point. You have more than a lot of people do. We can't be the only ones adrift out there."

"They have services out there that help people meet and function."

"Those 'gaggles for stragglers' services are not the same. Some of the stragglers are actual freaks who would be stragglers no matter what social landscape they were in. So when those blind date groups happen, there are bound to be total misfits-for-a-reason who mess up the dynamic, and then the normal people get frustrated and more discouraged than before, and then they're set adrift again—lonely as hell."

"Sounds like you speak from experience?"

"I do. Yeah, I didn't say anything earlier, but I paid a lot of money to a service to get placed in a pod of my peers."

"The Pod People? They're a Cerulean client."

"Yeah, well they suck. Has that come up in your analysis? Because it should. Anyway, at the first gathering, one girl spent the whole night gnawing on her fingers, not her fingernails mind you, but her fingers. Another guy was so nervous, he couldn't stop farting. Another guy seemed cool, but he excused himself to go to the bathroom, and never came back. And there was a really beautiful woman, I think she's why the guy was farting, anyway, she'd just moved to San Francisco, but she was just flat out mean. It was awful. Trey is better than every single one of them. So will you do this with me? You could be our queen . . . the fairy godmother of an entire movement."

"Or I could lose my job, and not only become more of a social pariah, my family would get a conservatorship to take care of me, and move me back to Chicago, and spend every moment managing my psychiatric care."

"Maybe, but probably not. No wonder this imaginary friend thing is working so well for you—your imagination is very thorough and super-specific. I think you should do this. You can either write the article with me and Trey, or you can let the article be at least in part, about you."

"I don't know. I'll have to think about it. Some days, I can't even believe I ever told you and Etta in the first place."

"Just think of how many people you can help. You even work at that company that's kind of to blame for this weird atmosphere. Like those banks who started the housing crisis, and those other banks that started the next housing crisis. You created this extroverts' nightmare. You have an obligation to try to fix it, don't you think?

Two episodes of *Eleanor*, four shared bottles of rosé, and two spaghetti and meatballs dinners later, I read Ty's article.

What IF?

By Ty Banks

It started for me, when I closed my eyes. That's when I became free, truly free, from my unexpected oppressor, loneliness.

I had been so tired . . . tired from a career that provided money, notoriety, and a platform for my voice to be heard, as well as the honor of using my voice to speak for others whose voices weren't as loud as mine. It also gave me all the fulfillment that came with being out there in the world, among the people. I hadn't even turned thirty and I knew to my core that I needed a break. The plan was to step back from the work, the noise, and the parts of my life that were overwhelming, taxing, and exhausting. I didn't intend to take a break from my whole life, mind you, but that's what happened. I hadn't realized what a precarious house of cards I'd constructed for myself to live in with all of the grace and self-awareness of a wild dog.

My social life, my day-to-day existence, my happiness, habits, and emotional well-being were so intertwined, and downright dependent on my career, that once I extracted myself from the work, everything else fell apart without even the satisfaction of a powerful explosion or the plume of smoke, dust, and rubble that would have served as the evidence that something significant had once been there. No; instead each card simply fluttered and floated away, wispy, light, insignificant, and with none of the weight I thought the parts of my life had carried.

San Francisco, the city I love, and live in, and fought to preserve and also to progress, seemed to move on fine without me. The people I interacted *with regularly—people I thought were my friends—didn't bother returning my calls. Nobody inquired about why, when I had everything going for me, I jumped off the hamster wheel into the abyss of anonymity. And with everybody my age so aggressively abandoning the superficiality of mass online friendships, for the intimacy of intense, small, personal interactions, I found my social life was just one of those cards fluttering about with nowhere to land. When I should have been having the time of my life, making just as many questionable decisions as good ones, I was lost, lonely, depressed, and desperate. I never imagined that it would just take a short time to descend to such a dark, dark place.*

I'm a man of action, and even in my intense pain, I was determined to not give in to my problems, but fix them. I signed up for a matchmaking service that promised an introduction to my new best friends, but there were no connections and I just felt worse. I smiled at everybody on the street, I went to bars and restaurants, and pick-up kickball games. I tried tracking down childhood friends whose relationships with me were rooted only in a mutual hate of both math and that know-it-all student body president, Trina.

Finally, I stumbled upon the solution that had been right under my nose, or more accurately, just downstairs. Quite spontaneously I befriended my neighbor; I'll call her Nancy. Even though Nancy and I are about the same age, I did not make the effort to welcome her or get to know her when she first moved in to the building. I felt no guilt about my lack of hospitality, because from what I could tell, she was very much in-demand with her dime-a-dozen-in-this-city job, and certainly did not need me—a progressive, mouthy, artistic intellectual. When I stumbled into her beautifully appointed apartment, I wasn't expecting to find someone who, like me, was layered, complicated, and mysterious. It only took a little wine, a little time, and a little Eleanor, *to peel away Nancy's layers and discover, that not only was she interesting, but that she had been in my same boat—alone, sad, and as she so aptly put it, abandoned by her own generation.*

This woman, who I had mistaken for a basic girl, obsessed with book-club-selections, chilled wine, spin class, and cashmere throws, turned out to be a funny, hard-drinking, hot-dog-eating, binge-watching fast-talker with one hell of an imagination.

I'm thankful for her love of wine, because without it, I don't think she would have let me in on her secret to newfound happiness. You see, when I came to her, I felt terrible, and hated myself and pretty much everybody else. Nancy had been in my same position, but she was no longer wallowing in a pit of despair and loneliness. She had recently been pulled out by a savior of her own creation—an imaginary friend. Nancy's a grown woman—successful, pretty (in a sweet vanilla kind of way, sorry Nancy!), and very reasonable—with an imaginary friend. I know that her telling me about this could not have been easy for her.

She and her friend spend hours talking like any two friends would. They cook together, and watch movies, and walk the neighborhood. If you passed Nancy on one of these walks, you would think she's on a call, when really, she's sharing her thoughts and expressing herself, to someone who only she can see walking right next to her, listening.

And now I have Trey. *Nancy, and her IF— that's what we call our Imaginary Friends—opened my eyes to the fact that I already had everything I needed to cure my own loneliness. I was worried because, though I knew I was interesting, I wasn't sure I was interesting enough to keep myself company for hours and days and weeks on end. As it turns out, I'm amazing. Trey is black and I'm white. He embodies everything I wish I was. He represents every unexplored corner of my personality. He says the things that even I wish I could get away with, but can't, and he sounds so cool when it's coming out of him. Once I got over the awkwardness of speaking out into the silence, our relationship came easier, and turned out to be one of the most natural things in the world.*

When I'm feeling down, Trey lifts me up. He doesn't just pander to my whims—he's honest. He understands me. He lets me talk as much as I want to. Just as anybody does with their best friend, I want to share my day, and my frustrations, and all of my innermost weirdness with him. Every morning brings the excitement of exploring my own imagination for how the day will go, and often, our conversations and activities take a direction that I never could have planned. When I'm creatively spent and can't maintain the conversations, we sit in silence, and neither of us grows bored with the other. It's comfortable, and I am happy.

Why write this? Why come out to the world with something so private and potentially embarrassing? Why go out of my way to talk about something that lives wholly in my head anyway? What do I have to gain other than humiliation and a potential 24-hour psychiatric hold? I'm doing this because Nancy and I know we are not alone. We are not the only ones betrayed, and yes, abandoned by our generation that was once so arrogant about how accessible, global, inclusive, and connected we were.

Only a privileged few get to carry the torch for the pseudo-sexy, gimmicky, and acutely exclusive and unconnected Generation Connect, a moniker that should be scoffed at, and left only to use by its precious members, and the clueless mainstream media. The rest of us? We need each other, but we don't. We're accepting, supportive while respecting both each other's space and choices. We are the Friendlies; we are here to open our arms—whether you can see them or not—to you who didn't make the cut, or missed the boat, and find yourself adrift, lonely, and doubting everything about yourself. We want to let you know that you are never alone, you just need to open your eyes and your mind to see it.

"You think I'm pretty? But also vanilla? I don't know what to say, I'm flattered but also a little bit pissed?"

"That's your takeaway, Flossie? You studied literature, and you're some kind of analyst, and that's your expert critique? You're better than that."

"In all fairness, the literature I read was not usually about me. Ty, I think it's beautiful. I do. I'm nervous for you because I just don't know how many people you are actually going to reach with this. I'm afraid you might be overestimating how many people need this level of encouragement. I think it's basically you, me, Etta, her stoner brother, and those Pod People matches—the farter and the girl who chews her fingers; I think we're the ones who need this. And the Friendlies, that's what we call ourselves? We have to call ourselves something?"

"It's the perfect counterpart to the term, "Imaginary Friend." Are you an IF or a Friendly? All the great sub-cultures have identities. "Friendlies," . . . it's catchy, but not cliché."

"How can anything about our lifestyle be considered cliché? This whole endeavor feels like a very big risk for little reward. What did Trey think?"

"He thinks it makes us—me and him—sound like a couple."

"Are you?" I had wondered, myself.

"No, Flossie, we are not a couple." He shifted his weight, and continued, like I knew he would. "Flossie, I have met someone else . . . another IF. It's not serious, but it could be. It's too new and freeform for me to write it into the essay. Neither of us are ready for that. Her name is Iggy."

"You have an imaginary girlfriend now? An IG? Oh wait, I get it Ig-gy. Are you bored with Trey?"

"Not at all; he's the one who encouraged me to see where things go with Iggy. I don't want to betray her trust about it yet. I'll tell you more and introduce you, if and when we get to that point. Can we please get back to my essay? Did it do you justice? I want to make sure I convey how thankful I am that you were willing to share this important part of your life with me, and that I think you are a visionary."

"I'm honored. I'm a bit cynical about the word visionary, but I appreciate the kind things you wrote. Also, don't think I'm going to forget to follow up with you about this Iggy situation. Ty, I have to tell you I am a little worried that your name is on this thing. It would take two seconds to find out who your neighbor Nancy is. Maybe, you could make me your cousin, or the person who delivers your organic meals, or your dry cleaner or something."

"Why would I get involved in the private complexities of my dry cleaner's life?"

I thought of my affection for the artisan butchers, and Etta's attachment to the baristas. "It happens."

"You can be a generic neighbor. I'll take out any references to us living in the same building. A neighbor can be from the building next door, or down the block."

"Fine. And how are you going to get this in front of your intended audience? These bare-your-soul, look-at-me articles don't go viral anymore."

"I'm not saying we're the underbelly of society or anything, but we're down at grassroots level, and grassroots is what I do."

"Okay. Are you ready for whatever comes from this?"

"I am. Tell me when you want in."

CHAPTER EIGHT

I've described it as eclectic. Bohemian. Vintage. Future Vintage. And also Bohemian Vintage meets Eclectic Future Vintage. No corner of the room was ignored. Though the space was full, robust, and a feast for the eye, it was not cluttered. I hate clutter. I had painstakingly curated every inch of it utilizing my fractured, frantic, all-over-the-place teenage sensibility. If you were to shrink my childhood home, and remove one exterior wall, you would immediately be drawn to my room as the most interesting room in the unusual choice of a dollhouse. You would be in awe of the detail, the little handmade quilt, the tiny art books stacked in the corner, and the itsy-bitsy framed photos of a blurry San Francisco taken from a cable car. Olivia stood speechless in the middle of my childhood-turned-adolescent-turned-teenage room, taking it all in, mouth agape. I knew better than to think she was impressed. She described my canvas of angsty, yet innocent self-expression as, "if an owl on a pillow, threw up more owls onto pillows, and they gave birth to pompoms and burlap and polka dots and homemade soaps and candles. What is happening in here?" She hadn't even put down her weekend bag. If I had that gorgeous bag, I would never put it down. She looked like she was going to Monte Carlo, instead of bunking down in the Midwest's most luxurious owl vomitorium.

"I told you, I was really into crafting," I remembered to drop my voice to a whisper, in case my mom was in the hallway, waiting for the appropriate amount of time to pass until she could come in and ask me if I'm dating somebody.

"I see that," she whispered back.

I transferred my things from my suitcase into the drawers that had stayed empty while I was away, and Olivia inspected every surface.

Olivia pointed at a picture from graduation. "Who's this?"

"Camila."

"She's pretty, where is she now?"

"Miami, I think?"

"And who's the boy by her? Oh. That's uh . . . that's Robby, Camila's brother."

"You guys were cute. Like 'matching clothes, super basic,' but still cute. Remind me; why aren't you friends anymore?"

"Just teenage drama after graduation. Then we went to different colleges, and that was it. Very cliché. I've told you this, haven't I?"

"Probably, I don't know. Oh, here's Charlie. So pompous and obnoxious. He's not even looking at the camera, and you're smiling like a maniac and holding onto him for dear life."

"He never looked at the camera—he was always mentally on to the next thing, and wondering where else he could be and what else he could be doing. I can't believe I didn't see that as a red flag."

"Speaking of red flags, have you heard from Ty?"

Three days after Ty's article started to make the rounds, in whatever grassroots rounds something like that travels in, Olivia and I boarded a plane to Chicago. She was not thrilled about having to stay quiet and isolated in my parents' house, but interested as an amateur anthropologist. I had put off the trip for months and months because I knew that any sign that things weren't going well for me in San Francisco, and I'd be pressured to come to my senses and move home. My big fear was that the telltale signs of a girl in distress would not be very difficult to spot. The timing of my visit was not entirely accidental. Not that I expected anything to happen with Ty's big reveal—but I didn't want to sit around and see him disappointed that nobody cared. Nor did I want to see him bullied by nasty neighborhood middle schoolers who would certainly be able to smell his vulnerability and desperation, and mine by proxy, from a mile away.

I presumed Olivia opted not to join us for dinner so she could spend the evening rummaging through all of our dresser drawers. I did that a few times as I grew up, but the most interesting thing I ever found was a photo that had been shoved toward the back of my mom's nightstand drawer—it was of my college-aged mother wearing a flannel shirt, fishnet stockings, and combat boots, flipping off the camera with one hand, and holding a beer in the other while a cigarette dangled from her lips.

At the restaurant, I looked across the table to my dad, then to my mom. It had been so long since we had gathered around any dining table, I shouldn't have been so surprised at how happy it made me. They stared back at me. I smiled weakly at them and threw myself into the wine list. I sat up straight, and ordered a bottle from California. I started regurgitating what I'd learned about wine while living so close to wine country. I was able to talk for about two minutes before running out of wine facts. I loved my parents. I'd missed my dad and my mom in different ways. Time had gone by at such an irregular, jagged pace that I hadn't realized just how much I missed them, which is why I was scared to death of the unavoidable questions I was expecting. I was scared of scaring them. It hadn't taken me much to tell Etta and Ty my secret. Who knew what I would tell Tom and Jen with even a little bit of probing? I couldn't tell them about what Ty was convinced was a lifestyle choice. They wouldn't understand. My mom might, but I couldn't really take that chance. I was ready to respond to their inquiries with, "I'm fine. I'm good, I'm really good, actually. I do get outside. Yes, I'm taking care of myself, I have farm fresh organics delivered to my doorstep every Tuesday, and my lean protein delivery comes on Thursdays. Cured meats are my guilty pleasure! Work is great. No, I'm not working too much, I'm an important part of the team, I got another promotion, so dinner is on me. Yes, I'm sleeping. I would love to get home more often too, but I'm constantly on deadline. It's a competitive atmosphere—the harder I work now, the easier it will be later. No boyfriend, but I'm not looking. I don't need those kinds of complications at the moment."

I didn't want to waste all of my speech at once, so I got as far as the "farm fresh organics" before I said, "Enough about me! How are things here? Work? What are you doing for fun? You should come visit me! San Francisco is especially beautiful in October. It doesn't have to be this October. Are you eating right? Exercising? Getting outside? Making new friends?"

Before our main course arrived, my phone buzzed.

"Who's calling you?" My dad asked gruffly. "I thought you didn't use the phone anymore. Who gets to call you, if your own father doesn't get to call you?"

"Dad you can call, I told you that. I loved getting your letter, and I love writing to you, because by the time I get a chance to call, you're fast asleep." I told him all of this as I peeked to see it was Ty, and before I realized my dad could no longer confiscate my phone whenever he wanted, it had stopped buzzing. A few seconds later, Ty called again. "I'm sorry," I said as I pushed back my chair, "it looks like I've got to take this."

I stepped outside, and was surprised by the warm evening air. Stepping out of a restaurant into a San Francisco evening usually felt like stepping out into a film noir scene, and chilled you to the bone. "What's the emergency?" I said in a rush to Ty, skipping a greeting. "Did the building burn down?"

"No, calm down."

"I'm at a family dinner. But actually thank you," I said, relaxing. "I think I was going to have to answer questions about my dating life."

"You'll be fine, that's not a long conversation. Listen, Flossie,

I'm sorry to bug you, but I absolutely had to tell you the news. I've heard directly from three hundred people in the last four days, and more than one hundred of those have reached out by letter, and almost two hundred are in the Bay Area. Only forty or so were threatening. This is amazing. I told you we were on to something. I can't believe you're not here right now to celebrate. Everyone's dying to know who Nancy is, even the threatening ones!"

"Wow, what do they want?"

"The threatening ones? Mostly to like, beat me up, or put me away in a psychiatric hospital for my own good, or murder me, or murder you. The usual."

"Ty, are you serious? Maybe you need to get out of town, or move, or get security or something."

"Flossie, any time you put yourself out there, you are going to hear from psychos who want to make a suit out of your skin. They just want attention. Threats are par for the course for a public figure, which, may I remind you? I was."

"Were you, though? I mean were you, really?"

"Most of these people," Ty continued, confident in his notoriety, "just want help, and assurance, and permission."

"Permission for what?"

"Permission to take a drastic step with their lives! Permission to knowingly go from being sane and lonely and miserable, to being happy, but a little bit crazy! They want assurance that everything's going to be okay. Wait, that's good, I need to write that down."

"I still don't know, Ty—"

"Okay, enjoy your family," he said, cutting me off, "Let them spoil you, or whatever. While you're gone, I'm going to brainstorm, and strategize, and collect myself, so that by the time you get home, we'll have a clear sense of where to go next. Give Liv my love, and tell her Trey misses her . . . and we miss you too."

"Liv? You gave my IF a nickname?"

"She's her own person, Flossie. Once you gave her life, she no longer belonged to you; she belongs to herself and the universe. You wanted a friend, right? Not a concubine. Ooh, I'm writing that down, too. Okay, bye! Yay, us!"

I returned to the table and made it through the rest of dinner without being asked about my love life, which was not at all on the same trajectory as my parents' when they were my age. They met at Indiana State. The story was that they met in a cafeteria on Halloween day. My mom was dressed as Courtney Love and my dad was Bill Clinton; but I think by "cafeteria" they meant "party," and "day," was actually "night." And after that magical Halloween day/night, Bill and Courtney stayed together the rest of college, got married the minute they graduated, and had me five years later. My mom gave me the leather jacket she was wearing in the "cafeteria" that day. She said it still smelled like teen spirit. I thought it smelled like the L train on a bad day, but I kept it, and wished regularly I could go back in time to see Bill and Courtney in the "cafeteria."

I asked as many questions as I could to avoid talking about myself and end up accidentally spilling my secret, like I had so easily with Etta and Ty. My questions though, revealed what I had already suspected; life at home was frozen in time. I wondered if at some point, I too would become frozen in time, and if so, what stage of my life would I be stuck with forever. What if it was this one? I wasn't in the mood for dessert.

After a convincing-because-it's-true plea for sleep on the way back to the house after dinner, I went straight upstairs. I had to kick Olivia from my bed to an imaginary trundle bed. To be a jerk, I covered it in a loud quilt and more owl pillows. "I can't sleep in this," she said groggily. "Owls are nocturnal, and they will keep me up all night." After I turned out the light in my room, I whispered, "When I was on the phone with Ty, he called you Liv and told me to tell you that Trey misses you. What do you think of that?" It reminded me of all those sleepovers when I whispered to Camila in her sleeping bag.

"That's sweet. I like Trey; he's sexy," she whispered back.

"You're not . . . you know, with him? Are you?"

"We're not 'you know?' This room feels like a reversion chamber. You are eleven right now, Flossie. And no, he and I aren't doing it," she sputtered as if she were talking through a mouth full of braces. I laughed out loud, and quickly covered with a cough.

"Not right now, anyway," she continued. "We're friends. That's what all of this is about, right? Having to invent totally boring friendships that would otherwise be a basic function of humanity? Except for Ty, and his freaky girlfriend, Iggy. Even I think that's weird."

"That's kind of mean, Olivia."

"It's not mean. Ty set himself up for that one."

"No, the part about friendships being a basic and boring function of humanity."

"Flossie, it's nothing you haven't thought before."

"But you're not supposed to say that stuff. I am, and then when I say it, you're supposed to tell me how great I am and how much you treasure our friendship."

"You wanted a real friend right? Not a concubine?"

The next morning, I woke to find Olivia stretched out on the trundle in her silk pajamas. She lit up a cigarette, and took a long drag.

"Really? And when did you take up smoking? You look so . . . so . . . French. But like, 1980s French, when Roger Moore was James Bond." He was my mom's favorite Bond.

"I am so bored, Flossieeee," she purred in a French accent. "I'm stuck in ze house, surrounded by hundreds of photos of you, and your parents, but zis place is smozering me. Your childhood is my prison, and I'm going to create my own IF, if you don't get me out of here."

"It's just two more days, and you are certainly not in prison. Don't be so dramatic. Anyway, today Mom's taking me to get a haircut—don't say anything mean right now, I don't need that— but you should go out and explore."

Olivia sat up and looked at me, forgetting her accent. "Your mom's taking you to get your hair cut?"

"Yes. I need one anyway, and it might be nice to have some alone time with her."

"Okay, well, we did come to Chicago quite a bit when I was in college." She was back to Michigan Olivia. "Yeah, I'll go out. Have fun at the mall with your mom. Olivia propelled herself from the bed, holding her cigarette between her fingers as she opened her bag with a burst of enthusiasm. She looked at me and flicked ash onto the trundle's comforter.

Shannon, the hairdresser from my youth, was still holding court across from the food court in the mall. The smell of hair chemicals and pretzels were such a powerful olfactory memory, that every time I stepped in a salon, fancy or not, I craved carnival food. Sadly, it looked like both Shannon and the shop were struggling to keep up with everybody else. Shannon hugged me and led me back to her station. She wore the same style of studded boot as the young stylist next to her, a girl who looked like she was fresh out of both the womb and beauty school, and already dreaming of moving to a better salon further away from a food court. Shannon's face was pancaked in so much "natural" makeup, the matte texture made her look like a mannequin in a movie about mannequins who come to life to cut your hair. She was wearing a flowing sweater on top of a small vest layered on top of a large t-shirt, with the straps of a camisole clearly visible. As I imagine anybody would in that outfit, she was sweating. By the time my shampoo was done, Shannon had stripped down to the t-shirt and camisole, and her mannequin makeup was beginning to run.

Shannon regaled me with tales from her action-packed trip to Branson, Missouri, and snipped away at the remnants of my expensive California haircut, while I held my breath. When she was done, it looked the same as it did at the hands of Agnes, my British stylist back in San Francisco. I didn't worry about whether Agnes would think I cheated on her with another stylist; I had to reintroduce myself to her every time I had an appointment. I was relieved that Olivia was out strolling Michigan Ave., smoking up a storm, and not around to make fun of Shannon, who blushed when she saw the huge tip I'd left her.

My mom and I walked slowly through the mall, then onto the sidewalk, then into my favorite art museum experiencing none of the awkwardness that sometimes comes with time and distance. She listened as I chatted about art, food, puppies, the weather, and what we should have for lunch.

Later, as my dad was downstairs somehow happily and angrily watching a Cubs game, and Olivia and I were packing for our return trip to San Francisco, my mom came into my room and stretched out on my bed, right in the middle of Olivia's perfectly folded clothes. I didn't remember her ever doing that.

"You okay, mom? Are you tired?"

"I'm fine."

"Are you sure? You look tired."

"I'm just already sad about you leaving tomorrow, that's all."

"I'm sad too," I said automatically, while continuing my folding. Olivia frowned from the corner where she was now looking through my yearbook again.

"Then don't leave."

"Mom."

"I know you need to leave. I mean, I want you to leave, but don't. I want what's best for you, but I want what I want, and they're not always the same thing."

"You don't have to worry about me."

She sat up just far enough up to prop her head in her hand.

"Flossie, I think you're old enough now for me to be straight with you. I'm not really worried about you. I don't want to hurt your feelings, or make you think I don't care, because I do. I want you to be happy and healthy, but all that fretting I do over how much sleep you're getting, and whether or not you're eating a balanced breakfast? It really felt like the right mom stuff to say. It's not you I'm worried about; you seem fine and frankly, better off without us."

"Mom, don't say stuff like that. If you're not worried about me, is it Dad? Does he have cancer?" I sat on the bed next, clutching the t-shirt I'd been folding.

"No, Dad doesn't have cancer. He's fine. He's frozen in time. Did you see him? He's had the same twenty gray hairs since you were born. He says he's going to the gym, but I think he goes to a cryogenic chamber, for a quick *schvitz*." I knew it . . . frozen in time. I needed to get to a place in my life where I wouldn't mind being frozen. This was not that time.

"Then what's the problem, Mom?""Oh, it's nothing, I'm just being dramatic." She collapsed back on the pillow, and stared at the ceiling. Her thick dark hair swirled around her head making her look like she was floating in a pool. I watched her from my spot at the edge of my bed, wondering if I was doing a good job of being present, then internally chastising myself because trying so hard to be present was making me not very present at all. The scene made me think back to when I was fourteen and fifteen, in this very spot where she and I did this exact same thing. Only back then, I was the one sprawled out on the bed, and I certainly wasn't waiting anxiously for her to open up to me. We'd usually end up sitting on my bed together, because I'd said something at the dinner table that made her take notice. She'd wait a few minutes before wandering into my room with the excuse of putting away laundry. Then she'd sit, right where I was sitting, using mom body language to convey that she was ready to help with whatever was troubling me. Boys? Eating disorders? Peer pressure? Bullies? But I'd probably made a meaningless off-hand remark at dinner, like I had started to ask if we were having dessert, then realizing I didn't really want dessert, muttered "never mind" and retreated to my room to think about nothing, or more accurately everything, which provides the exact same results as thinking about nothing at all. And all the while, she was sitting on the edge of the bed, hugging the decoy laundry and probably panicking about my happiness and whether she would once-and-for-all lose me to a black hole of adolescence. Maybe, back then, as I stared at the ceiling, stubbornly refusing to engage with her, she silently said a prayer that if "she's not willing to confide in me, her mother, please don't let her turn to promiscuity and drugs."

Sitting in the mom spot at the edge of the bed, I stared at her staring, and raced through all the things she might want to talk about. Money? Bullies? Eating Disorders? Peer pressure? I carefully stretched out in the space next to her, and while staring at the familiar ceiling right along with her, asked, "Are you sure, Mom? What's on your mind?"

"Nothing, I'm fine."

"Moooooooom," I growled. It was like muscle memory. It was the sound I had made when I was fifteen and out of ideas on how to get my way. "Please."

"No Flossie, that's why this is so ridiculous. I don't have cancer, in fact, I just had a check-up, and I'm totally healthy. Dad's totally healthy. We'll finish paying off the house in less than a year. You're in a good place. I have no reason to complain. Everything's fine."

"I'm confused."

"Me too, Floss, that's the problem." She sounded like the mom again. "I guess, seeing you out there taking the world by storm, makes me . . . jealous? Proud? Both? I was looking at her, but she was still staring at the ceiling. "You don't need me anymore. You are out there, living the life I could only dream about at your age, and in California where I always wanted to live, but you actually made it happen. You created a whole world for yourself."

"Mom, please don't say that. I need you. I've always needed you." But she was right, I really had created a whole world for myself.

"Don't get me wrong, I'm so proud. I'm just feeling senti-mental. A little wistful. Maybe with a 'what if' sprinkled here and there. I'm sure that's normal for a woman like me. I should look that up." She rolled over and swung her legs off the bed lithely.

I reached for her; desperate for her to turn around and stay in the room with me a little while longer. "You did everything right, Mom. We're all sentimental and wistful and envious some-times. I get that, but please don't be envious of me. That is a major waste of your time, and a major waste of envy."

Her hair was sticking out all over the place, disheveled from her stunt roll off the bed, and she'd gone from not looking at me at all to looking at me with a furrowed brow, like she was waiting for me to say something that wasn't just an empty platitude. I remained silent though, still unwilling to provide the specifics that would let her know I was a shell of a person dependent both on a job where I was essentially invisible, and a best friend who was actually invisible.

"Listen, Flossie. I'm so sorry I said any of that," she said, loos-ening her brow, and smoothing her hair. "I was having a moment of weakness because I'm sad you're leaving, and it's so wonderful to have you home."

"Come to California with me!"

"You are so sweet. You know I can't, as much as I would love to. It wouldn't be good for you, or for me. I miss you, and I can't believe how fast time goes. It's probably hormones. Let's say it's hormones. The last thing you need is to worry about me. How about we do a quick load of laundry, like the old days?" She kissed me on top of the head, and slipped out of the room when I shook my head no.

Olivia was sitting in the corner, observing and smoking.

"Don't say anything," I whispered at her, "and put that out."

"It's okay, I think I smoke in Chicago. Like some people

smoke when they drink, or have a different lover in every port, or use an English accent when they go to Vegas."

"People don't do that."

"How do you know? Anyway, next time we go to Vegas, we're using English accents, and in the meantime, I'm a Chicago smoker. Let's go to New York, I'm dying to see what I'd do there."

From the Diary of Jennifer Martin O'Brien
January 1, 2015

Happy New Year! I'm up early, Tommy and Flossie are still sleeping, so I'm ahead already!

This is going to be a great year, but in order for that to happen, I have so much to get done. There are literally a million things I want to accomplish. First, be a better parent, followed by being a better wife, friend, citizen, employee, etc. . . Then there's health, money, and doing something for myself . . . go to see more bands live maybe? Go to a music festival with my college girlfriends? I don't know, I'll get to that after the whole "being a better parent" thing.

I'm trying to keep my cool with Flossie, but she is making it very difficult. It's like trying to parent a hormonal zombie. Yes, she's wonderful, adorable, nothing delights me more than being her mother, yada yada yada, but the girl is making me crazy. Had Tommy and I had been able to have another child, I don't know what I would have done, because I am really struggling with the one. Again, I love her, she's great, but I'm losing it over here.

The phone. The social media. The videos. I can't take her phone because she needs it for school, and to keep in touch with all her friends (who I rarely see in person by the way, except for Camila, of course.) I think she's well on her way to getting a hunchback. What if her phone has ruined her brain and her posture forever? I am sickened by the sight of my own phone now, because I know what I must look like when I stare into it, even if I'm reading the news, or checking my work email. I don't want to read a book on a device. I want to feel paper and turn pages. I called my friend Liane the other day, instead of texting her, and she immediately asked what was wrong. I forgot my phone at home (maybe on purpose?), and it was terrifying and liberating, and it felt like I left my left hand at home, if I had a love–hate relationship with my left hand. I don't know how to fix this for Flossie. She's missing out on so much.

Maybe I should not have started the year thinking about this, because I've already lost a little optimism for 2015. Maybe I should have just started by making French toast.

CHAPTER NINE

"Five hundred Flossie! I've heard from five hundred people. Now is the time to turn this into something."

"Slow down, partner, how many of those were threats?"

I was sitting in Ty's apartment. Though our apartments had identical layouts, our living spaces couldn't be more different. Where my place was light and bright, his was dark, and dusty, and made me feel anxious. "Busy intellectual lumberjack" weren't the words that came to mind. It felt as if he was fifty years ahead of his own time, as in he was already fully prepared for his twilight years to be spent as an eccentric shut-in. I thought Trey might have done more to up Ty's style game a bit. And if not Trey, then Iggy, but I hadn't met her; maybe she aspired to be an eccentric shut-in too. Any time Ty and I made plans to hang out, I tried to lure him to my place with the promise of food.

"One hundred threats, tops. I know it's not the sexy viral numbers of yesteryear, but I think we're really on to something. We have to take advantage of this enthusiasm, shape it into what we want it to be. I'm talking about shaping a message, do you follow?"

"You've done nothing but make fun of my job, and now you're trying to explain the exact content of my job to me. I'm losing my patience." I went right into the executive analyst mode I knew was there waiting for the perfect moment to spring forth onto a condescending know-it-all. "What is the feedback you're getting? Do you want to give me the correspondence? I can take a look, dissect what they're really saying. I'm pretty good at quantifying the unquantifiable. I think my abstract literary background really helps. I'm not a black or white math type. I kind of harness all those gray areas."

"Now I'm losing patience, Professor."

"Aw, my dad used to call me that."

He ignored my reminiscing and flipped open his notebook. "A few people birthed their IFs just after reading our story, but aren't sure if they're doing it right. One person has an IF that sounds a little dangerous, and I'm going to put that in a special pile. And I heard from quite a few people who were already doing IF variations before they read the article, but in really sad ways, nowhere near as good as what we're proposing. They were telling people they had pods, and best friends, bull rider boyfriends in Dallas, model girlfriends in LA, but all of that was to appease others, with not even an IF at home to back it up, let alone a real bull rider boyfriend. Those are the stories that break my heart because they were just compounding their loneliness with the lies, getting none of the satisfaction of the relationship that we experience with our IFs—wait, I'm writing that down. These are the people I think that we can help the most. They have the imagination, the need, and they were already so close . . . almost there, you know? They just needed a little guidance from us."

"Really? I mean . . . really? You want to reach out and personally help these total strangers?" I felt anxious, and not just "in Ty's apartment" anxious.

"Yes, really. Anyway, you should probably take a look at these." He handed me a stack of letters and continued, "As I suspected, what most people are looking for—desperate for—is assurance they're not crazy, not alone in their loneliness, and tips on how to maximize their IF experience."

"What do you have in mind, exactly? We have no budget. I'm used to clients, and projects with budgets, really healthy, padded, budgets."

"We don't need a budget. We're grassroots, remember? And I have a ton of imaginary money, so we're good."

"Yeah, but remember even your grassroots work was part of a real-life budget."

"Ty?"

"Yeah?"

"You really want to help these people?"

"Of course."

"It's not about getting your name out there?"

"No, Flossie. I know we go back and forth sometimes, and I can be a bit brash, but really it's because I care. A lot. About a lot of things. I burned out because I care. I got into advocacy, and disruption, and activism because I care."

His face looked red, even in the dark, and his voice was

shaky. My ability to read people's emotions had probably been stunted by my new lifestyle choice, but he seemed sincere to me. I sat down next to him. "What was the issue that got you started?"

"I don't feel like talking about it."

"For the first time ever."

"Flossie . . . ugh, fine. My twin sister died when we were eighteen. She was messing around with her phone while she was driving, which still makes me so mad because she knew better. And there had been years of warnings and legislation and new technology so we wouldn't touch our phones in the car. There were a million cautionary tales of people who died years before she did. Sierra wasn't perfect—but she could have been great. She was so confident, but really selfish. She didn't care about anything that didn't have to do directly with her. I realized most of my friends were like that, too. If a problem didn't directly touch their life, they had a hard time caring, let alone getting riled up to work hard and fix it, that's what my mom calls it. She says I get people riled up about problems they didn't know they had. And I correct her and say, 'I get them riled about problems they don't have . . . yet.'"

"Wow, Ty. I'm sorry about your sister." He was still teetering on the brink of crying.

"Yeah, so I was on every TV station in Reno, talking to people about driving and texting. I was in a PSA that ran on TV at four in the morning, but online, it was shared more than a million times, and I was totally viral for a few minutes. Remember those posts that maybe your cousin or somebody would share, and it would start with, "make you sure you have a box of tissues ready?" It was that. I spoke at high schools and kids would throw pencils and garbage at me—nobody wants to be preached at by a kid who looks like a leprechaun—but I would talk about my dead sister and they would stop, and listen, and give me a standing ovation at the end. Then one of the community centers where I spoke was being forced to close down, so I fought for that. Girls playing on boys' baseball teams were getting harassed. But eventually, I needed to get out of Reno. I had to let the ghost of my sister go, and I needed different problems to solve, and different people to solve them for. I even blamed that town for Sierra's death, like if we lived somewhere else, she wouldn't have been driving where she was, she would have been smarter, or would have had a better phone or a better car. That's the . . . that's the version that pretty much nobody knows; you and Trey know. I haven't even told Iggy."

"Well, thank you. I'm sure Sierra would be very proud."

"Probably not. She wasn't very nice to me. She was meaner to me than anybody." He laughed, and stood up to grab the bottle of rosé.

"Hey," I said casually as he emptied the bottle into my glass, "so what's happening with Iggy? You've had enough space to figure out if you are a couple, don't you think? And when can I meet her?"

"Oh, I suppose you can meet her now if you want." He seemed happy to move on from talking about his mean, departed sister to his imaginary girlfriend. "Igs! Igs!" He hollered toward his bedroom. "She's here, and Flossie, she's pretty fabulous. She's

British, and so smart, and sophisticated, and funny. She's tiny, so she thinks I'm tall. She has long blonde hair and a raspy voice. She's very independent, and full of passion. She has a lot of causes, like I do, but hers are global . . . refugees, clean water, vaccinations, fair trade. She wears my button downs and cardigans, and loves French films, Japanese pop music, and a good pint. She's well-read so you guys should have a lot in common there."

"I'm not as well-read as I used to be."

"She's not jealous of our friendship, Flossie, which was important to me. She admires what we are doing and she is supportive of the movement even though she doesn't have time for a lot of it. She and Trey get along well. You'll have to let me know if you think she and Olivia will hit it off. I have a feeling they'll either be kindred spirits or mortal enemies. Okay, she's here."

"Nice to meet you, Iggy," I spoke into the air.

Dear Flossie —

It's been a while! How was your Chicago trip? I'm sorry I didn't send a card from Hawaii! It was a whirlwind, but it was an amazing time. Guess what? Nevermind, you will never guess. Emma and I are engaged!

I know it was fast, but I fell in love. Emma is everything I didn't even know I wanted in a life partner, and I've never been happier in my life. I popped the question on the beach at sundown, totally unplanned. And she said yes, and we cried, and cried. We're still figuring out ceremony details . . . it will definitely be an intimate affair, and I would love it if you could be there. The wedding will be for Friendlies only, obviously; the world isn't ready for anything beyond that—so maybe, if as a champion of our people, and if he's interested, Ty can come too, along with your IFs. (By the way, thank you for sending me a copy of the article that Ty wrote about you. I loved it.) And I'll make sure Robert and Kyle are there. I wanted you to be the first to know about the engagement, but I saw Robert, and was so excited, I told him. He's weird about it. I'm not sure what bothers him the most, the fact that I'm marrying an IF, or that the IF is a girl, but it's probably that I expect him to leave the house for an event. I know I didn't exactly tell you I was falling in love with my IF, and I'm sorry about that. Honestly, I was afraid talking about it would ruin it. I didn't want you to think I was on my way over the deep end, and turning into an awful human being who you couldn't be friends with anymore. But after reading Ty's article, I realized what a safe space I have with you, so thank you.

Anyway, I'll be in touch soon about wedding details.

Love,

Etta and Emma

Olivia and Ty were each reading over my shoulder.

"I can't say I'm terribly surprised," Olivia said dryly.

"Flossie, this is incredible," Ty gushed, grabbing the letter from my hands. "It's exactly what I was talking about. Etta's so happy! She feels safe! We are going to this wedding. I wonder if she'd be open to me writing about it. Or maybe, filming it? Yes! A documentary! We should really start thinking about a documentary. So many great subcultures throughout history have been validated and have secured a spot in the history books through documentary filmmaking."

"You read what she said, Ty. She needs it to be intimate and private. Friendlies only. You have to respect that. And anyway, I don't know how I feel about the wedding."

"Because Emma's a woman." Ty looked like he was wanting a fight.

"No. Because Emma's not real, and this wedding will be. I mean, we talk about lifestyle, but this is her actual life. What if it stops Etta from opening herself to real love, with a real person?"

"A wedding's symbolic, it represents a commitment. And Emma probably represents a lot of things to Etta. It's beautiful. You can tell from her letter, Flossie, this is real love to her. It jumps off the page. Iggy and I aren't talking about marriage, but I get it. You are Etta's friend, her one human friend, and you will support her. She needs you. We are going to that wedding. In the meantime, you are going to the first ever gathering of Friendlies."

"What?"

"Yes, I'm hosting—or we're hosting, if you're interested—the first ever mixer of Friendlies and IFs."

"We—you—are?" I was still kind of reeling from Etta's letter. Maybe Ty was trying to slip this in when I was distracted.

"Yes, next month. I have a venue, a low key pub out near the ocean, Friendly-owned. Help me finalize the event name, Flossie. 'A Friendly Gathering' or maybe, 'What IF? A Friendly evening of conversation . . . and,' I don't know? 'Friendship?'"

"Friendly Friendship? No. Let's forget the name for a second. How is this event going to work?"

"Ok, well, I have a group distribution list that could be, dare I call it, the start of a new social network? Chills, Flossie! I have chills! The event is part fun, social mixer, and part workshop and sharing about our IFs. Then, maybe a ceremony, like a coming out for our IFs, like a debutante ball? I want to celebrate these relationships so our IFs become one more shade of real."

The first "Friendly Fete: An Evening Celebrating our Wild Imaginations," was hours away, and I still wasn't sure I wanted to attend. I'd prepared a rousing and heartfelt speech, declaring to the world, or this small group of people, that I was the Nancy everyone had been asking about. I'd also packed a bag, so I could blow off the whole thing and jump on a Portland-bound plane with Olivia.

As I was pulling my new beautiful Italian leather overnight bag out of the closet, my doorbell buzzed. The delivery guy confirmed I was Flossie of Flossie and Olivia, and handed me an arrangement of pink peonies. *"To the mother of a movement . . . Nancy, you are amazing, and Olivia, you are an iconoclast of the highest and most invisible order. Tonight we celebrate! Love, Ty, Trey, Iggy"*

Olivia read the card over my shoulder and sighed into my ear, "That little moppet is persuasive. I don't want to go to Portland, Floss. I want to go to this party. I'm an iconoclast. Sure they're oddballs, but Flossie, these are *our* people. You will be a goddess there. They will worship you. Finger chewers or not, wouldn't it be nice to be actively admired by other human beings? This is your night. We are going. I'm not taking no for an answer." And so, at 7:30, Olivia, Ty, Trey, and Iggy and I shared a ride to the pub, where Ty handed me a subpar thyme beer, and told me to prepare myself.

Ty handed me an obnoxiously large custom nametag.

My name is:

My IF(s):

They are:

"This thing is confusing, Ty. What goes in the 'they are' section?"

"That's the beauty of it. Whatever you want. We are dealing with people who are totally okay without borders and rules. These are people who are not only comfortable in the abstract, they are living in it."

I watched Ty fill out his tag:

My name is: Ty (your humble host!)

My IF(s): Trey and Iggy

They are: awesome, super social. Trey: 25, smart, cooler than all of us, DJ, entrepreneur; *Iggy: 30, British, tiny in stature, large in personality, well-read, saving the planet*

I wrote mine.

My name is: Flossie

My IF(s): Olivia

They are: graphic designer, mildly intimidating

"That's it? What would Olivia say?"

"She's fine. She likes the part where she's mildly intimidating."

I could sense he wanted me to change it, but I was saved by the first guest to walk through the door, a middle-aged woman with dark, wild hair, and a long pale face. She was wearing a skirt that grazed the floor, and she clutched her bag to her chest. Her eyes darted around the room from behind her round spectacles. She stopped just inside the door, and yelled, "Am I in the right place? Is Ty here?"

"I'm Ty, and it sounds like you're in the right place." Ty was moving quickly across the bar, "And you arrrrrrrre . . ." He stretched the word long enough to get him all the way over to her. I trailed behind him, not knowing what else to do.

"I'm Simone."

"Did you bring a friend Simone?"

"Um, I don't know . . ." She glanced at me, and I smiled.

"Never mind," Ty said, waving his hand around, "don't worry about that, right now. We just want you to do and say what's comfortable for you, okay?"

"I'm not comfortable right now." Her eyes darted to me.

"I understand," he said softly, nodding.

"Is this for real? I mean. This isn't for a practical joke show, is it? I sent a letter after I read your article. Then I started to think it might be a ruse to lure lonely women. And Terry said that I could possibly be kidnapped or killed if I showed up to this fake sounding party, but I hadn't been to a party for a while, so I thought it was worth the risk."

"And here you are! I'm glad you thought our little party might be worth being kidnapped and possibly killed for. But you won't be!" Ty tried to sound cheery.

"Good. Then that means Terry was wrong."

"Terry? Is Terry your—"

"I don't want to talk about Terry," Simone snapped, and clutched her handbag even tighter.

"Okay, Simone, why don't you grab a seat, or mingle. I see more people coming in. Have a good time, okay? We're glad you're here."

"Hi! I'm Ty!" I heard it over and over as he worked the room like he was trying to sell every party guest a sports car. I rotated around the bar that occupied the center of the room and seemed to be everybody's first stop. I white-knuckled my warm beer, and made sure to keep the growing crowd on the other side of the bar from Olivia and myself. Simone sat in a corner, still clutching her purse, murmuring to herself, or maybe to Terry. I examined the crowd closely. For a few minutes the crowd skewed male, then female, then older than I expected, then more racially diverse than I expected. Olivia took it upon herself to evaluate why each person there was lonely enough to need an imaginary friend, "socially awkward, tragically socially awkward, annoying, dumb, new to town, naïve, boring, arrogant."

"Olivia, stop; we don't know these people. Be nice."

"Well, if you want me to stop guessing about their lives, then get over there and confirm stuff for me. You're making Simone look like the bell of the ball the way you're lurking over here in the dark."

Olivia was right. In a room full of potentially unstable people, I looked like the least stable of them all. I took a deep breath and moved through the crowd, trying to come up with a reason I needed to find Ty.

I tried glancing at people's nametags as I passed, but most of them were so crammed with tomes of tiny handwriting, I couldn't read a word. I was thankful for big, bold "Jolene" whose friend "Maureen" was a "nice woman."

Ty's face lit up when he saw me. "Hey, look who it is!" I quickly shook my head, to let him know I was in no way ready to be Nancy. He nodded, and finished, "another guest!" On one side of him was a young Asian woman, who was gulping down her glass of white wine, and on the other side, a tall, lanky guy with messy brown hair, and a flannel shirt. "I'm Flossie," I said with a half-wave to the group.

"I'm Mary," the woman sputtered after gulping down the wine, "and I can't believe I'm here."

"I'm Flossie, and don't worry, I think half of us can't believe we're here, and the other half don't know they're here." The guy on the other side of Ty laughed.

"I'm Henry," the tall guy said, "and this is our host, Ty," he politely gestured toward Ty who was raising his eyebrows at me.

"Oh, we've met," I said nodding at Ty, who looked almost giddy.

"Oh, I'm sorry," Henry said, turning red, "I just . . . Sorry."

"It's fine, Henry," Ty put a friendly hand on Henry's shoulder, and looked at me, "Flossie, I was just telling Mary and Henry about Trey and Iggy."

"Already?" I immediately started sweating. "I mean, didn't we just kind of get here? Shouldn't we warm up to that?"

"Somebody's got to be first, right?" Ty looked around the group, nodding at each of us. "And our IFs are the elephants in the room, are they not? Actually, I think somebody's IF *is* an elephant. So, let's have it. It's safe here."

"Is this for real?" asked Mary, "Does this end with a mass kidnapping, or brain washing? I can't believe I got out of the car. The whole way over here, I expected to see someone I knew from Stanford as a graduate student conducting a psychological experiment that will reveal me as a total loser, and everybody who already thought I was the worst, will be overjoyed to see me like this."

"Mary," Ty transferred his hand to Mary's shoulder, "this is not an experiment. This is real. The party is real, the friends are not. Relax."

"It's just so weird."

"I know it is, Mary. It's okay."

"Alright then, what the hell?" She swallowed the rest of her wine. "I'll go first before I chicken out. I did have friends at Stanford, and yes, they all went to graduate school, and I wanted to get some work experience, so I moved to San Francisco, got a job and a terrible apartment. I only have my dad and a couple of aunts, and all they wanted was to be proud of me for having a successful career. I work all the time and with people I hate. I'm in finance, and it's me and all these guys who, if they're not being misogynist pricks, are totally ignoring me. I used to be nice. And then, one of my old friends told me I wasn't very nice anymore, and I realized she was right, but it was too late. My old friends had podded up without me, and I realized I was alone and mean, which was actually making me meaner, and making it even harder for me to make friends, so I got a life coach, but I think she hated me too. She had a copy of your article Ty, and she gave it to me. Can you believe it? What a bitch! To suggest to a client they get an imaginary friend! So guess what? I fired her ass, and got an imaginary friend slash life coach. Ha!"

I looked closely at Mary's nametag. And there it was at the bottom in perfect block printing, her IF? "Tina, Imaginary Friend/Life Coach."

"Tell us about Tina, Mary." Ty was facing Mary, nodding in his pre-prepared amazing listener way, and providing Mary with scads of unbroken eye contact.

"Well," Mary took a deep breath, "Tina's older. She's not like a grandma, but she's matronly. She's kind. She loves manners, but she has a really dirty sense of humor, and she drinks pisco sours. She bakes. She's frumpy, but she's so easy to be around, I just don't care what she looks like. She wants to know about my day, and makes sure I go to bed early. She tells me I work too hard, and keeps trying to get me to introduce myself to the young guy who works at the bodega across the street from my office. She cares about my life and wants me to be happy."

"Wow. She sounds great Mary. Is Tina here right now?" Part of Ty's amazing listener-and-unbroken-eye-contact package was "meaningful follow-up questions."

"She's not standing here, no. She's not who I would have pictured taking to parties, you know? Not at all. I thought if I was going to go out on a limb to create a friend for myself out of thin air, I would go with someone really amazing. I tried adding a couple of other, younger, cooler people, or what do you call them? IFs? But, they didn't stick. They were really into travel, and glamour, and spoke a dozen languages and worked in fashion and the entertainment industry, but they kind of ditched me too, I guess. Wow, that's pathetic. Anyway, I always come back to Tina."

"Maybe Tina's just exactly who you need right now, Mary." Ty had his hand back on Mary's shoulder.

"Yeah, maybe. Can someone else please talk now? I need to know this isn't a practical joke."

"I'll go." Henry raised his hand a bit before shoving it in his pocket. "So, hello, I'm Henry. I'm obviously new to this too, but I'm kinda pumped to be here. This room has a really weird, but really good, happy, but messed-up energy. I'm a systems architect and I work from home, which sucks. I have a roommate, and he's okay, and by okay, I mean I don't think he'll kill me, but we have absolutely nothing in common. I grew up on a farm in the Central Valley, and I could not wait to get to the city. My parents lived in San Francisco before my sister and I were born, but they had these notions of cashing in their stock options, selling their Pacific Heights Victorian and their nice cars, and getting chickens and growing organics, and homeschooling me and my sister. People threaten to do stuff all the time. But those jerks actually did it. Anyway, I would get so resentful when they would talk about their old life, because I would have killed it as a kid in the city. I hated that farm. I was allergic to every single thing within three miles . . . pollens, grasses, every animal, and I was even allergic to dairy and nuts . . . on a farm! So I went to college in Sacramento, then moved here, with notions of greatness, and finding myself, and where nobody blinks if you're nut-free. Sorry, I'm talking too much."

"No, go ahead," I blurted, surprising myself.

"Yes," Ty nodded, "please continue, Henry, we're listening, that's why we're here." Henry had a really weird, but really good, happy, but messed-up energy, and I weirdly couldn't wait to listen to him talk some more.

"My parents sold the farm while I was in college, and moved to be near my sister in Pennsylvania, where they now own a bed & breakfast, and where they're each writing memoirs." He was talking faster now. "Oh, and did I mention, that throughout my whole childhood, my mom wrote a blog about how hard it was to parent a child with so many allergies? She had a whole commiserating community of moms out there swapping ideas about snacks that wouldn't kill their kids. They created this army, waging with school districts and doctors, local government, and allergy insensitive parents. Well, who was my mom talking about when she talked about her plight? Me . . . I was her plight. She was an inspiration to thousands of parents out there, she reminded me constantly. Anyway, my timing's just the worst. So I get to San Francisco and everybody's already paired off or whatever, and it didn't help to try to find anybody with the same interests, because everybody in this town has my same interests: technology, good food, good drinks, and being snotty about books, music and movies, and taking great pride in being first to do weird stuff, which I guess is one of the reasons why I'm here."

I snort-laughed. Olivia looked like she wanted to kill me. "Sorry." I cleared my throat, and sipped my hot, and still subpar beer.

"No it's cool," he said without missing a beat. "I tried woodworking and fishing, thinking that might set me apart in the friendship pool, but oh, yeah, I hate that stuff. But guess who doesn't? My buddy Abe."

"Is that your IF, Henry? What's Abe like?" Ty was full-on facilitating.

"Kind of like what you said, Mary. Abe was not who I meant to invent for myself. But there he was. He's got a beard, and he drives a truck. He's really strong, and he makes furniture for a living. He likes sports, but he's not obsessed. He's not obsessed with anything I guess, which is why he's so cool. He has a big hairy dog with tons of imaginary dander that I think I might actually be developing an allergy to, in real life. He has a fishing cabin. I think maybe he hates me? I don't know, but he hasn't ditched me yet. Maybe because I'm a really good cook, and sometimes he doesn't even notice that what I've made is vegan. Oh yeah, I'm a vegan, and Abe isn't allergic to anything. So that's it. Sorry I talked so much. I guess, I haven't talked like that in a while."

"That was really cool, Henry," I said without thinking. Olivia pretended to barf for a second before mouthing 'cool?' "I mean, it was great for you to share that."

"Flossie, how about you? Will you share?" Ty said, looking at me, both eyebrows raised.

I took a deep breath. "Sure. Um, I'm Flossie. I'm an analyst with . . . that doesn't matter, I'm an analyst. I'm originally from Chicago. I went to Northwestern, and moved to San Francisco after graduation. I like books and museums, and interior design, and DIY projects, but I haven't had the time to do that stuff as much lately. I'm just kind of a regular person, or maybe I've always just felt regular, and really, I'm not? I don't know. I worked hard in college, and I surrounded myself with people who were hyper intense and serious about their goals, and their work, and so it was easy to scatter and disappear into our lives without anybody really noticing. I feel like I slept through the parties, brunches, ski trips, friendsgivings, happy hour thing I just thought would always be there. Only I wasn't sleeping, I was working. And when I looked up, I was alone, and work wasn't enough. I couldn't make work fill up every corner of my life."

"Same," said Mary, "What's your family like?"

I hesitated. "My parents were only children too. They, uh, they think I am absolutely killing it in every way out here. If my dad found out about this, he would forcibly move me back to Chicago. I talked to my mom, she even told me she was jealous of me, because I was living her dream life."

"Right, right." Ty nodded, facilitating me. "So tell us about your IF, Flossie, how did you two meet?" He nodded at me, like he was nudging me. He wanted me to out myself as Nancy. I pretended I didn't know what he was doing. "Olivia is my IF, and she's cooler than me. She's a graphic designer. She started out sweet, but she's kind of become a tough-love friend. She doesn't let me get away with anything. I was going to fly to Portland tonight, but Olivia made me come here. Honestly, I feel honored sometimes, when she hangs out with me. Oh, and I met her after a day of intense introspection and feeling sorry for myself. I work from home, and I was about to fall into being a full recluse. I was going to board myself in my apartment forever so I could just accept my fate and die alone and go undiscovered for weeks, maybe months. But then Olivia showed up and made me get outside again. Sometimes I hate her for it, but I end up appreciating it." I smiled at Olivia where she stood at the edge of the circle. She smiled back and fidgeted with her drink.

"Powerful. Thank you." Henry smiled.

"Yeah, thanks." Mary kind of smiled too.

Ty clapped his hand, bringing an end to the nice moment. "This is exactly what I hoped would happen. Thanks everybody. I'm just going to take a quick spin around the room, and make sure everyone's comfortable and getting to know each other, then we'll gather everybody." Ty whirled away.

"I'm getting another glass of wine." Mary turned and followed Ty away, leaving Henry and I to stand and fidget.

"So, that was interesting, Olivia. In addition to the whole IF thing, it's kind of nice to hear from someone else who hates working at home."

"I'm Flossie, Olivia's my IF."

"Oh no, oh no, I'm so sorry."

"It's fine. It doesn't bother me. But back to your point, yes, I hate working from home. It messes with your mind."

"It totally does . . . where in the city do you live? If you don't mind me asking. If that's too personal a question, or you're not comfortable in any way, please refrain from answering."

"It's fine. I live in Noe, and you?"

"Potrero Hill."

"Cool, cool. Hey is Abe here right now?"

"Oh, yeah, he's here." His eyes darted to my right. "Is Olivia?"

"Yeah, she's here."

"Um, maybe, you and Olivia, might want to grab coffee or something with us one of these days? It would be nice to talk to somebody about all this. Again, only if you're comfortable."

"Did Abe make you ask me?"

"Kind of, yeah. Sorry. Well, technically he didn't, but I knew if I didn't ask, he would respect me even less."

"No, it's fine. Olivia's making me say yes."

"Sorry to interrupt, kids, but Henry, I have to steal Flossie for moment." Ty had his arm around my shoulder and was leading me away before he even finished his sentence.

"But Ty," I protested.

"It's okay," Henry called after me, "I'll catch up with you."

"Work the room, Flossie!" Ty whisper-yelled into my ear as he continued leading me to the other side of the bar. "If I hadn't popped in there, you would have stood there mumbling and apologizing back and forth with that human pencil, all night long. The guy's probably allergic to pencils." Ty dragged me through the room introducing me to the bar owner Rowan and his Imaginary sober companion, Morris. There was steampunk Shay, and her IF Benson, a poet. Lily and her IF, Julius, who was half cat, half human. "Does he look like Mr. Mistoffelees?" I asked, "From 'Cats?' The musical? Nevermind." I happily allowed Ty to move me along to George and his IFs, Salt and Pepper, performance artists, and to point out Simone in the corner, swaying and dancing with who I guessed had to be Terry.

"Friendlies! Attention Friendlies!" It was Ty, who was suddenly gone from my side and yelling at us from somewhere with an ancient, crackling microphone. "Glad you are all having a great time, but can I get you over here in the corner? Hey! Come here! Sheesh, for a bunch of socially awkward freaks with no friends, you sure do talk a lot." There was silence in the room for a split second that felt to me as if it was heavy with doom, but quickly dissipated into whooping and clapping, and a very impressive whistle from Henry, whose last name I did not know, and who I could see above the crowd, almost hovering like a charming ghost. We all migrated to the corner where Ty was standing on a small stage that was just big enough for him, and a drum set and a keyboard. I pictured him singing, Iggy playing the keyboard, and Trey, the drums.

When the noise level evened out a little, Ty started in with what I knew was the inspirational speech he'd prepared to make us all feel better about ourselves, the hands the universe had dealt us, and our unusual but brave life choices. Much of the crowd was well blitzed by all of the liquid courage and social lubricants they'd consumed throughout the evening; nobody seemed equipped to listen to a speech, but they did applaud for themselves, and their imaginary friends, and yelled the occasional self-deprecating joke about loneliness. After what felt like the twentieth interruption in the touchiest-feeliest portion of his pep talk, Ty shrugged his shoulders, and skipped to the end where we are supposed to go forth into the night and celebrate our perseverance and ingenuity in a lonely world, and look around at this new community! The world just got a little less lonely.

I felt a deep sense of relief that the opportunity never arose for me to reveal myself as Nancy. "Let's come back next week!" someone hollered from the crowd.

"Um, well how about next month?" Ty called out into the bar's crackly microphone.

People cheered again and started chanting, "Friend-ly, Friend-ly." It was like they'd never been around people before.

I saw Mary writing down her number, or maybe a recipe, or a citation, and giving it to a guy in a fisherman's sweater and cowboy hat, and realized I never made it back to Henry and he would have no idea how to get a hold of me for our coffee. Olivia was in the corner laughing with a half-cat, half-person, Salt and Pepper, and the very androgynous Terry. People were trickling out, and I couldn't see Henry hovering above any of them. I was trying not to feel desperate, and panicky about how hard I was looking around the room when I felt a tap on my shoulder.

"Flossie, are you looking for something?"

"Oh! Henry! I'm looking for you actually," I blurted, knowing I would hear from Olivia later about being too eager.

"Really? Oh, good. Um, we talked earlier about maybe getting . . ."

"Coffee? Yes. Let me write down my info."

"Nice pen. I have one just like it in Midnight Velvet. What is that? Indigo?"

CHAPTER TEN

Many of the books I read through the years spent pages and pages detailing new love, broken love, forbidden love, dying love, undying love, and the most painful love of them all, unrequited love. But all that love had to start somewhere, (or not, if it was of the unrequited variety.) Literature love is often born of incredible circumstances like danger, hatred, trauma, hardship, or the gradual realization that your soul mate has been under your nose the entire time. Literature, however, hasn't been very forthcoming with perfectly turned phrases describing first dates. Beach reads, and young adult novels, are far more helpful with the anxiety and even logistics of what to expect on a first date, or in my current case determining what even constitutes a first date.

I had plans to meet Henry. He sent me a message five days after the party, and two days after Olivia had convinced me that he had likely died of a panic attack before getting up the nerve to reach out. In our logistical back and forth, neither Henry nor I used the word "date" in our correspondence. Date felt like a dated term that nobody really used to describe whatever they, themselves were doing. I would never say out loud, "I have a date." But if you pointed to any two people sharing a bottle of wine, leaning toward each other to hear what the other is saying, maybe reaching out to gently touch an arm or a face while tilting their heads and laughing or smiling or glowing from the inside out—and you and asked me what *they* were doing? I would either say, "torturing me," or "they're on a date."

My first outing with Henry wasn't the low-key coffee meet-up with our IFs we had haltingly talked about that first night. Olivia pointed out that if by some chance Henry was not dead of a panic attack, and we were to get together, his height and his job were already very Charlie-esque, and if I saw him drinking Charlie's favorite pour-over coffee, my ovaries might just shrivel up and die. So, at her suggestion, I pushed for happy hour drinks in the Financial District. Olivia gave me the plan like we were getting ready to raid a drug den with the rest of our SWAT team. "You'll both be slightly out of your element, out of your neighborhoods, and your mutual discomfort with social situations will force you into each other's arms, which seems to be something you want. Are you sure that's what you want? You're kind of taking the first thing that comes along. There might be something just around the corner. Something better. Something with muscle tone and a passport and dairy tolerance."

"Are you serious? You've been trying to get me to go out and meet guys for months!"

"I know, but different guys. Whatever. You're a grown woman."

"Is it my imagination, or are you being weird right now?" I cocked my head to the side.

"It's your imagination. Remember, Flossie? It's *all*

your imagination."

"Very funny. Anyway, Henry's nice, and his IF Abe sounds like someone you might get along with."

She rolled her eyes at me, straightened her short skirt and stepped into her tall shoes.

When I arrived at McCallaghan's, I found Henry waiting at a back table, fiddling with the buttons on his shirt. He stood up, and pulled a chair out for me. Olivia threw her hands up in the air, annoyed that he'd forgotten her.

"I didn't know what to wear here. I've never really spent time around so many bank people, and I've worked at home for so long that I almost forgot how to use buttons." He was still thinking about his buttons.

I told him he looked nice, and he blurted out that I looked nice the moment I began talking, as if he was trying to beat me to it. His knee bounced as we both scanned the room for a server, as two owls might scan the room for a chubby and distracted mouse to share. The mouse spotted us finally, and seeing the desperate looks in our owl eyes, came straight over, perhaps anticipating a social emergency that she might be able to fix.

"So, Henry, did you bring Abe?" I asked after our waitress scrambled away leaving Henry and I as alone as two people with imaginary friends could be.

"I did. And speaking of Abe, I have some questions," his voice lowered, and he leaned in closer.

"How long have you and Olivia been friends?"

"I met her on the plane when we were moving out here."

"No, not like that, I mean, how long have you been friends with Olivia, in the *friendly* way."

"Oh, um I guess, like ten months."

"What?"

Oh no.

"Ten months? Ty's article came out not that long ago. That means . . . Wait . . . are you . . . are you, Nancy? You said at the party you'd already met Ty. You have to be Nancy."

"I am."

"No! I can't believe it!" he yelped, then leaned in with a whisper. "You're a legend. Wow, I suddenly feel very weird. And like a giant idiot. And very self-conscious. But also, proud, maybe? Honored? I don't know. I should stop talking."

"Please don't. The only thing about my being Nancy is that I was the quickest to snap after being even a little bit cut off from meaningful human contact. I'm Nancy because I was the weakest."

"Or the bravest. Listen. Let's just assume you're awesome, and creative, and a visionary."

"I'm so sorry, I don't mean to be a pain, but I hate the word visionary."

"How visionary of you. Sorry. Anyway, I thought I had questions before, but now I have soooo many questions."

"Go ahead."

And so I pretended to be delightfully surprised at all the same questions Etta and Ty had already asked.

"How do you interact with other people's IFs? Like, what

are Abe and Olivia doing right now?"

"Okay, based on your description, I see my version of Abe, sitting here with Olivia, intently listening to our conversation. Abe keeps looking at Olivia, she's kind of eating up the attention, but not really reciprocating, because she thinks that will keep him interested. Now he's smirking and she's giving me a very dirty look. Sometimes I talk to Ty's IFs, or I kind of picture them in the room interacting, but I generally follow his lead, on what his IFs do or don't do."

He was nodding, "Do you think, now that the Friendlies have met, and might meet again, do we still get to keep our IFs? I'm sure you would never have guessed but it's been a while since I've hung out with humans, let alone a pretty girl."

"Wow, thank you. Oh no, you may not have even been talking about me."

"I was."

I could feel my cheeks turn red. I hadn't felt that in a long time. Once, back when I first met Frank, he complimented my sweater, so, maybe then. "Since I've been friends with Ty, and now meeting you and the other people at the party, I feel like I actually need Olivia to help me process it all, and she's kind of inserted herself even more into my life."

"Really? What did she think of me?"

I glanced in Olivia's direction. She was sipping a martini and looking sidelong at Abe, who was very rugged, confident, and handsome. "She thinks you're sweet, maybe with just a small chance of being a serial killer, but probably not. She's tough, remember? Protective."

"I'm not a serial killer."

"Great. And, anyway, I let Ty know I was coming here in case Olivia and I disappeared. Did you tell your roommate you were meeting me?"

"I mentioned it, yes, but not so he would know where I am in case you turned out to be a serial killer. You're not are you? Not that it's an immediate deal-breaker."

The waitress finally arrived, and came back two more times delivering increasingly complex cocktails. When I noticed Henry starting to slur, I suggested we call it a night. I enjoyed his company, and I didn't want to not enjoy his company.

"Wait, I have to tell you something," he said as I settled the bill and ordered our separate rides home. "I had an imaginary cat when I was a kid. It was the fluffiest cat. I let it crawl all over me and it never made me sneeze, or wheeze or itch. I even named it Fluffy, and I imagined playing with it, and fur flying every-where, and me kind of spinning around in the flying fur, like it was snowing. I grew out of the cat. And now, here I am, a grown man. Actually, I think I still might be growing. Anyway, now I have a dog. Really, it's Abe's, and it's so fluffy, too. Did I tell you that? I made an imaginary dog, with so much hair and tons of dander. Did I tell you that?"

"You did, but that's okay," I assured him. "I'm considering a cat, myself. Or maybe a baby giraffe? Or a unicorn? I don't know."

We stepped outside, and my ride whirred to the corner almost silently. The driver stuck his head out of the window. "Flassie?"

"Flossie, that's me." I tuned to Henry. "Well, bye." He was rocking back and forth. "Are you okay, Henry? We can wait for your car to get here."

"I'm fine. Can I give you a hug?"

"Sure."

And we hugged. It felt like I was holding him up a little, but he smelled nice. Non-relative, totally human hug #3. "Can I see you again?" he slurred.

"Yes, I would like that," I said as I climbed into the backseat, feeling like I was at the end of a beach read first date, probably not a literature first date.

"Good night, Olivia," he called into the space next to me.

"Come on Abe," I could hear him yell, as we pulled away from the curb, "let's go!" Never mind, not even a beach read first date.

"Who's Olivia? I thought your name was Flossie," the driver said.

Olivia

I did not feel compelled to inform Flossie that I already knew Abe. I had mentioned him to her, but in a low-key, generic way, like "I flirted with a lumberjack at this work thing," but I'd left it at that because she did not need to hear about my social successes when she could barely even get off the couch. My thing with Abe was never going anywhere anyway; talking to him was like trying to maintain a riveting conversation with an actual log. It also wasn't a good time for me to be fretting over a random guy when Flossie so desperately needed me. I had not thought about Abe in forever, so I could not believe my non-existent eyes when I saw him walk through the door at the IFs party. I managed to avoid a run-in with him by busying myself with Salt, Pepper, and the lovely life coach, Tina, who helped me work through some stuff.

Once Flossie made plans with Henry, I knew I'd have to see Abe again, and I would have to talk to him. At the bar, when Henry and Flossie were making their awkwardness worse with all that alcohol—it was cute how good they thought they were doing—I tried talking to Abe. I asked him how he'd been. He said "fine," and spent much of the night staring at Henry with palpable disdain. At one point, in the middle of Flossie's story about the time she left a deli without the very sandwich she went in to purchase, Abe aimed his stubby thumb at Flossie and said, "You're stuck with a real winner there." I threw a drink in his face, and suggested another place he might like to put his thumb.

CHAPTER ELEVEN

By the time the next Friendly Fete rolled around, Henry and I had hugged five more times; once following happy hour in Japan Town; once, post-burritos in the Mission District; one time after a food truck rally; and the latest hugs came before and after dinner at last year's hot spot, Fish Face. When he hugged me after Fish Face, I thought he might kiss me too. I almost asked him if he wanted to, but I didn't, and so of course he didn't, and I wondered if it was because my face smelled like fish, since he's a vegan whose face probably smelled like Japanese Eggplant.

I made plans with Henry to meet up at the next Friendly party. Ty and Iggy were still together, and much to Olivia's dismay, Ty had given Trey an IF girlfriend, Mabel. Mabel was an artist, and intensely everything—intellectual, sexual, musical, beautiful, and conveniently, Iggy's best friend, which meant double dates every night of the week. On our girls' nights in our college sweatshirts, Olivia and I spent at least half the time talking about how much we hated Mabel. Olivia wasn't exactly thrilled with Henry, either. One minute she was ridiculing him for his awkwardness, the next she was chastising me for not throwing myself at him. "If you don't at least kiss that loser at this party, I don't know what I'm going to do with you."

Ty didn't ask me to ride with him to the party, and he didn't send peonies, and he didn't seem particularly interested in whether or not I planned to reveal myself as Nancy. That week he'd taken his IFs to the beach and to six different parks throughout the city. Ty was quickly ruining his reputation as a hater of the outdoors. I heard him in the hallway one afternoon, engaged in what sounded like a very real telephone conversation with a human person, talking about the party and how passionate he was about his new community.

Henry was waiting outside the bar when I arrived to the party, and hugged me hello (hug #7). As he and I sipped our dill beers at the bar, a woman waved her hand between us, and hollered her order of a root beer and rum. "Oh, hey guys! It's, me Mary!" She clasped a hand down on each of our shoulders.

"Mary! I almost didn't recognize you!" I said, surprised. It was true, I did not recognize her, until she said, "It's me, Mary." Since the last time I'd seen her, she'd swapped her dour, anxious expression for a smile and a face full of pink makeup, and her drab business casual outfit for a bright sundress.

"I'm so glad you're here. Tina's here, too! Are you going to say hello?"

"Hello, Tina," Henry and I said in unison, like we were children responding to a request from our mother. I scrambled to try to remember Tina's details. Matronly, I think? I imagined a nice nanny standing next to Tina, in ill-fitting slacks, sipping on a pisco sour.

"Ok, well, I already know you," Mary said throwing money down for her root beer and rum, "Tina's making me mingle before Anthony gets here. Did I tell you? I met a guy here last time. Anthony. His IF is his grandpa. Isn't that sweet? We thought maybe he and Tina might hit it off. Wish me luck!"

"Did she just bounce away?" Henry asked.

"I think she did."

Unlike Mary, Simone did not look any more relaxed than she had at the last party. Her hair was still wild, and she was clutching her purse in one hand, and a piece of paper in the other. I was guessing they were questions and feedback she and Terry had for Ty because she followed him around the room as he networked. Ty knew she was there, but masterfully kept his back to her, and never lingered long enough to allow Simone, or Terry, to corner him. I was comfortable on my stool not networking, and satisfied knowing that if I wanted to, I could talk to absolutely anybody in the bar, because I was one of them. And Henry was relaxed next to me, chatting a little about work, and a little about his roommate, who had decided he was over minimalism, and really going for a maximalist lifestyle. The roommate had purchased a life-size brass tiger to guard the fridge that was full of champagne, cheese, and chocolate covered cherries. "I almost died, Flossie, tripping over the tiger," Henry said animatedly, "then I almost died from sheer terror, then from what I think was a rage-induced heart attack. Then when I didn't die, I wanted to kill the guy, with his own tiger. Oh, sheesh, look at those guys," he said forgetting the tiger, and gesturing across the room.

I looked over to where Henry was pointing. And there, one adorned in the tightest yellow pants I had ever seen, and the other in painted-on mauve suit, were Frank and Bob.

"No. No. No. Oh, God no. Why?"

"Flossie, what's wrong?"

"I know them."

"You do?"

"I do. I work with them. Why are they here? They don't need imaginary friends. They have pods. Pods of really beautiful, well-traveled, artistic, active, stylish, human friends."

"Maybe their pods dropped them when they saw those pants."

"No, Frank and Bob are rock stars."

"They are? I've never heard of them, and I've literally heard of everybody. What kind of music do they make?"

"No, not music rock stars, rock stars in their field. They are the reason I hate the word visionaries."

Frank and Bob scanned the room. They didn't only stand out because I already knew them, they were just that different than the rest of us. I was confident a casual bystander would be able to guess that they were not accompanied by imaginary friends. I blocked my face with my beer, so I could still peer over the top of the glass and keep a watchful eye on the scene. Ty descended on the pair, shaking their hands with too much force, then waving his arms around as if he were showing him the vast reaches of his odd little kingdom. I could tell by just the enthusiastic and animated hand motions, that he was telling them how much our community had grown in the month.

Frank and Bob looked in our general direction following Ty's arm flinging. We made what seemed to be disinterested, accidental, momentary eye contact, before they turned their attention back to the rest of the crowd.

"They don't recognize me," I said, sighing with relief.

"I take it people at work don't know about your . . . about Olivia."

"No, they do not."

"Well if these guys are here, they probably have IFs, and don't want to reveal themselves by ratting you out."

"No, not those guys. They're trend-spotters. They're ahead of everything. They're here for reconnaissance."

"It's just our second party."

"That's how good they are. I didn't tell you, but my firm basically drove the whole "Introverting of America" thing, and those two had the keys and the traveling snacks. They don't live in the now, they live in the six-months-from-now."

"Got it. We'll have to talk about your company later, but in the meantime, we'll just keep you on the other side of the room."

"Flossie, is that you? Long time no see." It was Frank, close enough where I could feel his breath on my neck. I froze for a moment before turning around.

"Hi Frank. Bob. What are you doing here?"

"Research. Is that why you're here?"

"I'm Henry," Henry stuck out his hand, with a very valiant,

time-buying handshake.

Both Bob and Frank shook his hand, without losing the confused, but not-confused-enough, looks on their faces.

"Flossie, is this imaginary friend thing for real? Were you ahead of this? Have you been working on this?"

"Not really," I gulped my dill beer looking for confidence and an idea.

"Flossie, are you . . . do you," Frank leaned in to whisper, very gentlemanly away from Henry, "are you here with an imaginary friend?"

"I'm not imaginary," Henry said with a laugh. "Can we order you fellas a beer? I hear their sage is pretty good."

"Oh, are you guys *not* here for the party? Oh . . ." Bob said, nodding. And just as I was about to agree, Ty showed up.

"Bob, Frank, this is my dear friend, and one of our founding Friendlies, Flossie O'Brien. Flossie, this is Bob and Frank, and they are about to take us to the next level."

"Please don't tell Dave." I had left the comfort of my barstool next to Henry, for a much scarier small bar table a few feet away with Bob and Frank.

"Do you think we're going to tell Dave that you were this far ahead of us?" Frank said, frowning at the room temperature water and lemon slice, "We need *you* not to tell Dave."

"Deal," I said, "Oh, and guys, do not tell anyone from Cerulean, please. Not Fiona, not anybody. My involvement here has nothing to do with work."

"We heard about this party, and are trying to figure out if this is going to be something, or if it's a one-off, or if it will fizzle before it starts, or if it's already happening out there. Are you guys the first to organize or what? Is it marketable? Billable? Is it cool? Or Is it just sad? I'm not getting a read. I usually get a read." Bob's brow was furrowed. He was thinking out loud.

"Flossie, how did you end up here? How were you on the ground floor of this?" Frank rested his chin in his hand as if he was striking a thoughtful pose for the dust jacket of heartbreaking novel about one man's quest for meaning in a meaningless world.

I gave them the most glamorous version of the story that I could come up with. Overworked! Solitude! Society's sudden obsession with intimacy! A lifelong active imagination! I did it to prevent myself from losing my mind, not because I'd already lost it! And, little did I know, I wasn't actually alone, I was surrounded by other avant-garde individuals fed up with the artificial precepts about what constitutes reality and relationships and mental health! Frank and Bob wanted to know every detail about Olivia, but I told them nothing, citing the privacy that I suddenly cared deeply about.

Henry watched protectively from his barstool. He was flanked by Abe and Olivia, both frowning, and for different reasons. Abe was visibly/invisibly bored, and Olivia was not happy with how I was handling myself. Ty circled our table jealously. Frank and Bob had dismissed him. Trey really needed to talk to him about how generally off-putting his desperation for cultural relevancy could be.

"I just don't know what to do with you. I don't know how to feel about you, Flossie." Frank kept his chin in his hand.

"You made that clear."

"I mean. Are you the coolest? Or, are you the saddest?"

"Maybe the coolest of the sad?" I suggested straight-faced, sipping from my drink.

Frank and Bob laughed harder than I knew they were capable of, which to people who did not know them, would have appeared to be one facial muscle beyond a smirk. I tried using the same mind muscles that willed Olivia into existence to wish Frank and Bob away from me. Not seeing them for so long made me start to forget how I'd felt before I met Olivia. But now we were sharing the same air, and they were mauve and yellow reminders that I was supposed to be busy hating myself, and trying to figure out if I was alone because I was inferior, or inferior because I was alone.

Frank and Bob waxed poetic about next-level lonelies being unintended casualties of their paradigm shifting work and I kicked myself, figuratively, as the world was truly not ready for a new subculture of literal self-kickers. I had brought the moment upon myself earlier at the bar, feeling arrogant enough to be comfortable and confident in a room full of like-minded oddballs, surveying them as if I was their benevolent queen. I was surely being punished for my self-satisfaction.

"We'll have to digest this," Bob's voice was directed back to me, but I wasn't sure what they were about to digest.

"When we do," Frank continued, "we'll get back to you, so

we can pick your brain a little more." And without looking at me again, they stood, nodded at Ty, and weaved their way through the crowd that did not seem as impressed by them, as they might have otherwise been used to.

"Are you going to get fired? Is it bad?" Henry asked, looking concerned as I climbed back onto my barstool.

"I don't think so. I don't know. Maybe."

"Do you want to get out of here?" He nudged my elbow with his.

"Sure," I said, trying to contain the simultaneous anxiety, excitement, and dread I was feeling at the moment.

Getting out of there to Henry, meant another hug outside, and each of us departing separately into the night. Olivia didn't look at me at all during the long ride home. Every once in a while she'd chuckle to herself. If we passed a bar, or a group of people on the street, she'd look back at them longingly.

"Maybe he was tired," I said breaking the silence as I unlocked the door to my place, kicking my shoes off before I was even all the way in the inside. "Or," I continued, "maybe he thought I looked tired, and he doesn't want me to get sick so we can go on a proper date. Maybe he thought I was emotionally fragile after seeing Frank and Bob, and he didn't want to take advantage of that. That's actually pretty sweet."

"Maybe," Olivia said her voice full of passive aggressive doubt. "Or, maybe you're just not his type. Maybe he's never had a girlfriend. Maybe he doesn't want to date anyone in the lifestyle. Maybe he's married. Maybe he has an Iggy of his own."

"You think? I don't know. Maybe, I guess. Listen, I'm going to bed."

"You dragged me all the way over here, for twenty-eight seconds of watching you mope? Fine. Good night. Oh, and I have to work tomorrow, so I can't hang out."

She kicked at my shoes that blocked the door, and opened it without looking at me, and slipped out.

Was she mad? At me? What did she have to be mad about? Was it jealousy? Did she think Henry could come between us? Was she afraid I was moving on without her? Friends get annoyed and fight. She would get over this. I had real things to worry about.

I had a message waiting for me when I woke up.

"You okay?"

It wasn't Olivia, my mom, Ty, or Dave. It was Henry. Some difficult-to-identify part of me fluttered. If I were ever to go on a walk and disappear, there was someone else on the short list of people who might notice my absence.

I messaged him back boldly that I had not been okay, but felt totally okay when I got his message. I also mentioned my desire for brunch foods, and that Olivia was working, so maybe, if he wanted, he could leave Abe sleeping, or chopping wood, or building a credenza, to join me.

I was a block away from the restaurant, but spotted Henry. He was taller than the throng of brunch appreciators milling about on the sidewalk. I walked faster. He didn't look uncomfortable. He looked relaxed. He wore an expertly buttoned shirt

I had never seen, and faded, soft-looking jeans. He'd gotten a haircut at some point in the last fourteen hours. I'd met him out in public before, but it felt different today. Olivia wasn't there.

Abe wasn't there. It was just the two of us.

I didn't wait for him to hug me, I hugged him first.

"You look happy," he said.

"I am. It's gorgeous today. I don't need a coat. I'm about to eat Eggs Benedict. Thanks for meeting me. What did Abe say when you left without him?"

"Oh, he came with me. But he's taking the dog to the park while we eat."

My disappointment surprised me. I'd left the house just fine on my own that day. Sure I was annoyed at Olivia, but mostly because she was annoyed at me. Maybe it was just enough space to propel me out here into the world to meet a tall, real boy for eggs. He couldn't do the same, but I guess leaving Abe and the dog at the park was a start.

Henry hadn't picked up on my disappointment, because he was chattering away about how we only had an hour wait and even though San Franciscans are so used to instant gratification, they are still willing to wait for brunch. He'd taken his hand out of his pocket, and it was just dangling there. Olivia wasn't there, but I could almost hear her telling me to grab it. Either grab it, or stop thinking about grabbing it. So I did. I grabbed it. I hadn't asked Henry for permission, and almost immediately regretted it, because he stopped mid-sentence and stared at our clasped hands as if my grabbing it had made him suddenly realize that he even had hands.

We stood there in some kind of suspended reality, me staring at him staring at our hands. I waited for him to do something, and after what seemed like forever, I started to let go, and mutter, "I'm so sorr—" but he squeezed my hand back, so I didn't let go.

"Is this okay?" I finished.

"Yeah," he blurted, louder than I expected, then quieted after our fellow brunchers turned around to look. "It's just been a long time."

"A long time?"

"Since I've held hands with someone. A really, really long time. So stupid, I'm sorry Flossie, forget I said anything."

"No, it's been a long time for me too. Olivia held my hand once, when she helped me to my bedroom after we polished off a couple bottles of Zinfandel, and I couldn't walk straight. Well, I guess that was all me, wasn't it? But this feels different than that time."

"Yeah, I guess it would." It looked like he was blushing, though he might have been getting a sunburn, along with the rest of us on the sidewalk. I think our skin had collectively as a generation become sensitive to any light stronger than the glow of our computer screens, and whatever rays made it through the fog.

We chatted about the weather a little, and all the parts of the previous evening's party not involving Frank and Bob. As happy as I suddenly was, I still found myself drifting off, wishing Olivia was here to see this . . . me standing on the street, holding hands with a guy. I thought about what Henry and I must look like to everybody standing around waiting for a table. Did we look like a normal couple? Like holding hands was what we did all the time? Maybe we looked so normal that nobody thought anything about us at all. Maybe people assumed we were college sweethearts, or met in a bar, or that mutual friends had introduced us at my college roommate's destination wedding in Palm Springs. Maybe we met at a coffee shop, or at the park, or at the finish line of a marathon—my first, his third—where we were exhilarated not just by our individual accomplishments, but that we'd met our soul mates as we reached for the same cup of water. We could totally pass for a couple who met at cooking class, or interning for the same law firm, or on a blind date. I was so lost in all of the places we could have met, I almost forgot he was there in real time, and not the uneven timing of most of my social interactions. He seemed to be waiting for me to say something.

"What? I'm sorry, I'm distracted."

"That's okay," he said, squeezing my hand tighter.

I was sad when our names were called, and I had to let go of his hand so I could sit across from him.

"Does your mom still write?" I peeked over the menu, and asked with a familiarity that startled even me. I'd been in a restaurant with him many times now, and we'd talked about work, and our IFs, and Ty. But I'd just held his hand, so it was definitely time to talk about our mothers.

"I think she's holding out hope that she gets a grandchild

with an allergy or some kind of disorder she can champion. If she could get an adult-onset something, she would be the happiest woman in the world."

"Does she know about Abe? She could champion your cause, start a whole thing for family of Friendlies. Family & Friends & Friends—I think we're on to something. I'll send her a button and a bumper sticker tomorrow."

I raced through my breakfast, so we could get back to handholding. But then, concerned I'd eaten too fast and was forcing Henry to get back to Abe and their magic-dander dog, I ordered a cappuccino and stirred it for fifteen minutes. Abe was a survivalist; he should be fine roaming around for a while longer. I wished we were in my neighborhood, and not all the way over in North Beach. It would be nice if a neighbor, or someone from the artisan meat place could see me with Henry, flirtatiously stirring for the benefit of a human being with skin; talking out loud to a person, who somehow kept getting more handsome every time I saw him.

Once we had covered my mother and her inability to let go of the 1990s, we stood to leave, only to be replaced at the table by a couple who for sure met while interning at the same law office.

Henry grabbed my hand as we made our way to the exit, and I tried to contain my smile as once outside, he steered me in the opposite direction of the park. Abe could wait. Henry wasn't saying anything and neither was I. I could hear him every time he swallowed. It helped that his Adam's apple was the size of a golf ball. I didn't know what to say. If I talked about us—the he and I, us—that would be weird. But if I talked about the weather again, or breakfast, or asked him another question about his parents, that would be weird too. So I said nothing. The more we strolled, and the more nothing we said, the more I thought about how much nothing we were saying. The blocks started slanting upward to the sky, and our stroll turned into a climb. I focused on breathing and not hyperventilating, though I was basically summiting Everest, if Everest was dotted with multi-million dollar homes occupied by rich, urban Sherpas who probably had to use the special altitude instructions when making boxed brownies.

Not very long ago, I was so desperate to stop saying nothing all the time that I willed Olivia into my life, and I started feeling normal, and happier because the silence had stopped. But as we climbed, I enjoyed very much saying nothing. Quiet + nobody = sad. Quiet + somebody = weirdness. Quiet + somebody + strolling + holding hands = comfort, and comfort > weirdness. But strolling + hand-holding + quiet + equations = ridiculous. If Olivia was there she would have known I was thinking about math, and she would have been disappointed, in that intimidating, guilt-inducing way of hers that suggests I'm hopeless. But she wasn't there, and I wouldn't tell her what I was and wasn't thinking about. And I didn't spill my inner ramblings to Henry, so all of my stupid thoughts stayed tucked away as we climbed skyward.

Our path became more narrow and so steep that the sidewalk

became a concrete set of stairs, and we had to drop hands. I was relieved only because Henry didn't need a palmful of my sweat as a memento. I trailed behind him and quickly wiped my hands off on my hips. When we'd wound our way to the top of the hill, Coit Tower loomed above us. Tourists milled about, aiming their cameras up at the tower, at the statue of Christopher Columbus who was standing guard in the parking lot, and furiously left and right, trying to catch the panoramic views of the bay and the colorful buildings jutting from the rolling hills. "I love it up here," I said. I was going to say something about how winded I was, and how much I needed to spend a solid week in spin class, but I knew Olivia wouldn't say anything like that, and I kind of needed to think about what she might do at this moment. Instead of taking me by the hand, he wrapped his long fingers around my wrist, and pulled me gently to a spot at the edge of the lot that looked out over the city, then moved around to stand in front of me. I saw the golf ball in his throat bob around.

"Flossie, I'm just going to say this. I've wanted to say this for weeks, but I think I'm ready to say it. I would very much like to kiss you. But I haven't kissed anybody for a long time, and I'm probably worse at it than I am at holding hands. But if I don't say anything, I will always regret it. If you don't want me to kiss you, I understand that, and I respect you, and your womanhood."

"My womanhood?"

"Yes, I'm sorry, asking your permission felt like the right thing to do. It is, isn't it?"

"No, I mean, yes, it's fine. It's good. I respect you, and your manhood. And, yes, I would like for you to kiss me."

He smiled, and breathed a sigh of relief, and then did not move.

"Is this a right now thing?" I asked. "The kiss? Or for another time of our choosing?"

"Oh, right now, I thought. There are a lot of people, but nobody's looking at us, really. We've learned that, right? I do probably smell like coffee and vegan bacon, and again, I'm woefully out of practice."

"Me too, on all of the above, except swap the vegan bacon for Hollandaise."

"Okay. Here goes." He placed his hands on the tops of my shoulders, like he was preparing to tell me the truth about something. I aimed my face upward toward him, and from the angle I was standing, it looked like he was the same height as the famous Coit Tower. I closed my eyes.

"Before we kiss," he said softly. I opened my eyes again. "Did your breakfast contain any tree nuts that might still be lingering on or near your general mouth area?"

"No."

"Are you wearing a lip product—gloss, stick, or balm— that may have been produced in a factory where nut products are also made?"

"No, it's just honey, wax, and shea butter, and it's been hours since I've even applied it."

"Oh, you have naturally pretty lips." He bent over at the

waist, as if his lanky body were on a hinge, and kissed me gently.

"Hot," Olivia said rolling her eyes, as I relayed most of the details to her. "So after the allergy checklist, he kept his hands on your shoulders? The whole time?" Olivia was wearing her Michigan sweatshirt and sitting cross-legged on my couch. She still seemed kind of mad at me when she walked in the door. I immediately blurted out, "Henry kissed me today," but instead of running giddily to the couch to hear every juicy, sordid detail, of which there were none, she picked apart the kiss that I had not been able to stop thinking about.

"Yes, he kept his hands on my shoulders, and his butt was sticking out in the walkway because he had to bend over so far to get to my face."

"How long did he kiss you? A couple of seconds? A minute? There's a big difference between the two."

"It was the middle of the day. I was sweaty from walking to the top of the universe. Tourists were everywhere. Children were everywhere. It was very appropriate for the circumstances and for the stage in our relationship. He kissed me for the most appropriate amount of time, and honestly it was very nice. I had braced myself for terrible, or uncomfortable, but it wasn't. I felt bad that he had to bend over so far, but it was nice. And I didn't even think about anything else, while he was kissing me. I didn't even think about the fact that I wasn't thinking about anything."

"Ugh, stop that."

"Stop what?"

"Stop thinking about *thinking* about everything. It's not

cute, and it's not the mark of superior intelligence. It's just annoying. For God's sake, don't tell anybody else that's how your mind works, especially a guy. Unless he's on drugs. A guy on drugs might want to hear about that. Wait, are *you* on drugs?"

"You are really ruining my mood right now. I thought you would be happy for me. You were so frustrated about how slowly things were going with Henry. We've finally taken charge of the situation."

"I'm just being real with you, Flossie, which is ironic, isn't it? What you're doing isn't taking charge. You took charge when you brought me in to your life. You didn't take charge when you let the pencil kiss you in the day time. I'm just trying to protect you, a little from yourself, and a little from other people who could take advantage of you."

"You're the one who needs to stop. I don't need this right now. You're not making any sense anyway."

"Listen carefully. She came over to place her hands on the tops of my shoulders, and look into my eyes, surely mocking Henry. "You can do better, Flossie; but to do better, you might need to step up, and *be* better. 'kay?"

"I'm tired, Olivia, good night."

"You're not tired. You're just going wrap yourself in a blanket and think about how you're thinking about this fight, telling yourself you're right and I'm wrong, but really, you'll just be delaying the obvious, which is acknowledging that I'm right, and by proxy, you're right too."

Olivia

I couldn't even get any real satisfaction out of being right, because that meant that she would still get credit for it anyway, which made crazy. I was still mad at her. I'm not sure if it was jealousy, or resentment, but I was due both. I am capable of doing absolutely anything; as in, anything. I am not restricted by the laws of physics, or morals or even a court of law. I was saddled into the most mediocre of fantasies. I should be sprouting wings and flying around the city. I should time travel, steal a diamond, or bed a movie star. I should design clothes for giraffes, or be part giraffe, or dig a hole to China. I should turn the world into an oyster, and eat it. I would be absolutely killing it, if this girl was capable of using her imagination for anything other than wondering what people were thinking about her at any given moment. I was supposed to be sophisticated and worldly and beautiful, but I was following Flossie around, giving in to her every whim. I was not making any traction with these weird pathetic guys that kept hanging around. Trey was cool, until Mabel came along. Mabel sucks; I hate her.

Maybe it's time for me to move on. Maybe I should move to Paris, or New York. Maybe I'll find Camila in Miami. Maybe Flossie and I are just growing in different directions. Or she's growing, and I'm left to stagnate, or worse, I'm left to be the shrew . . . the jealous, resentful shrew.

CHAPTER TWELVE

The first few days after the Friendly party with Frank and Bob were the same first few days after I kissed Henry, and the first few days after my fight with Olivia. I expected to hear from Frank and Bob during that time of rampant emotional highs, lows, and overthinking, but I didn't. Their silence wasn't entirely comforting. Waiting to hear from them morphed into waiting for a summons from Dave to meet him at the office, or one of the little outside tables in our shipping container office park, where people drank their coffee and ate their hot dogs, and made plans to go canoeing or gold panning up north, while laughing, and laughing, and laughing. That is where Dave would sit me down, and wonder aloud if I might be more comfortable in another company, or maybe even another part of Gamboge? He could probably arrange for me to take an analyst position in Santa Fe or Sioux Falls or Tampa. I wondered what I should wear to my yet-to-be-scheduled firing. A power outfit that would communicate that, though rarely seen by human eyes, I would not disappear into the night? Or maybe, something mousey to remind him that I was of no threat to anyone, and firing such a sad little creature would only mean bad karma for him.

So while I was waiting to be fired, I was waiting for things to cool down with Olivia and heat up with Henry, but those things didn't happen either. Olivia came over, but we didn't talk about our fight, or Henry, or work. We read articles about celebrities, and healthy living and toyed with the idea of making our own yogurt. Henry was on deadline, and I said I also was on deadline. He called me twice to remind me of his deadline, check in, and hint around to see if I'd been fired yet.

The only other human contact I had that week was when Ty slipped a note under my door. His calligraphy was so swirly and ornate, it looked like a royal decree, and took me fifteen minutes to decipher.

> *Hello Neighbor,*
>
> *I'm writing to inform you that I've been interviewed for Hills + Water + Sky + Fog magazine, about the Friendly lifestyle. I'll be gone most of the day for a photo shoot. Per your request, your name was not mentioned. As you know, Hills + Water + Sky + Fog magazine is a legitimate mainstream publication, and not at all focused on subversive, alternative lifestyles, societal disruption, etc. Iggy, Trey, and Mabel look forward to being introduced to the world, and having this magnificent movement we've created together get some legitimacy (not that we needed it). I do hope Olivia is fine with you hiding her under a rock . . . that girl deserves to shine. Wink!*

*I'll let you know when the piece comes out. Let's
catch up! The countdown to season two of* Eleanor
*has begun.
Wink + Air Kiss + Awkward Hug +
Complicated Handshake,
Ty Banks*

He wrote out "wink," twice, surely enamored by how it looked
in calligraphy.

Olivia read over my shoulder. "Hmmph," she said.

"I know, right? This is so obnoxious." I wanted to tear it up,
but the calligraphy was beautiful so I put it in my growing box
of letters.

"Well, actually, Flossie, I think he's right. I do deserve to shine,
and you have been hiding me."

I wasn't looking at her, but I could sense that she was waiting
for a response of some kind. I took a deep breath and spoke
calmly. "Olivia, no matter what I do, you seem frustrated. You
would be mortified if I was out there talking about you—like
out there, out there—not just to Friendlies, but to everybody."

"Maybe, I don't know. But I would be kind of famous, and
maybe not so . . . stifled."

"Now you feel stifled? Please. You can't even be happy for me.
All you're worried about is yourself. You seriously have one job."

"And what's my one job? Keeping you company? Affirming
you? I'm a creative, Flossie, you know that, you made me that
way and now you can't handle it. I wasn't meant to wither away,

surrounded by cozy throw blankets and empty bottles of chardonnay, and with not an interesting man anywhere? You want my only connection to be to you! Pathetic you. You're a cliché, and now, I'm a cliché . . . a total waste of an imaginary person! At least Ty is out there DOING something interesting!"

"Shut up!" I screamed into the silence. My head vibrated. I hadn't screamed in years.

"If I shut up," she said quietly, and emotionless, "and go along with every one of your sad, timid, lackluster desires, you will be here forever, pining for affection from a clammy man-child, eating and drinking away your days and wishing you were friends with your fashion icon, Eleanor Roosevelt. Or maybe you'd wander the streets in your high heels, waiting for the meat store guys to remember your name and invite you out for drinks, or maybe you'd meander up and down the streets, hoping a real person will notice you, and invite you to be their best friend. And you'll work and work and work, and then one day, you will realize, that all of that work was meaningless, and you wasted your life making other people's dreams come true, and all those people you toiled away for, didn't even remember that you worked there, or that they knew you, or that you existed. You'll have no one."

"Stop," I said without screaming, but with tears starting to present themselves. "It's not true."

"You said it yourself; if it weren't for me, you'd be miserable."

My hands were up over my ears, pressing them shut, but I could still hear her. I squeezed my eyes shut, but could still see her. I felt the urge to scream again, but decided to just cry instead.

"Listen. It looks like this is getting too real for you right now, so why don't you get yourself together, mmkay?" It was syrupy sweet, but cutting.

When I opened my eyes, she was gone. I sat on the couch. The room felt emptier than it had a few minutes earlier, though there were the exact same number of skin-covered humans present. I pulled one of the throws that had stifled her over my head hoping it would stifle my stupid, pathetic crying.

CHAPTER THIRTEEN

Thoughts of Henry came and went, but the promise with which the week had begun wasn't enough to take away from my new brand of misery.

Olivia was wrong. I wanted so badly for her to be wrong. I fell asleep only after exhausting myself by trying to figure out whether or not I hated Olivia.

The next morning, I woke up to see Henry had texted me.

Just thinking about you.

Guess you're busy. Talk tomorrow? Good night.

Everything ok? Let me know. Did I do something wrong? Never mind, you're busy.

I texted him back.

Hey, sorry I missed you. I just had a fight with Olivia, and went to sleep early, that's all.

His response was immediate. *A fight? Really?*

I guess so. Weird, right? Yeah, so what are you doing later?

Tonight? Working. Sorry. Maybe you and Olivia can patch things up though. I'd hate for you guys to be fighting. What are you fighting about?

Everything. Maybe I need a break from her.

The phone rang, it was Henry. "Hey," I said, trying to sound nonchalant.

"You can't take a break from Olivia."

"What, why?"

"I mean, you can't. You're you. If things with Olivia fall apart, what hope do the rest of us have? Abe turned my life around, and that was a direct result of you creating Olivia. We can't go back to the way things were. No. we can't."

"Henry, are you alright?"

"Sorry, I just don't want you to give up. Are you bored?"

"No, actually, and maybe that's the problem. I'm not bored."

"Am I in the way?"

"You in the way? No, Henry. You are a human. Humans take precedence. Always."

"Is that a rule? Did I miss the rules? I didn't know there were rules."

"No, I'm talking about me. Henry, don't worry about it. Friends fight. It's normal. It's not a big deal. I'm sorry, I didn't mean to drag you into this, okay? It's fine. I'll let you go, so you can work. I would like to see you again."

"Okay," he said, sounding relieved. "Me too."

I could feel Olivia out there, somewhere, sitting in a design team meeting, or wooing a client, or leading a pack of her cool co-workers down the street for happy hour. Whatever she was doing, she was smirking.

I sat down at my desk, and pulled out some fresh stationary.

Dear Etta,

I'm so sorry it's been so long since I've written. I'm mortified. It's been weird here. I'm glad you got the engagement card. (Should we quit our analyst jobs and start a line of Friendly greeting cards?) How are you? How is wedding planning going? Have you finalized a date?

One of the aforementioned weird things is that I've met someone, too. A fellow Friendly, Henry. It's new . . . it's not so new that I've met him, just that I am kind of seeing him. Well, I've seen him a few times. But it's different now, I guess. I'm not sure I'm a huge fan of his IF though. I can't really relate to him, and now that I think about it, I don't get the feeling that the IF likes me, or is very nice, or even particularly nice to Henry. I don't know what I'm complaining about, Olivia's not particularly nice, either. Don't tell me Emma's turned on you? Just kidding. Emma's a gem, I'm sure.

Ty, the neighbor, the self-proclaimed champion of the Friendly lifestyle? He has now been interviewed for a mainstream magazine, but was kind enough to leave me out of it, though I don't know how I feel about that, and I am trying to withhold judgment until the article comes out.

Olivia thinks I'm stifling her. Ty thinks I'm stifling her. Not to drag you further into my drama but a) do you think I'm stifling Olivia and b) do you and Emma ever fight? How do you handle it? Am I crazy? I mean, am I crazier? What does that say about me, that there is an entire segment of my imagination that I can't get along with? Today, as I write this, I'm almost relishing the silence, though I have a feeling Olivia could come rushing back in at any moment, just to berate me some more.

Henry (see above), is still really into his IF, and in the honeymoon period if you will (ooh, no offense intended to the happy couple, any honeymoon plans?) Henry doesn't seem to want to see any of the realities of the Friendly/IF relationship, and I just wanted to check in with you to see what your experience has been? Have you run into anything? Any advice that you might have? I should probably just call you, but I cannot bear to say any of this out loud.

Oh, and you should know, Bob and Frank, yes THE Bob and Frank were at our latest Friendly gathering. They were snooping around and they recognized me. I was floored they even knew who I was, and then after being floored, I was horrified. I have not been fired, and nothing has come of it, yet, and of course, I did not mention you at all. But if you hear of anything through the greater Gamboge gossip mill, please let me know, and I will do the same for you.

So, I know we languish between letters because

of our now flourishing social calendars, but if there
is any way for you to get back to me soon, I would
really appreciate it. Thank you for your friendship.
All my best,
Flossie, just Flossie

I threw myself into work for the rest of the day. I called Dave twice, once with an idea that I'd had about market segmentation, and again with well-rehearsed questions about a client's new project. I would not toil in vain, and I would not be forgotten. Also, I would not allow myself five extra minutes to fume about Olivia or worry about Henry.

Dave eventually called me back. Though first he'd seemed exasperated by being reminded of my existence, he finished our conversation with "Nice job today, Flossie. Good stuff. Good stuff." His voice suggested neither imminent mandatory counseling, nor an imminent firing.

I was facing another evening alone in my living room, so I dressed in my exercise clothes, left my phone at home, and ran down to the 8 o'clock drop-in spin class, arriving early enough to get Bike 3, in the front of the class. I didn't notice who else came in and I didn't care. I didn't pine for chit chat. I just rode my heart out, went home, and fell into bed without a word from Olivia or from Henry.

Henry and I shared a few benign text exchanges, until he finally decided he could tear away from his project for lunch. I was aiming for dinner. I suggested we meet at Husk, a tamale shop a few blocks from his house. I hoped lunch would end with him holding my hand all the way back to his place, and him deciding he could take a few hours off from whatever project he was working on, and I could see the brass leopard, or cougar, or tiger that almost killed him, and maybe kiss him again.

Henry was already sitting at the table when I showed up, so there would be no loitering on the sidewalk waiting for a table and innocently touching each other, the way couples just naturally tend to do if they have a few minutes to kill. He smiled when he saw me walk through the door. It looked like a real smile. I knew what an imaginary smile looked like. His was wide and inviting, not just polite. He stood up, and after what felt like a few seconds of contemplation, he leaned down and kissed my cheek. I could feel my whole face flame up.

"Hi."

"Hi."

He pulled out my chair for me, and I told him he looked nice. It didn't look like he'd rolled out of his apartment after a four-day system architecture bender just to meet up for a tamale. He'd showered. He'd shaved. He smelled good. His shirt looked new.

He told me I looked pretty, and that he should have said it sooner because he thought it the moment I walked into the restaurant. As it turns out, I had also showered, and I was confident that I too, smelled good.

I had hoped that Abe was out foraging for food or something. But no, he was walking the dog around the block.

"Abe's bummed Olivia's at work. I think he's warming up to her," Henry said as his long fingers plucked a blue corn chip from the basket.

I asked Henry about his systems architecture project. I didn't know what to call it, really or even understand enough of what he was talking about to ask meaningful follow-up questions, other than, "Oh, yeah?" I caught myself racing through my vegetarian green chile, 100 percent nut-free tamales, and slowed myself down before I would be forced to order a coffee to stir. As much as I didn't want to, I did talk about Olivia. I had to. Henry asked direct questions that made it really hard to avoid, like "how are things with Olivia?" And when I told him every-thing was cool with her, I felt bad, because I liked Henry, but I was already lying to him. Things were not at all cool with Olivia.

When I asked him how things were going with Abe, he laughed. "Abe did the funniest thing this morning. I told him I was having lunch with you today, and he said . . . he said . . ." I leaned in, curious as to what he was trying to say, "He said . . . 'listen Harry, or whatever your name is, I could steal her away in a second if I wanted to.' I mean he probably could, he's that manly, or whatever, but he's always saying crazy stuff like that, you know . . . when he talks. I almost didn't bring him today, because, what if he tried? You know, to steal you? Not that anyone can steal you. You're your own woman. I respect that. I respect your—"

"My womanhood?"

"Yes! Your womanhood!"

I was flattered. His laughter was nervous laughter.

"That's not going to happen, Henry. I'm having lunch with you, not Abe. I was looking forward to spending time with you, not Abe." His laughter dissipated, and his golf ball Adam's apple bobbed dramatically as he swallowed.

"I just wish Abe and Olivia had hit it off. She doesn't really like him, does she?" he said, not making any mention of how much I'd just put myself out there. We were back to Abe and Olivia.

"Just like real people, not everybody clicks." I shrugged my shoulders.

He gulped again. "Thanks for meeting me today. I . . . uh . . . I was hoping you wanted to go out again."

"I did. I do."

"Oh. Good. Me too." His nervousness made me feel oddly calm. "I have to go. I'm sorry."

"That's alright, I understand." I'm sure I sounded disappointed, because I was.

He paid the bill without us saying much else. He put his hand on the small of my back as we left the restaurant, though his long arms meant that he didn't have to stand very close to me to do it. He did not ask me to come over to look at the big brass cat I'd been dying to see. Instead, once we were out on the sidewalk, he put his hands on my upper arms, down from where they were on my shoulders before, and leaned in and kissed me. People streamed around us without saying anything. For a pretty reserved guy, he sure wasn't shy about kissing in public. Maybe he felt so invisible that he figured he was actually kind of invisible.

When he stood back up, I said, "You didn't ask. What about respecting my womanhood?"

"Oh, no I'm sorry . . ."

"I'm kidding Henry. That was nice. Thank you for lunch, and just so there is no confusion, I would like to go out again, or maybe you can come over and I'll make you dinner. Or you can make me dinner. I'd love to try your cooking. People do that in real life still, right? It's not just for people in those movies my mom loves . . . those movies with Reese Witherspoon, or what's-his-name, Will Smith? People make dinner for each other, right?"

"Yes, I'm pretty sure people still do that. I'll call you. I should be done with my work project soon."

In a moment that was maybe from a Reese Witherspoon movie, I hooked my hand over his shoulder, stood on my toes, and kissed him, again. It was longer than a peck, shorter than a linger; it was a familiar, genuine, spontaneous kiss.

"Thanks," he said, when I let go of him and returned to my regular height. "I mean, great. Okay. Bye. Great. Um. Thanks, again. Talk to you soon. Thanks."

"Bye Henry," I twirled on my toe and headed in the opposite direction. I glanced back over my shoulder, to see he was looking back at me as he walked away. He waved a little, but then ran into a lady with a stroller, and had to focus on profusely apologizing to her, and as far as I could tell, to the stroller's infant occupant.

I wasn't sure if I should tell Olivia about the major development in my love life . . . well, my like life. I wanted to maintain realistic expectations about where things would go with Henry after I caught myself picturing what our wedding would look like, and how happy my parents would be. Without realizing it, they would be thrilled I was marrying a human being with both skin and a social security number. For a quick second, I pictured him moving in with me, and putting up our Christmas tree, and how we'd laugh every year when he would put the star on top without having to use a ladder, and how the artisan meat guys would notice him, and the paperie lady would notice us, and tell us we looked so in love, and it would sound so romantic in her French accent. And then she would say that she would someday like to make our wedding invitations, and I would blush. It seemed like our first getaway would be to the wine country, or maybe Big Sur. Maybe we'd go to a music festival, or maybe I'd take him to Chicago, and we'd go to a Cubs game with my dad. And for all of those reasons, I knew I could not call what I had a love life, not even to myself. It had to be a like life, or maybe I might just get carried away.

From the Diary of Jennifer Martin
November 1, 1993

I met Bill Clinton yesterday. Well, the next best thing. His name is Tom (but I heard his friends call him Tommy), and he was at this party I went to with my roommates. He's cute, funny, and smart, in a very down-to-earth way. He had the rubber mask pushed up to the top of his head, so he could drink his beer. It was fine with me though, because then I could see his real face. He didn't get my

costume at first . . . he had never heard of Courtney Love. He
thought I was just wearing a slip, leather jacket, a tiara and red lip-
stick because it was Sunday. He doesn't know who the Pixies are either
which would normally by a deal-breaker, and he's more of a jock than
I usually like, but there's something about him that captures my imag-
ination, and makes me hope he'll call me. I am Courtney Love though,
so I could totally call him.

Olivia

Flossie hasn't wanted me around much, which is fine, I suppose.
That was the goal, right? For her to not need me anymore?
But she dismissed me for all the wrong reasons. I might seem
harsh, but I'm tough on her for her own good. I really do want
her to be happy and healthy. Is it healthy for any of us to be
surrounded only by people who agree with absolutely everything
we say and do? No. What would she learn from that? She and
I would still be sitting under those luxurious throws (I do miss
those) watching movies, drinking rosé by the liter. She would be
hiding from the world, while secretly wanting the world to come
knock at her door and ask her to play.

I admit, if it wasn't for her, I wouldn't exist. Well, technically,
I would. I mean, the real me is out there somewhere, the woman
from the coffee shop with the diamond earrings and the friendly
smile. She probably doesn't have an IF. I'd love to meet her. My
guess is she's an investment banker or a real estate attorney.
She's engaged either to an investment banker or a real estate
attorney. Bali's her favorite place on Earth. She loves sushi

and kickboxing. She speaks Spanish and Japanese and visits her grandmother and she earned a perfect score on her SATs. She squeezes her own grapefruit juice. See? I can do it too.

I'm not a quitter. Flossie's not going to create me, and then dump me. Also, let's be honest, she's not ready for me to go away. She's not there yet. Sure, her sad little band of Friendly oddballs is a good start. She's relearning how to exist in the world. But, when babies take their first steps, they don't go straight to getting their own apartment. Maybe they do, I don't know very much about children.

I just want what's best for our little Flossie.

CHAPTER FOURTEEN

Olivia came over to pick up the scarf she'd forgotten, and as I looked around the living room to find it, she asked if Ty's new article had come out yet. It had not. She did not invite me to the place where she would be wearing the scarf. She looked around at my apartment and up and down at what I was wearing—yoga pants—then excused herself, slipping out the door with her scarf and a barely audible goodbye. I tried forgetting about her, and not worrying about what she had been thinking about my outfit and my life in general, but it was more difficult than I liked. I could only maintain full brain distraction with work and exercise and house cleaning for so long before my thoughts would drift back to her.

Time spent with Olivia as of late wasn't exactly fun or filled with laughter, but I didn't like thinking of her out there in the world, loving life without me. I didn't have a clear picture of what she was out there doing, but I felt that she was doing a lot, and that she was doing it all with just a little bit of spite. Maybe if she and I could spend more quality time together, we could get to a better place and I could stop thinking about her so much.

Maybe things could be fun and easy like they were in the early days of our relationship. Things were good then. I mean, things were weird, and pretty dark, but good.

Over a two-week period, I called Olivia but she didn't call back. She no-showed for our movie night. She canceled on me right before we were supposed to walk through Crissy Field. I invited her for a spa day, my treat. She texted back, "Yeah, no, can't. Sorry."

When texting with Henry, I skirted around his Olivia questions, knowing that whatever I was going to tell him about her would be a lie. I hated that she was a factor in my brand new, real human relationship. Henry was worried that he was getting in the way, but he wasn't. Olivia was in the way. She was in the way, even by not being around. Just her being out there was stifling. I was the one who was stifled, not her!

I was in bed, actively not sleeping, when I realized I was angry. So angry. Where along the way had I forgotten that I was the one who was really in charge? Not her. Me. She'd tricked me into things and out of things. I was mad at myself, but furious with Olivia. I wanted to kill her. Maybe I should. I could . . . I could kill her if I wanted to. I hated how she had taken absolute advantage of my natural kindness and goodness . . . two qualities I lost claim to the instant I considered murder.

Olivia was mean and rude, and it was her fault that I wanted to kill her. It was rude of her to have made me think such a terrible thought. Nobody else could hear my murderous inner monologue, but I thought of my mother, and there's no way that she would approve of me killing somebody simply because they were rude. Olivia would have to do something worse.

"I got the weirdest note. It wasn't in calligraphy."

"Not everybody does calligraphy, Ty."

"I know, but it was from Olivia."

"Oh?"

"Yeah."

"Well, Olivia thinks calligraphy is a waste of time. What did it say?"

"You want me to tell you what the letter from Olivia said?"

"Yes, please tell me what it said. I'm sure she wouldn't mind."

"Are you okay, Flossie?"

"Me? I'm fine. I would just like to know what the letter said."

"It was not really a letter. It was a note, shoved under my door while I slept which was between approximately 3 am and 6 am."

"Oh?"

"Flossie?"

"Yes?"

"Are you sure you are alright?"

"I'm fine. What did the note say?"

Ty looked down at the creamy expensive paper that still appeared smooth and beautiful even after having been brutally shoved under a door in the wee hours of the morning. Expensive stationery is totally worth it. He looked back up at me, and I smiled and nodded at him, gently nudging him to get on it with it. He cleared his throat, "The note says, 'I thought you should know that Flossie thinks you are a pathetic weirdo perv.

Depending on her mood, she sometimes says you are a pathetic pervy weirdo. But don't listen to her. You're not the pathetic one, she is. Isn't it sad? I am totally on board with your lifestyle, and I just wanted you to know what you were dealing with, and to watch your back. You are too good for her. You've done all the hard work with the IF community, and she is preparing to just come in and brush you aside, and take all the credit. Do Frank and Bob return your calls or your letters? Probably not, and it's because of her. She talks to them all the time. Anyway, I'm sure you can work through this, you are neighbors after all, and that's a very strong everlasting bond that nothing can get in the way of, ever . . . unless one of you decides to move a couple blocks north. You're a great guy who really wants to help people, so I feel that I should tell you to take care of yourself first. Also, please tell Trey to call me. I'd love to see him. I think that if Flossie hadn't been in the way, he and I would have had a chance."

I let my jaw drop. I covered my mouth daintily. "Why would she do such a thing?"

The day after a very confused Ty returned to his apartment with no answers, Henry called to tell me that Olivia had sent him a message begging him to run away with her. He didn't ask me if I was okay. Instead, he laughed. "Good one, Flossie. Please tell Olivia that I am not interested."

On Thursday, a letter from Etta arrived by overnight delivery. In it, she asked if what Olivia had written was true. Did I really think her marriage was a bad idea? She was starting to have second thoughts herself. She and Emma were fighting over the wedding details. Etta wanted it to be a small affair, maybe deep in the woods, or high on a mountain, or in a field somewhere with a barn in the background. Emma had always pictured herself at a country club, or in a ballroom, an exotic beach, a villa, or an English garden. If they couldn't overcome a venue difference, how were they going to handle the demands of an IF/Friendly mixed marriage? She wished, however, that she had heard it from me directly, instead of from Olivia. Nowhere in the letter did Etta inquire about my emotional well-being.

My mother called me on Friday. "Who's Olivia?"

"A friend."

"Well, your friend has written me a letter that she is worried about you. I'd like your take on this because she doesn't sound very stable."

"She's not. She's jealous. I'm handling it. I'm sorry she dragged you into it."

"Is she dangerous? Is she stalking you? Do you need us to come out there? Do you need to come home for a while?"

"No Mom, it's not a big deal. She's just desperate for attention. What did the letter say? Some nonsense about me hanging around terrible people who have turned me against her?"

"Yes. That's exactly what it said."

"She's very immature. I'm seeing a guy. I haven't told you about it yet because it's so new. But she hit on him, and he turned her down, and she's mad. I have new friends which she doesn't like, and I guess I said some things that she found upsetting."

"She sounds unstable. Please notify the police."

"No mom, I think she's probably leaving, anyway."

There. Olivia was now not just rude. She had revealed herself as a backstabber who was actively trying to sabotage my relationships. She had practically outed me to my mother. She had crossed the line. She was nuts and out to destroy me. What I was considering was drastic, and not something to be taken lightly. I scrawled out the pros and cons of homicide on my grocery list notepad.

Pros:

Won't be berated by her anymore

Kind of curious about murder

Murder outside of my personality and

natural inclinations = growth opportunity

Better chance of having a real life without her

Olivia would probably kill me if our roles were reversed

Normal people don't have imaginary friends

Cons:

Will have to explain her absence

Will be alone with my thoughts

Could get lonely again

Possibly not a Friendly anymore (perhaps this

should go on the pro list?)

Dynamic with Henry, Etta, and Ty might be weird

Homicide outside of my personality and

natural inclinations

Murder is bad

I read the pros and cons a dozen times, and committed them

to memory before ripping the list from the notepad, along with the three pages underneath, in case anybody stumbled on the pad, and tried to make a rubbing with the backside of a pencil. I tore the paper in smaller and smaller bits, recycling just a few pieces in my home bin, before tucking the rest into my purse to scatter in recycling bins throughout the city.

When I was little I would pretend to shoot the neighbor kids, and they would pretend to shoot me and we would die dramatic deaths complete with jarring, full-body shudders and more nuanced leg twitches and masterful and realistic (to us) guttural sputters that preceded our last breaths . . . breaths held in as long as we could stand it. Camila was the best at it. She could hold her breath to the point where her brother would be forced to check on her to make sure she wasn't actually dead. We'd lay there for a while then get up and do it all over again.

A whole world existed in the Clue board game; exotic rooms connected by secret passageways, a suspicious cast of characters, and easy access to a tiny, shiny little knife, an old-timey revolver and a lead pipe. ("If a blow to the head by the pipe doesn't kill you, the lead will!" my mom would joke . . . every time.) When my parents weren't playing the game with me, I played on my own, immersing the game's characters into storylines—affairs, failed business ventures, stolen family fortunes—that all ended in . . . murder! The characters were all so dishonest and tangled up in each other's lives, it was a miracle that in a mansion with a conservatory, a library, secret passageways, and handy cache of weapons, there simply weren't more murders!

In the light of day and in the company of dirty little neighbor kids, I could be blasé about death. But at night, when I was tucked alone in my bed—whether it was my childhood bed, my dorm bed, or the bed that was just a few feet from Lola's in my old apartment—it wasn't unusual for my thoughts to wander to strange places. If I couldn't distract myself with the murmur of the television show my parents were watching, or the murmur of Kira and Kelsey gossiping in our shared living room, my mind would end up cataloging the books I hadn't read but should, countries I would like to visit, and all the ways I could be murdered. I might be pushed from the platform in front of a speeding L train, strangled by a stalker hiding in the backseat of my car, caught in the crossfire of a botched liquor store robbery as I shopped for wine, or poisoned by a sinister old lady who lured me into her musty parlor for some hard candies.

With so many murder mysteries, games of Clue, and imagined dramatic homicide scenarios under my belt, I could certainly kill one traitorous, snide, back-stabbing, life-disrupting, imaginary enemy.

I called Olivia and asked her to come over. She told me she was busy. I said I needed to see her. Another time, she said. I promised I wouldn't be weird, and told her I had something to give her. She said she could swing by.

I straightened the apartment and lit the eucalyptus candles that always made Olivia gag. I opened a bottle of Riesling, or pee-zling as she called it, heated store-bought spinach dip, and dumped the creamy mess into a bread bowl I'd hollowed out by hand. I turned on the home decorating show I'd once loved but had abandoned at her urging. If she could make it through this mine field of her pet peeves without being terrible, I wouldn't go through with killing her. I would give her another chance. I knew from the second she came through the door, though, the second chance was not to be. She breezed in and stopped in her tracks, just as I imagined she would. She took in the pedestrian tableaux I'd created and snickered.

I smiled and asked her to sit. "I can't stay." The snickering stopped when she saw my smile. "I'm meeting up with some people."

"Please, sit. Just for a minute. I'll grab you a glass of wine."

"I'd rather not."

"Vodka?"

"Fine."

I moved toward the kitchen, but turned back. I slipped the scarf from around my neck and quickly hooked it around hers. If I was going to go this far, you'd think I would want to look her in the eye so I could see her acknowledge that I was strong and in control. But the murder wasn't for her benefit, it was for mine. So I didn't say goodbye. I didn't offer a villainous monologue explaining to her why I was killing her right there on my couch. Instead of looking into the eyes I had given life to, I silently stared into her perfectly glossy hair. The hair was what had struck me about the real version of her in the coffee shop. She was wearing the same diamond earrings she'd been wearing that day too. Olivia had been dressed to spend an evening out. She wasn't dressed up to see me, I was just a stop for her on her way to somewhere else. Her beauty was effortless, just like everything she did. And ending her—apart from hollowing out the bread bowl—was fairly effortless as well.

I wasn't sure when to be done with the task at hand, the strangulation of an imaginary person. It seemed like it had gone on the same amount of time it does when it happens in a movie, where it's also imaginary, and therefore an appropriate guideline. The entire process was far less dramatic than what I'd expected, and maybe even than what I'd hoped. I was expecting an adrenaline rush, but it never came. There was no intoxicating, cathartic release to propel me into ever wanting to murder again. I only felt weirdness, like if you mixed relief, with disbelief, pride, shame, and delusion. I put the scarf back around my neck, without a worry of DNA or epithelial transfer, and wondered what I should do next. Olivia's body wasn't slumped over on the couch. I mean, I guess, having no body to dispose of at all, was the biggest perk of murdering an imaginary person. I dug into the spinach dip and poured myself a generous glass of Riesling which I have to admit, was terrible. I poured the Riesling down the sink, opened a merlot, ate a pound of spinach dip and the better part of a crusty sourdough round, and lost myself in countless homeowners' quests for turnkey homes with terrazzo counters, new appliances, space to entertain, and a drought-friendly, low-maintenance outdoor space for their dogs. Finally, bloated from my post-murder meal, I made myself go to bed so I wouldn't awake the next morning on the murder couch while still wearing my murder outfit.

My apartment was quiet in the morning . . . truly quiet. It wasn't that I had become accustomed to Olivia clattering about in the kitchen making me coffee and eggs, chirping about what a beautiful day it was, and how the world was my oyster. It was always quiet. That morning though, the morning after, was oddly, unusually, specifically quiet. The world had not changed. A light had not been dimmed. A bright star had not flamed out. The world would be fine. I just hoped I would be fine, too.

As I took a shower then drank my tea, I thought about how I wasn't a Friendly anymore. I was definitely an UNFriendly. I'd intentionally disqualified myself from the only community I had. I didn't know what I would tell Ty and Henry. I could lie. It's not like they would know any better, would they? I hated that it would take an imaginary friend to maintain whatever odd reputation I had created for myself.

I didn't put on my tattered work-from-home yoga clothes, but instead dressed in normal adult clothes and got to work. I sent Dave a message to let him know I was ready to take on anything interesting or complicated he might have in the pipeline. I was drunk with confidence, which was a nice change from being drunk from rosé. I sent a message to a Persian cat rescue organization, and said I would make an ideal, emotionally mature companion for one of those little flat-faced beauties. I reserved a spot in an evening spin class. I made a reservation for one at the pigs in a blanket restaurant. Granted, it was for two weeks from now, at 5 p.m. but I was in the system. I bought a jacket online, as well as high thread count sheets, and a professional grade chef's mandolin. I dashed off a note to my parents that I was feeling great, and would be scheduling another visit soon, and then I even looked at flights to Chicago. I didn't book anything, but I looked. I scheduled a visit with my dentist, and decided that as a newly independent adult, I was absolutely crushing it. By two o'clock, I hadn't been assigned any new or interesting work projects, and I had run out of ways to crush it. I went to the mailbox. I walked through the stationers, but the woman who owned it was immersed in a phone call, and only nodded in my direction. I walked to the artisan meat shop, and smiled at the guys behind the counter who were apparently too busy to smile back. I came home with my $35 artisan summer sausage, and returned to my desk to find a message from Frank and Bob. It was an electronic message, and not a hand-written missive, so I immediately began to worry.

"I think we're ready to deal with this IF thing. We'd like to meet with you, in person, not at the office. We're in Austin— Tempe—San Diego—SF. We'll be in touch with dates." I sent back the elegant reply I knew they wanted, "Fine."

I didn't know whether to be happy or terrified.

Days went by as I waited for them to contact me. Their vagueness and cloak and dagger approach made me anticipate a note slipped under the door, or a benign statue delivered to my doorstep that I would instinctively know to smash open for a coded message. But nothing. Dave said to stand by for an interesting project he'd soon send my way. Henry was on a deadline, and reeling from seasonal allergies, but promised we would get together as soon as possible. But even the promise of a date, and a pig in a blanket, couldn't take away from the fact that there was nothing new to fill the void left by Olivia's absence. She had been the newest, and most mind-bendingly time-consuming change in my life since I was eleven and got my first e-reader loaded with all of the Harry Potter books. But there was nothing new to take away from how quiet it was, and how quiet I was.

I busied myself with cooking so I could be fully prepared to entertain humans once they became available to me again. I was in the middle of a seemingly endless recipe for a French-Japanese-Brazilian fusion Treasures of the Sea dish, when there was a knock on my door. I was just to the part where I was to carefully cut the world's thinnest cucumber slices, and glanced longingly at my mandolin as I went to the door, already knowing who would be on the other side.

"Hi Ty," I said as I swung the door open.

"Hey! What is that smell? It was wafting under our door, and Iggy thought it might be a decomposing body, but Trey and I smelled fusion food. So in the interest of making sure you're not dead, and me having exactly zero dinner plans, I thought I would come over to see what you were up to."

"Fusion."

"A-ha! Iggy owes me twenty bucks. Nobody's dead."

I gulped.

"Well, then, are you expecting company? The human legume perhaps?"

"Stop that, Ty. You sound like a jealous ex. Henry's busy and I'm teaching myself a new recipe."

"Olivia talk you into doing that? Is she tired of exotic sausages from those meat bros down the street?"

I stood firmly in the doorway. "I haven't seen you for days, or weeks, and you wander in here, talking like that. It seems to me, that you've forgotten your manners."

"Are you being serious right now? We joke around. That's what we do. You call me a leprechaun and I make fun of you being a spinster. It's kind of our thing."

"It doesn't need to be our thing. Can't we be civilized adults?"

"Occasionally. Speaking of civilized adults, is Olivia here? Can I come in?"

"Yes, come in, but I have to get back to cooking. Timing is very important with this recipe. I suppose you want a glass of wine . . . and dinner."

"I don't want to impose, but that would be lovely. Iggy won't be jealous considering she thought it smelled like a rotting corpse. See? I said it smelled delicious, how many more manners do you need than that? So, Olivia's not here?"

"No."

"Where is she?"

"Not here."

"Are you guys fighting? I haven't heard you talking or laughing for days. Things were weird with that note from Olivia, but I just assumed you were drunk. It was so quiet, I thought you were out of town or something, or staying at your new boy's house, but then I smelled cooking. What's going on?"

"I've been very busy with work."

"So Olivia's at her place?"

"She's not here, and I don't want to talk about her."

It was after three glasses of wine, and three bites into my masterpiece of a meal, and the thousandth question about Olivia when I finally told Ty, "Olivia's not coming back." Ty had pestered me into revealing Olivia's existence, and he pestered me into revealing Olivia's non-existence.

"Come on, Flossie."

"I killed her, Ty."

"What?"

"I killed her. It was the only way I could really be done with her."

"What?"

"I was feeling messed up, Ty, and I needed her to go away."

"I don't understand."

"You were busy. Too busy to notice she wasn't helping me anymore."

"What are you saying?"

"Not only was she not helping me, but she was hurting me."

"You killed her?"

"Yes. And Ty, it's okay."

"No, it's not. I can't even look at you right now." Ty's voice was shaky.

"Ty."

"I feel sick."

"Ty."

"How could you do this?"

"I needed to kill her. I needed her to be gone. Even when I wanted her to be gone, she kept coming back, just to torment me."

"Do you hear yourself right now? This is sickening. How selfish can you be? She was real."

"She wasn't real."

"So what if you couldn't touch her? The minute you created her, she was real to you. She was real to me. She had friends. She had a life. She said things. She went places. She existed. So what if it was in another plane? You created her; that's special and wonderful.

But you destroyed her and that's awful. How did you do it? Wait, don't tell me, I don't even want to know."

"The how is not important. Ty, I had to do it. I'm not exactly proud of it."

Ty pushed his chair back, and the corners of his eyes were glistening. "How could you, Flossie?"

"She was going to kill me."

"She was trying to kill you? Like with violence?"

"No, that's not what I'm saying."

"Then there's no excuse. She was a friend, Flossie. Are you going to kill me next? Oh no, you might. I'm going to be sick." And with that, he threw my door open, and rushed straight through his own unlocked door. There's no way I could use him as a character reference to get that cat.

Frank

The sun leapt off the bay in playful ways you don't get to see under San Francisco's oppressive fog. I was just across the Golden Gate Bridge in Tiburon, looking back over the bay, toward the city. I was drinking a Bloody Mary, and keeping an eye on the seagulls that were keeping an eye on my crab Benedict. Bob was drinking a root beer. Actually, he was drinking six root beers, and peeing every ten minutes.

"I'm drunk from root beer," he said. "I had root beer once when I was little, I think maybe with ice cream in it. Then we didn't drink soda, and I never thought about root beer again. *Like, never. Why would I? Then last week I had this dream* about it, and I couldn't relax until I had one. It's providence, because this root beer is the most amazing thing I've ever had. It's so ridiculously creamy and bubbly, and it does something weird to my tongue. And for maybe two seconds, every few minutes I feel like I could vomit, which makes me think that maybe I am technically drunk from root beer."

We were supposed to be idea birthing, but we weren't getting anywhere. It was our third birthing session in a week—the first with root beer; the second with crab Benedicts; the third without Fiona, at my insistence. She was supposed to be in LA, but always seemed to be wherever we were. Anytime she accompanied Bob, she tried to slyly contribute, and pretending not to notice became exhausting for me. Bob also pretended not to notice her unoriginal, overly rehearsed spontaneous thoughts. "You know what I was thinking about yesterday?" she said after obviously waiting for the perfect moment when nobody else was speaking. "Pogo sticks. My dad used to have a pogo stick, but I mean, when was the last time you actually saw one? But you can see it right? You can see it becoming a thing?" Her ideas were the worst. She was acceptable and tolerable to a certain level, attractive, well-educated, and she had a decent apartment in an acceptable neighborhood. Then, like most people, she stalled out. At Bob's recommendation, she was tapped to set up the LA office, because Dave will do almost anything Bob thinks will be strategic, resourceful, and innovative. It wasn't going well though, and Dave had to send Gamboge vets down there to make her look good. I couldn't decide if she was vapid with intellectual undertones, or intellectual with vapid overtones. Whatever it was, she was intentionally intense. Like it didn't come naturally to her, and she worked fruitlessly to make everything seem natural. I called that two years ago, Intentional Intensity, as being the most desirable trait in a short-term romantic partner. I also predicted that relationships built on Intentional Intensity would flame out quickly because while temporarily interesting and affirming, they are also emotionally draining, and eventually hideously boring. Intentional Intensity could be especially tough on a pod. I desperately wanted to excise Fiona from ours. I'm sure burned-out pods all over the place were casting these people onto the streets to roam, which was what brought Bob and I out on to eat crab Benedicts by the water.

"How Can Lonely Be Sexy?" was written neatly across the top of a page in my notebook, right above the realistic lone wolf I had sketched while Bob was in the bathroom. "Lonely Chic" was already happening and we were behind in addressing it. Loneliness was driving the creation of new sets of social norms. Loneliness had created desperation, and desperate people will pay anything for anything to feel less desperate. We just needed to shape that. Under the wolf, I carefully penned, "Does loneliness reveal your inner strange, or does it create it?" and under that I wrote "Flossie" in the most beautiful handwriting I had ever done. My s's were absolute perfection, and s's are hard to do.

Flossie had become a thousand times more interesting to me. I no longer forgot her name and I wondered what she did at night when she wasn't analyzing things. I wanted to know what her home looked like, and what she ate for breakfast. Whenever I found myself surrounded by people anxious to hear my every manufactured thought—people who were unsure if I was Frank or if I was Bob—I was surprised my thoughts drifted to Flossie, who was probably somewhere quiet, wrapped in a cashmere blanket, not thinking about me. I thought about how it would never even occur to her that it was an option to think about me.

The stake-out was my idea, and Bob agreed, because of course. Her neighborhood was nice. I befriended a French lady, who said she didn't remember ever having seen Flossie. She gave me a business card from her paperie, and touched my arm. She was about ten years older than me. The artisan meat guys didn't know Flossie either. Bob and I ate dumplings and sausage rolls, and drank coffee in his car. He wanted to quit after six hours, mostly because the smell of sausage rolls and dumplings doesn't just go away. After two days of sleeping in shifts, cycling through public restrooms, and moving the car twenty feet at a time, Flossie finally left the house. We followed her to a tamale shop I had never even seen before. Tamales had never occurred to me, and I hated myself a little bit.

I waited for her to emerge with a greasy bag full of tamales, but it became obvious she was eating there. I wanted to go inside. I wanted to know what she'd ordered, and why after being inside for two days, she suddenly needed tamales. But I waited. She wasn't alone when she came back outside. She was with a lanky guy, and then they kissed. It was very normal. I think it was the same lanky guy I vaguely remember from the imaginary friend party. Part of me thought he was perhaps somebody's imaginary friend, like an imaginary brother, or an imaginary tutor. But there they were . . . two lonely hearts kissing in front of a tamale shop. I went from disappointed to jealous. It was a pure moment. Not manufactured. Not strategic or lustful. I realized I cared a lot more about them than either of them cared about me. Were their imaginary friends there? What did they look like? How unencumbered they must be without suffering from social confines and prolonged unbroken eye contact with the tiresome people from their pods. They had all that time to create and imagine and form whatever lives they wanted. Physics and reality wouldn't hold them back. They had discovered a new level of existence. I thought I had no rules. I was looking at the freest people in the world. I imagined kissing Flossie. I wondered what it would be like to have a secret with her. My biggest secret was that I wanted to share a secret with her. I never got to be lonely. Never. I wanted to be lonely. I watched people all the time, but with a goal to be critical, and to observe, and on my very best, most optimistic days, to get inspired. The jealousy I experienced as I watched them kiss, physically burned my insides. I'd never watched anyone while experiencing such a yearning in my core. What's sexier than yearning? Literally, nothing.

Olivia

She can't kill me. I'm a ghost. I am an amazing ghost, still imaginary, but I get to haunt her.

I knew she was thinking about killing me. I found the faint scribblings of her murder pros and cons list on her notepad. If she had taken off just one more page, I wouldn't have been able to make that pencil rubbing. I was somewhat surprised, however, that she actually went through with it. That's admirable I suppose; I wasn't sure she was capable of that level of follow-through. I'm not thrilled about the letters "I" sent to her mother and Henry. As if I would ask Henry to run away with me! The letter to Ty was a little more on the nose. After she sent those letters, I did consider killing her. She made me out to be a pathetic woman tipped over the edge by jealousy. Why not go all the way with that cliché characterization? But she and I both knew that the most effective way to hurt her—more than murder— would have been to just disappear from of her life so I could live out a fruitful, social happy existence without her . . . in spite of her.

I can feel Flossie trying to will me back, but I simply will not go. I won't. But I have customized the perfect haunting for her. My total silence is driving her crazy. I am actively punishing her. I knew she would miss me. I am sucking the air and the life out of her. I like to think of it as slowly suffocating her with one of her cashmere throws.

CHAPTER FIFTEEN

Flossie,

I heard what you did. I couldn't call you. I want to, but I'm too sad. I'm disappointed. I'm confused. I didn't know what else to do but to write this letter to you. In addition to being somebody I enjoyed spending time with, I looked up to you for your sensitivity, your bravery, and your creativity. Ty reached out to let me know what happened. He's very hurt. He's concerned for the movement. He's mourning Olivia. This whole thing you created together was just starting to go somewhere, and he could never imagine something like this would happen. I know we live in a depraved broken world, so I could totally imagine something like this happening, I just couldn't imagine that you would be the one to perpetrate such a heinous injustice, and such an ugly act.

I am sure you have your reasons. Someday, I would like to understand those reasons. But now is not the time. I need space. I need time. And I suspect you

need to sort out whatever is going on for you—what-
ever darkness or trauma in your past that would
lead you to do something like this. So I'm not say-
ing goodbye, nor am I really trying to change things,
because I do like you Flossie, and not just for your
IF, or your place of honor in the IF community. But
maybe things are going a little fast, and I need to re-
frame my relationship with you. Abe and I are going
to the mountains. I'm going to think. You are real to
me. You brought depth to my new understanding of
real, and I don't want to feel as though you are the
least real part of this entire experience. Does that
make sense?
I'll be in touch.
Henry

I tried to bring Olivia back. I spoke out into the thin air, thinking she'd show up on my couch in a top knot and a Michigan sweatshirt. She did not.

I set out some figs and a bottle of really good wine. The next night, I set out a design magazine, a vodka tonic, and lit a candle that smelled like cashmere and confidence. Then I set out peonies. I put all of my offerings together in an attempt to summon her, but all I did was create a shrine to a murdered girl. I wrote a letter confessing and apologizing to Etta, unsure whether I would hear back. I wanted to write back to Henry, but he was in the mountains, opting to spend time with allergens instead of with me.

After two weeks of Ty ignoring my knocks on his door, I woke to find a fresh copy of *"Hills + Water + Sky + Fog* magazine had been pushed under my door. There was no note.

Party of One

by Katie Baker

Historically, San Francisco has been on the leading edge of every social movement, and every notable trend, revered or reviled. The ideas conceived in and birthed from the city's Victorians, college apartments, street corners, cafes, parks, classrooms, salons, well-appointed break rooms, artist lofts, and Internet cafés, have left no aspect of the modern human experience ignored, and we as a city have pushed, pulled, and propelled progress in the sciences, the arts, technology, social justice, politics, philosophy, spirituality, and commerce.

And once upon a time, social media ruled until it didn't, and both of those phenomenon started here too.

We're two years into the Great Introverting of America, and where are we? Following years of phone addictions, internet bullying, trolling and scamming, our decimated attention spans and exhausted and meager human brains had reached their saturation points. Our desire for anonymity, intimacy, and depth over took our collective desire to be famous at all costs. And so we went willingly into our pods, celebrating our grandparents who knew how to behave and interact with each other and simultaneously lamented parents who led us down the path to intellectual and interpersonal ruin.

We podded up and found each other and ourselves again. We read books, and discussed them. We retreated into our curated and intimate worlds. We lived and communicated with intentionality. We carefully selected not just the people we would allow into our lives, but the people we would leave out. Out went casual acquaintances, online friends, old friends, and even perceived close friends that simply didn't make the cut. Those left behind were expected to find their own way in the world without having access to our vacation photos, big announcements, or the mundane daily minutia of our lives.

What happens when you are on the receiving end of the heartless curation of a friends list? Of many one-time friends' friends lists? You're a normal person with a job and a sense of humor. You have good hygiene. You're intelligent, and volunteer, and are concerned for the future of the planet. What happens when you juuuuust don't make the cut over and over again? When you haven't been on your own in a while? When you've been surrounded by people, and conversations and endless platforms to connect with your fellow humans? What happens when the world goes on without you? Only you're not dead, or stranded on an island. You just simply aren't quite good enough.

San Franciscan Ty Banks will tell you; you don't sit idly by, waiting to die, just because you're not in the small chosen group of people who enjoy drinking the beer they brewed together from the clay steins they fired together in a cozy kiln. Banks says, "You take matters into your own hands, and in your own minds, and you come up with your own damn friends."

"I'm a party of one, but my house is full," said Banks who lives in a Noe valley one-bedroom rental. He took a sabbatical from his career as a professional activist, and found that the world outside of his job contacts had changed. At the encouragement of a neighbor, who had become so desperately lonely she created a friend to talk to, Banks also created a companion, Trey. "He's the perfect friend, entirely custom designed by me, with every quality I look for in a companion," he said of Trey, citing their shared sense of humor, political leanings, hobbies, taste in music and movies. "He's funny as hell, and I never get tired of talking to him, and he never gets tired of listening," Banks said. "I bounce ideas off of him." Satisfied and *fulfilled with his burgeoning relationship, Banks went on to create another imaginary partner, Iggy, a woman Banks says he has become romantically involved with. And then to keep Trey from feeling as if he was a third wheel in Banks' new relationship, Banks created Mabel, a girlfriend for Trey. The foursome dine out, explore the city, and stay at home listening to music, talking, and watching movies.*

Seeing how an imaginary friend had helped him, as well as the neighbor who has chosen not to reveal either herself or speak publically of her imaginary friend, Banks felt the need to educate others who might be feeling left out and isolated by San Francisco's new exclusionary social landscape. Using his grassroots resources, Banks did spread the word, and hosted a turnout for this small group, IFs (Imaginary Friends) and the Friendlies (imaginary-friendly humans with skin you can touch) who created them. The second gathering doubled in size, and a larger event is currently in the planning stage. Banks is fielding speaking offers in cities such as Portland, Los Angeles, Chicago, Washington DC, and New York. He and Trey plan to write a book about their experiences.

When I met with Ty in his home, his apartment felt as if it were occupied by more than one person. Glasses covered the counter, dirty clothes were draped across the furniture, and notebooks sat in stacks around the living area. Colorful flyers advertising the friendly parties were tacked haphazardly on the wall.

H+W+S+F: "Is there ever a point where you feel like, maybe you're . . ."

Banks: "Crazy?"

H+W+S+F: "For lack of a better word, sure."

Banks: "In the beginning, I did. Not anymore, though. I feel empowered."

H+W+S+F: "How does it work with your girl-friend?"

Banks: "That's personal. Iggy is real to me. If you were asking an interview subject about his sex life with his girlfriend—well you wouldn't. People are connecting with themselves in new ways. They're unearthing their deepest desires. They're completing themselves in ways they never knew they needed. We (Friendlies) are not all perverts. Our IFs are just exactly who we need in our lives. A best friend. A girlfriend. A grandparent. A chess partner. For some people, their IFs are the exact opposite of themselves . . . bold, strong confident. For others, they need someone with a personality or temperament very similar to their own, quiet, judgmental, smart, dumb, what-ever. These are people who might look powerless, but they have all the power in the world. They

are utterly self-sufficient, independent, and interest-
ing. A large percentage of children at one time or
another have an imaginary friend. Child psy-
chologists have long touted this as a healthy part
of brain development."

H+W+S+F: "But at what point does it move
from healthy and playful to delusional, and maybe
dangerous?"

Banks: "We've all got issues, right? I mean,
nobody is mentally perfect. But this group of people
knows and understands that we have befriended
imaginary beings. We are not registering them to vote, or
applying for jobs with them, at least not that I know
of. I imagine Trey can drive, but I'm not sitting in
the passenger seat, expecting him to get me where I
need to go. IFs help Friendlies work out whatever
we need to work out. And they're fun. I like to have
a cocktail, but I don't want to sit in the dark and
drink alone, and I don't want to go to a bar where
I'm surrounded by pods of people I don't want to
know. I can enjoy a cocktail while surrounded by fun
people who find me profoundly interesting and hang
on my every word. It's perfect.

Through the IFs movement, we have basically
been saving lives. People who were once so desper-
ately lonely, not only have the day-to-day intimacy
of an IF of their choosing, but now they know they

are part of a bigger community of Friendlies that is becoming a force in its own right. A few Friendlies, since meeting through the gatherings, have begun dating and hanging out socially. Imaginary people have been bringing real humans together.

There's still a stigma for sure. Some of the privileged and podded have been quick to call us pathetic, crazy, and strange. But what those haters don't realize, is that they could become one of us in an instant. It doesn't take much to go from being a perfectly put-together person, to a desperate person, unhinged by isolation and abandonment. We were built to be in community with other people. We weren't built to be alone all the time for all eternity because some marketing jerks needed something new to do."

As for the "marketing jerks," many experts point to a boutique San Francisco firm as having created and lead the dramatic cultural shift away from lives lived out online to more face-to-face based interpersonal relationships. Cerulean Group, now a part of larger Gamboge Consulting, has bragged in the media about their role in the social revolution, with their in-house style and social forecasters, Senior Vice Presidents Frank Drexler and Bob Winn, and Cerulean Managing Director and now business author and visionary, David Chase, leading the charge.

Though trendsetters were already eschewing social media accounts and digital living, it is widely accepted in business circles that Cerulean was the first to monetize the movement, creating and shaping a new marketplace for their clients who were, thanks to Cerulean, uniquely prepared for the radical cultural shift, leaving competitors blindsided and scrambling to catch up.

It is unclear if the creation of a new class of citizens—the unpodded—was an intentional business move by Cerulean, or an unfortunate bi-product of their endeavors. H+W+S+F calls to Cerulean for comment went unanswered.

While matchmaking services have helped to some extent in creating pods for the podless, success rates are far below 25% for manufactured pods who remain together even three months after an initial match. Organic matches have proven to be most successful.

For a number of reasons, otherwise socially savvy people have found themselves to be amongst those who were left on their own.

Mary, her last name withheld for her protection from "UnFriendly Employers," has been to all of the IF/Friendly functions hosted by Banks. After attending a top-tier university, Mary was career-focused, and spent so much time at work

*in the financial sector that she unintentionally ne-
glected her social life. "It took a while for me to
realize how alone I had become. I wasn't friends with
the people at work, and my college friends had kind of
gone off in different directions without me. I hadn't
made time for them, why would they worry about
me? Things clicked for me when a life coach told me
about Ty and what he was doing. My new IF is an
amazing listener. She's kind. She's encouraging. It's
because of her that I connected with the other Friendlies—something I never ever could have imagined
doing a year ago. I've met some nice people, and I
have a new boyfriend. I talk to my IF every day.
I tell her what I'm worried about, what I'm excited about. She helps me crystalize my thoughts, and
get my priorities straightened out. I mean, I know
she's not real, but saying things out loud to a person,
even an imaginary person, ironically makes them
more real. When your thoughts are trapped in your
head they get too scary, strange and loud, and you
give too much weight to every ridiculous thing
you think. Putting them out there helps you sort
out what's good and what's not. I feel like a huge
weight has been lifted off my burned out brain."*

*Banks is still in contact with his neighbor, the
original Friendly, who like Mary, is not ready to
openly discuss the lifestyle outside of Friendly circles.*

Though seemingly frustrated at questions surround-
ing the woman, Banks said of her, "She and her IF,
are to be revered. They are fierce, wonderful people,
who are taking care of themselves. For people who
really needed somebody, they don't need anybody."

"Did you know about this? Dave was frowning, and looking expectantly over the top of the magazine to Frank and Bob. I sat in the corner with a notepad. Frank had requested my presence in the office, and I prepared for the firing I had envisioned for months. Maybe I was going to be the scapegoat. Maybe they wanted my ideas. When I'd hesitated at accepting the meeting invitation, Frank said they would like my professional input, and assured me they wouldn't out me to Dave. I trusted Frank as much as I trusted myself, so like, not at all.

"We did," Frank said confidently to Dave.

"How am I just hearing about this? Our names are in it. My name is in it. We should have been ahead of this."

"We've been working on it. We are working on it."

"We look like devils."

"No, no, no. These people are in the minority." Bob emphasized "these people."

"We look like assholes. The last thing we need is Gamboge second guessing us." Dave was rubbing his temples with his hands.

"I don't think we need to cater to the dregs of society," Bob replied.

"They're not dregs," Frank butted in.

I sat quietly in the corner. Neither Frank nor Bob looked at me, even though it felt as though Bob's use of "dregs" was for my benefit. I leaned on my elbow and tried to hide my face like I was reading the article for the first time instead of the fifteenth time, and so they couldn't see my cheeks fluctuate between shades of crimson, ruby, russet, and my favorite, vermilion.

"We need to address it somehow. Make light of it? Do something? Acknowledge that we already acknowledged it?" Dave was trying hard to sound calm, but was starting to spin out in his own special, Dave way.

"The monetization and ROI possibilities are still a big question mark for us," Bob said, trying to talk Dave down, "We're agile, and nimble, but I don't know that we need to go this small. Nobody's going to give up real people for imaginary ones, and might I remind you, imaginary people don't spend money."

"These are people's lives," I wasn't looking at them, but I knew it was Frank. I had never before heard Frank and Bob not wholeheartedly agree on something.

Frank only looked at me once that day in Dave's office. I wasn't sure if he was disappointed or relieved I stayed so quiet. I wrote Frank a letter after the awkwardly uncomfortable meeting played out, and the realization of my outdoor-firing fantasy had been mercifully delayed once again.

Dear Frank,
   Thank you for your discretion at work. I appreciate it, though I don't feel I entirely deserve it.

However, there is something I feel you should know. I'm no longer with my IF. If you really want to hear about it, I will tell you, but it's not pleasant or happy, or very well-received in the IF community. I have been through an unusual grieving process, and have decided to try it all over again with a new IF, though my efforts so far have been unsuccessful. This process has given me additional insights into the Friendly and IF communities. I appreciate you not wanting to take advantage of the good people of the Friendly community.

You have helped me, and I would very much like to help you. Here are some industries that would benefit from warmly embracing this misunderstood subset of the human race: hospitality, restaurants, travel, publishing. Immediate actions—whether for monetary gain or as a public act of goodwill—might include taking over the Friendly Fetes, and even hosting an IF/Friendly cruise, perhaps. Ty may already be putting this together . . . who knows? Maybe you should work with him. He's annoying, but passionate. He might make for a valuable consultant.

Regards,

Flossie

My phone rang two days later. "Flossie, this is Frank. Pardon my intrusion with the unscheduled telephone call, but I am so very intrigued after receiving your letter. May I please ask, what happened with your IF?"

"Hi Frank. It's fine. I got rid of her."

"It sounds like it was more than that."

"Not really. I'm sorry, but in a series of very weird things, this continues to be very weird for me."

"I'm genuinely interested. No judgment. At heart, I'm a researcher . . . a scientist."

"If you really must know, and if it's for science, in order to really get rid of her . . . I had to . . . I murdered her. She was destroying me, not because she's an IF, but because she was an IF that wasn't good for me."

"Wow. Okay. How was that? How is that?"

"Now that Olivia's gone, I miss having her around. Ty's furious about . . . what I did. I've heard through my clumsy unreliable grapevine that after Ty spread the word to the Friendlies about. . . what I did, there have been other IF homicides. I heard about one Friendly who was so furious with her IF, that the murder was really gruesome and pretty disturbing. Poor Terry. Anyway, it's quite possible now that just as fast as people are creating their IFs, they're killing them off. I think some people are curious about killing somebody. I can tell you, it's not all it's cracked up to be. I didn't feel great about it. I'm relieved there's not a serial killer lurking inside me. It sounds like there's going to be a rash of murdered imaginary people, so maybe there's a market for detectives specializing in IF cases?"

Frank laughed. "I tried it, you know."

"Tried what? Murder?"

"Making my own IF. I'm not very good at it, I think he ended up looking just like Bob. Maybe I should kill him."

"Bob? Or Fake Bob?"

"Ha. His name is Bill, and he's not worth sullying my spotless felony-free record."

"Frank . . . How mad is Dave? How bad is this situation?"

"He doesn't suspect you. Bob almost slipped, but I covered for you. Plus, Dave's distracted wondering how he can leverage this into another book. How about you? Are you okay Flossie?"

"You've never asked me that before. You haven't asked me much, outside of report related things."

"That's not true. I asked you a lot of things that night at the IF party."

"That doesn't count. I was a science experiment, not a person."

"I'm sorry about that, but are you? Okay?'"

"It depends on the day. Murdering my IF has lost me not only an IF, but the human friends I had made."

"You said you're making a new IF? Can you tell me about her?"

"It's a guy."

"Oh."

"His name's Jack. He's in finance. He knows what he wants. He's like the guy version of my last IF, but at least I know what to expect. I'm just getting to know him, so I don't know if he'll stick around. I thought I would end up with a sweet girl who works at the library, but I couldn't get any traction. Oh Amanda, created and then practically forgotten."

"Did you . . ."

"Kill her? No. I couldn't kill Amanda. Maybe we should introduce her to poor abandoned Bill."

My apartment was starting to feel cramped, and noisy with the constant chatter of conversations going on around me, but without me. Jack hit it off with Amanda. Naïve Amanda was obviously attracted to Jack's bad boy persona. She blushed when he paid her any attention. Esther was funny, but self-conscious about her weight and it came out in her passive aggressive demeanor. Penelope was an aerialist and took herself very seriously. Yadiel was a professional baseball player from the Dominican Republic. He was quiet and polite, and a teensy bit homesick. The best listener of all was Chester, a bright orange fluffy cat who purred and loved me and never ever shed fur on the furniture.

There were moments when the chatting stopped and the purring stopped and every room was squashed under a giant cashmere throw of silence. It felt like Olivia was trying to suffocate me under it. My new IFS only just knew a little bit about Olivia, and they never asked what, or who, was at fault for her demise.

Frank and I started meeting, at his request. Our first meeting lasted only fifteen minutes before he was called away on some kind of Bob emergency. When I arrived at the coffee shop two minutes early for the second meeting, I found Frank sitting with his legs crossed and hand in his chin, staring into the depths of his mysterious leather notebook. From all the way across the room, I could see swirls of ornate handwriting and sketches tease and flash for a moment as he flipped through what appeared to be expensive and velvety pages. There was no evidence of Bob anywhere; I wasn't sure if his absence would make the meeting twice as awkward, or half as awkward.

Frank saw me approach and called to the girl behind the counter, "Evelyn, we're ready whenever you are."

"Okay, Frank!" she yelled back.

I was wearing my Olivia outfit: tight, ripped jeans, a silk camisole, and a structured blazer. My oxblood pumps were as well worn-in and comfortable as they would ever be. Frank wore orange pants and a brown cashmere sweater that looked to be two sizes too big for him. It probably was worth about a month's worth of my rent. His dark hair had grown out a little, and it was slicked back, like mine was.

I slid into the chair, just as Evelyn arrived with our coffees. He looked at me and pushed one of the mugs closer to me when I didn't make a move toward it. "Bob's busy and we might have better ideas without him interrupting us to talk about how crazy it is that donuts were huge, then they weren't, then they were, and now they're gross again. I don't take a lot of meetings without him, but we have to act fast. I ran into an old acquaintance the other day who's nice, but basic and uninspired. This woman never found her way into a pod, and almost immediately gushed to me about her IF named Antonia, who's a high school principal and drives a Vespa. While imaginary Antonia sounds interesting, I found it disheartening that her very boring Friendly is ahead of us. You sitting here, makes me feel slightly less disheartened, I guess."

If that was a compliment, I knew I hadn't earned it. "I've said this before, but I shouldn't be doing this. Ty should be doing this. He has the passion. I *murdered* an IF."

"Oh yeah, about that. Ty has been relentless in keeping us updated on the increase in IF homicides. He's incensed that nobody at the police commissioner's office will take him seriously. He tried to make the case that IF homicide is probably the very last step before a person commits real homicide. If you could kill an IF—something you lovingly created—then what's to stop that same person from killing a real person you hardly know? He said he was going to write an article exposing you, but agreed not to when I offered to hire him on as a consultant. After we talked, I thought about killing Bill, but I couldn't do it. I put him on a plane to Toronto. Anyway, what was that like, really? Killing an IF?"

"Not great. It was not my proudest moment. Murdering an IF falls right below, or maybe above, inventing an IF."

"I get it. The symbolism of killing this thing. Self-defense. Morbid curiosity. Starting anew." And then he smiled a little. When he realized he was smiling, he said, "Okay, I guess we should get on with it."

Two hours later, and after the world's best cup of coffee from Evelyn, the artisan and coffee visionary, I had spilled every feeling and experience with my IFs: the challenges, the excitement, what we did for fun, where we would go, what we would talk about, and what it felt like after the short high you get when you forget your best friend in the world is a figment of your imagination. He took page after page of notes, sometimes circling something, sometimes underlining something. Sometimes he used a misshapen star, and a shaded arrow to highlight some mysterious point I must have made.

"Thank you for this, Flossie," he said, interrupting me while I talked about my relationship with my mother, "and for what it's worth, I'm sorry."

"Why? For what?"

"I feel responsible for this . . . for your . . . situation."

"For turning me into a spinster?"

"You're not a spinster. No. This is something that happened to you. I know that. You didn't do it. Not really. It sucks. I'm sorry, that's all."

CHAPTER SIXTEEN

I flew to Chicago for Thanksgiving. My new friends came with me, and quickly took up every corner of my room. They glanced at the same photos Olivia had carefully studied, and lay their invisible heads on my owl pillows without comment. Jack made inappropriate comments while Amanda blushed and swatted at him playfully. Yadiel sat with my dad and watched football. Chester bounded out of his invisible cage, and headed straight for Penelope, who ran her hands through his fluffy fur, and pulled him tightly to her chest.

While I liked having my new IFs around, I didn't necessarily like them as people. Frustrated and grieving my dead imaginary best friend, I rushed into creating my new IFs, and opted for quantity over quality. I would never have befriended any of them on an airplane, or in a bar, or in the neighborhood. I opted for quality over quantity in the friendship department. I had tried in vain to bring Olivia back from the dead, with no success. Olivia's long-lost twin Charlotte wanted nothing to do with me, but who could blame her? Charlotte was mourning a sister she never knew.

Carl and Larry wore on my nerves. Larry was tall and thin,

but he wasn't funny or endearing like Henry, and he didn't turn out to be nearly as smart as I thought he would be. Carl was clumsy and had terrible taste in clothes; he was not the loveable sidekick I'd intended. There was an underlying darkness to Carl's dry wit. I considered encouraging him to pair up with Esther and travel the world, but I wasn't sure they were the healthiest choices for each other.

I put on a brave face for family at Thanksgiving, and stayed busy in the kitchen showing off my new culinary skills with nary a mandolin in sight. While the turkey was in the oven, I excused myself for a quick walk. A California girl now, I wrapped up every inch of my body to face a Chicago November. Had Olivia been there, she would have happily joined me on my walk, and taken advantage of the opportunity to smoke outside, and escape obligatory chit chat. Without thinking, I started trudging down my old route through the neighborhood, as if I was headed to my high school. I could almost feel the weight of my phantom school backpack weighing me down. I crunched the dirty remnants of the last snowfall under the old winter boots I'd found in my closet, the same boots I did not throw into the Pacific Ocean. My route took me by the market where I was regularly dispatched for milk for Mom or candy bars for Dad. It would have been a beer and red wine run, had I been an adult under their roof. The shoe repair shop had become a deli, and the deli had turned into a furniture store. My steps slowed even more as I approached the corner and Camila's family restaurant. I could see their old sign had finally been replaced, and Casa de Lugo looked like a sleek modern restaurant rather than the old reliable neighborhood stalwart it was; I suspected Camila had everything to do with the new look. The lights were on inside, while the other shops on the block were dark. I hesitated. The Lugos were very nice people, but I hadn't seen them in years, and I wasn't in the mood to explain my life. They probably wouldn't notice me or recognize me anyhow, so I hurried along the icy sidewalk as best as I could without falling. As I passed the glowing restaurant windows, I peeked to see a sign that said, "Closed for private party," and inside, a room full of vaguely familiar faces.

"Floss? Flossie O'Brien?"

"Camila, is that you?" I don't know why I asked. Her beautiful face was not wrapped in a scarf like mine was. Her olive cheeks were slightly rosy, and her cascade of black hair looked like it was keeping her neck warm.

"Flossie, are you here for the party? Did uh . . . did Mama invite you?"

"No . . . no. I was just cooking at the house, and decided to get out of there and take a quick walk."

"Ah, okay, that makes sense. Are you living here again? You're not in California?"

"Just home for Thanksgiving. And you . . . you're in Miami?"

"For now."

It was quiet for a moment, then a voice inside the restaurant shouted, "Camila's here!" causing her to turn and signal to whoever yelled, that she would be just one more minute.

"You guys are doing Thanksgiving at the restaurant," I said, showing off my keen observation skills.

"Yeah, it was getting too big for anybody's house. My sister has three kids now, and my cousins have gotten married. Listen, I'd invite you in, but . . ."

"I get it. Don't worry."

"I'm in town until Sunday. Can I see you? Maybe lunch tomorrow? Go shopping for old-time's sake? I think I can sneak away."

"Yeah, sure, I'd like that."

I gave her my number—the same number I could have sworn I'd already given her multiple times—and she wordlessly turned and opened the door of the restaurant. The warmth and the aromas from inside came out in a generous fog that enveloped me on the sidewalk, just as Camila was enveloped inside by a swarm of hugs and kisses.

I expected to receive Camila's cancellation by eight that night. It didn't come until nine.

We'd attempted to make plans a few times over the years, but they'd never materialized. I felt bad about what had happened, but I didn't know what I could have done differently. Robby had been my friend, but when he died, seriously, what was I supposed to do? I was a kid when it happened, barely eighteen, and I didn't know what to say or how to handle myself. I still wouldn't know what to say.

Robby was dropping off his girlfriend Molly across town when he was shot on the sidewalk, thirty feet from where he said goodnight to her.

Robby was always nice to me. He was nice to everybody, but that didn't stop me from having a huge crush on him, and feeling slightly faint whenever he called me Saucy Flossie. He was three years older than Camila, and looked like a full-fledged adult to us when at sixteen years old, he could adeptly work every job in the restaurant including host, waiter, cook, and bookkeeper. The customers and the neighbors loved him, and they all knew what to say and do after Robby died. I put posters up in at least three neighborhoods, and I shared every one of the family's posts across every one of my social accounts. But what else could I do? Suddenly, Camila felt like a stranger to me, angry and defiant one minute, and sad the next. She wasn't just emotional, she was busy all the time, and she was surrounded by her sister and cousins, and their big supportive family. When I would see her, I couldn't think of anything particularly helpful to say. I'd swallow my words and not say anything, or when I did speak, I'd say the wrong thing, like how pretty all the flowers were that had been left on the sidewalk where he died. My dad didn't exactly want me hanging around their house anyway . . . the police still hadn't ruled out that Robby was targeted and he suggested that the shooter could show up again. Robby's funeral was the same day as my college orientation. I didn't send a note or tell Camila I wouldn't be there. I didn't think she'd notice my absence. She did. She showed up at my doorstep a few days later with a box of my stuff, like she was breaking up with me in a movie. She blamed her parents and her sister Ana for my dismissal from the Lugo family's graces. She promised I'd always be special to her, but it was going to be different. We were going to college, and our friendship was bound to be different anyway, she said. I looked up Robby's case every once in a while, but as the months passed there were fewer and fewer updates. I watched Camila from my laptop. She joined a sorority, and dated guys and made new friends and went to football games.

Camila called a few times freshman year, and we snuck out to shop the day after Thanksgiving of freshman and sophomore year, when we were both home. She was busy junior and senior year. The calls slowed down to exactly none. I didn't call either, but we both knew she was the one who was best about reaching out first. That was kind of our thing.

When I returned to San Francisco, I knocked on Ty's door, and presented him with a bottle of his favorite whiskey and a plate of perfectly decorated cookies. He didn't invite me in, but I introduced him to my IFs who stood behind me. To the casual Friendly observer, we would have looked like a ragtag group of carolers delivering our own brand of Christmas cheer. Ty took the cookies and said, "Are you going to kill them too? You can't make up for Olivia's death by imprisoning and endangering more innocents, Flossie. These are living people."

"One of them is a cat."

"Well I hope all of them know, the cat included, they are living with a murderer."

> *Dear Henry,*
> *I was just thinking about you. The Christmas season*

seemed like a good reason to reach out and apologize again for disappointing you. I was in a dark place . . . I know that doesn't make it okay. I'm not proud of how I handled things. Even though I have new IFs, Olivia's total absence is so stark and strange, it's almost like she's still here, torturing me. That would be so like her, to haunt me for spite. Anyway, I know the new IFs don't make up for what I did, but I think you would like them, at least Amanda. She could be your sister.

Speaking of IFs, were you at the Friendly Fete last week? I obviously did not go. Ty said he wouldn't burn me in effigy or anything, but that he would speak his mind and his heart about IF rights. And if you were there, did he? It's interesting, isn't it?. . . "in effigy." Is that basically what we are doing? Friendships in effigy? Maybe not. I'm not 100% certain of the technical definition of "effigy."

I think about you, and was wondering if you wanted to talk, or meet, or write me back or communicate in whatever way is the most comfortable with you?

Regards and Merry Christmas,
Flossie

Henry

I missed the purity of the first parties. At the last one, Abe immediately left me to find the bar and never came back. There were so many people there, most of whom I'd never seen before. I considered the possibility they were voyeurs, or more likely, people hoping for weird sex stuff. Ty looked thrilled, like he was a king welcoming his subjects. I looked for Mary, but didn't see her. A girl talked to me, but she didn't seem very interested in IFs at all. She mostly wanted to hear about my job, and even though I'm a farm boy, I knew she was really trying to figure out how much money I make. I heard the next party will be huge and corporate sponsored, which of course, might signal the beginning of the end.

I finally had to tell my roommate about Abe. He found my copy of *Hills + Water + Sky + Fog* magazine, with Ty's letter sticking out of it, and he asked if I had an imaginary friend, and then he asked if I was mentally ill. I said I wasn't crazy, I was an early adopter in an important cultural movement, so he should relax. He said that if someone else was living in our apartment, imaginary or not, he should pay a third of the rent, then proceeded to ignore me even more after that. He moved the brass cat into his room. Maybe he was afraid I was going to befriend it.

I think about Flossie. I think about when we kissed by the tamale shop and I think about when we kissed at Coit Tower and every once in a while I think about what it would be like to kiss her at the beach, or on the Golden Gate Bridge, or on my couch, or maybe, and probably better, on her couch. I asked Abe what he thought about the Flossie situation. He mumbled something about Olivia being a snob. I rephrased the question, because he appreciated brevity. "Should I call Flossie?" He said, "Call her, don't call her, I don't care."

Flossie wrote me a letter. It was nice. She sounds sorry. But do I want to be with a murderer? Would I be settling? How well do I really know her? I remember telling her the first time we hung out, that even if she was a serial killer, I wouldn't necessarily see that as a deal breaker. Maybe I accidentally planted that idea in her head.

I asked Abe if I should write back to Flossie, and he said, "Write to her. Don't write to her. I don't care." One night, I asked Abe if I should open a bottle of chardonnay, and he told me he was going to rub peanut butter on my face while I slept if I didn't shut up. I slept with the door locked, but of course knew I was being crazy . . . Abe could totally get in the door if he wanted, locked or unlocked.

CHAPTER SEVENTEEN

"We're using your idea and sponsoring the next IF gathering."

"You and me?"

"Cerulean." Frank shifted in his chair. He looked at me expectantly.

"Thank you Evelyn," I said diverting my attention to her as she set down our coffees. She stopped at me saying her name, and said "you're welcome . . ."

"Oh, my name is Flossie."

"You're welcome, Flossie."

I turned back to Frank. "Sponsoring it?"

"Sponsoring it. Planning it. Embracing it. Growing it. It's going to be great. Are you pleased? This is your baby."

It didn't really feel like my baby, but more like a lingering cold I was sharing with the world.

Frank and I had four more coffees together, and one afternoon, Evelyn asked me if I like to hike. Frank took me out for three dinners, two of which were in restaurants that had yet to open to the public. We had four lunches, including one where we shared a jar of his homemade pickles while sitting on a bench overlooking the water, and one at Husk at his urging. We went to one Sunday Brunch, and five happy hours. He paid for everything. It was a full month into our regular meetings before I realized I was basically dating Frank. I had been out more with Frank than I had with Henry, and maybe more than when I was dating Charlie. Only my outings with Frank weren't dates; they were technically work meetings. Frank's beautiful leather notebook was always at his side.

Frank had many questions, which over time resulted in me spilling my life story in clumsy increments of out-of-order anecdotes. I chattered away to him, feeling like I was contributing more to a clinical experiment than a getting-to-know-you part of a relationship. He complimented me, but in a sterile and professional way. The compliments would come quickly, and he would be on to something else before I even realized what had happened. We were reviewing hand-drawn flow charts when he told me my eyes were the same color as the water of Capri, and then he asked if I had the budget projections he'd requested. Frank and I both dressed well for our meetings. I bought a new pair of uncomfortable shoes. Frank never repeated an outfit. He escorted me to my door when our meetings ran late.

Nearly a month into our intensive work on the upcoming event, I called the venue with some questions, and they asked if I was Ali with Event-u-Ali. Upon further investigation, I found out that the big party we had been spending so much time planning, was being planned outside of us by actual event planning professionals.

"So, do you want to tell me about Ali?" I'd arrived to the table an hour early to make sure I could be seated when Frank arrived. I wanted to catch him off guard before he could take off his coat and his scarf and his hat and his gloves and his messenger bag. I'd never seen him look surprised.

"We're big picture, Flossie. Ali's just the details."

"I thought you needed me for this project? I thought that's what we're doing. What's the big picture exactly? And how am I helping?"

"When you have your serious analyst expression, your eyes glimmer, and your skin in this light looks dewy and sparkling like a forest fairy. Speaking of skin, our skincare clients are loving the possession of skin as a major differentiating factor between IFs and regular people." He then stopped the waiter to ask for spring rolls.

"You are an insider with unique insights. That is gold," Frank said, returning his attention to me, "but you also have trendspotting skills, and may I say, trendsetting skills. You can't teach that. You can coach it and coax it, and that's one of the reasons why I'm working with you. Bob and Ty are deployed with their whirlwind of self-flattery and we're moving forward. Plus, the help you are providing is for more than a party. It's a movement, remember? Oh and by the way, Ty floated the idea that Trey should also receive a paycheck. Dave said 'Sure!' and scribbled out an invisible check, ripped it out of an invisible checkbook and handed it to Ty and said, 'That's five hundred million dollars. And there's more where that came from!'" Frank smiled much wider than his standard smirk, which made me smile too and

I didn't ask him anything more about Ali.

That night, I came home to find a note shoved under my door. It had become common practice for Ty, who, depending on his mood, honored his thoughts with exquisite calligraphy on heavy resume paper, by scrawling them out across stray junk mail, or by printing them neatly on a piece of binder paper. This night at what I can only presume was Mabel's urging, his note was crafted with carefully cut out magazine and newspaper letters, ransom style. His notes usually heralded his fabricated IF homicide statistics, and served as a reminder that no matter Ty's employment status and my role in securing him a paycheck, he had not forgotten my transgressions or given up his fight for IF's rights. The magazine letters, spelled out, "Blood of countless IFs on your hands." It would have taken him weeks to cut out the letters to spell the contents of his previous note:

Through research and modeling, using Olivia as IF Zero, more than one million IFs have been birthed. That number is still expected to grow exponentially, barring another radical shift in the social landscape. Our research also revealed IFs tend to be extremely attractive, famous, accomplished, kind, caring, jet-setting, exciting, empathetic, compassionate, adventurous, and wealthy. Thanks to the murder of our beloved IF Zero, the wonderful life of an IF is now a high-risk one. The life expectancy of an IF is now a mere 8-12 months because the likelihood of their being the victim of a homicide, whether from premeditated murder or sheer negligence, is 300% that of a person with skin.

I added the ransom note to my box of letters, thankful one of my IFs hadn't picked it up off the floor to read it before I got home.

Between work-dating Frank, planning a party someone else was already planning, researching the un-researchable, and keeping track of my swollen roster of IFs, my days were truly full for the first time in months. I found a night to return to a grueling Spinster cycling class, and pumped my way through the entire hour on Bike 10 without once worrying I might die mid-spin.

When I returned home, exhilarated from the brief chat I had with the instructor about the weather, I heard yelling from Ty's apartment.

There was an "I'm sorry!" and a "shut up!" A "stop!" A "don't!" and an "I'm going to bed. Please leave." I didn't care, and wasn't curious about what was happening in his hovel.

I climbed in to bed to carry out my nightly routine of over thinking in the dark. That night I thought about Etta. I thought about my mom. I thought about Olivia. I wondered what Henry was up to. I wondered if I should finally ship Carl and Esther overseas. I wondered if Frank was planning to take me to Dip for a five-course meal of artisan chips and scratch-made dips. I was right in the middle of imagining what my favorite dip would be when I smelled the smoke. Even after I smelled it, I still lay there, thinking it was my imagination.

"Flossie! Flossie!" Ty yelled as he pounded on the door. "Flossie! Wake up! Are you in there? Get out! The building's on fire!"

Once my brain switched from my meandering self-centered thoughts to my immediate survival needs, I flew to the door without stopping for my shoes, purse, cashmere throw or computer. I didn't stop for Chester, Jack, Amanda, Larry, Carl, Esther, Penelope, or Yadiel.

I unlatched and threw open the door, and the smoke that had filled the small hallway came rushing into my apartment. I stood in shock for a moment, until Ty who had a t-shirt pulled up over his face, forcefully grabbed me by the wrist and pulled me to the street. I still hadn't said anything, but moved like a robot at his instruction to the front gate of the building next to ours and pushed all of the apartment buzzers over and over again, my non-robot heart pounding, and my hands shaking. Any time a voice barked, "What is it?" through the intercom, my voice squeaked back, "Fire."

It felt like hours before the fire trucks arrived, but they were there within four minutes of being called.

People poured from the buildings. I recognized some faces from the neighborhood, but mostly I was surrounded by people I'd never seen before who'd been sleeping just a few feet away from me all this time. Ty and I stood behind the barriers to watch the flames and the water and the professionals all carry on with their jobs. I was barefoot. I thought of my shoes, and my beautiful blankets and sweaters and coats, and wondered if they were all burned to a crisp or soaking wet, or both.

Our neighbors were eventually released to go back to their homes. Ty and I responded to a barrage of questions with slow, unsure answers. Someone gave us blankets and water and plastic sandals. We were offered shelter, and phones to call our loved ones, which left Ty and I to stare at each other blankly. We should have had dozens of people between us who we could call, people who cared that our homes burned down, and that we were cold and in shock. We should have had an endless list of humans at our disposal who would be willing to throw real shoes on with their real pajamas and drive right over to us in their real car. I could think of one.

When Frank showed up, his clothes were pressed and his hair was combed. He might have been out. It was only 2:30 in the morning.

"I'm so sorry, Frank," I said, "I'm realizing how wildly inappropriate this is. If you'd rather, we can stay at a motel, and I can pay you back."

"It's fine. It's fine." His coupe whirred into the garage of an industrial building near the waterfront. The building looked dilapidated, but the gates were heavy, and required a fingerprint and lengthy code, and maybe a retinal scan, for us to pass. Once Frank slid open the heavy metal door to his home, Ty found his way to a bathroom, and settled in for a full night of throwing up. Frank led me to a huge guest bed, where he pulled back the luxurious blankets and motioned for me to crawl inside.

"Thank you," I said, "I didn't know what else to do, obviously."

He leaned over me, like my parents did when they put me to bed in my childhood room. He smoothed my hair with his hand. "Do you want me to sit here until you go to sleep? You should sleep. We can deal with things in the morning."

"That would be nice, thank you." I surprised myself, and Frank looked surprised by my response too. I liked feeling the bed dip under his weight as he sat carefully next to me. I liked hearing his real-person breath. I liked hearing street noises and life outside, even if it was squealing tires, sirens, and drunks yelling at each other. I even liked the sound of Ty retching on the other side of the loft. I was sharing a space and an experience with all of these people.

Ty retched again and groaned.

"Maybe we should check on him," I said.

"I left a hand-crafted ginger ale, made with locally sourced ginger, by the bathroom door, but that's all I can do. I can't be around someone else who's throwing up. I'll throw up too. I've already contacted the cleaning service to come in first thing and de barf that side of the loft."

"I'm sorry."

"Don't be. That is literally a non-problem. Try to sleep. You need sleep."

And so, not because I was told to, but maybe because I was in a warm and lush cocoon and under the watchful eye of a person, I fell asleep. And because I was exhausted and depleted in every way, I slept. Not like a baby. Not peacefully. Not two hours in a row, but I slept. The first time I opened my eyes that night, it was still dark, and Frank was gone from my bedside. I woke again, with dreams of running to the door, and standing barefoot in the street. I woke for the day when I rolled over, and the overpowering aroma of smoke in my own hair startled me.

Sunlight scattered across the room and the smell of coffee from the kitchen overpowered the smell of smoke in my hair. I found a basket of toiletries in the bathroom and a cashmere sweater was folded neatly at the foot of the bed with a pair of brand new women's linen drawstring pants. Underwear was wrapped discreetly in tissue. It was 9:30 in the morning; I don't know where Frank got the brand new clothes in my size, but he could probably get anything, anywhere, any time.

I dressed and joined Frank and Ty around a kitchen island that looked like an operating table, where we ate egg white omelets in silence. Frank let the de-barfing crew in the door and drove us back to what was left of our building.

Ty's place was gone; the walls with the haphazardly hung posters and everything within them, had been reduced to wet ash and smoldering rubble. All of his weird little papers. All of that dust and his collection of dirty dishes. All those copies of *Hills + Water + Sky + Fog* magazine. His crazy scribble scrabbled notes about taking over the world with his IFs.

Only half of my home was lost to the flames, my kitchen, the mandolin, my collection of wine. As I had feared, my blankets were gone, as were the yarn pompoms from my college dorm room. My books were spared by the fire, but ruined by the water, which was the same story for my phone, computer, and any paper that wasn't in the fireproof safe my father insisted I buy when I moved in to the place. In the safe was a small antique tin box that held my few hard copies of photographs, and a thousand dollars in small bills I'd stashed in case there was a catastrophic earthquake and I had to incrementally pay people to help me escape the ravaged city in their kayak or rowboat. The cash was also my dad's idea.

Frank deposited Ty, along with a suitcase of new clothes, in the empty apartment of Frank's friend who was spending a month in the Maldives. Ty was gone from my side and his role as co-fire survivor, and homeless, adrift, in-shock stuff-loser. I hadn't even asked Ty if his IFs had made it out of the burning building. He hadn't asked me about mine either. I wasn't sure what had happened to my IFs. I didn't try to get them out. I didn't go back in for them, and I hadn't heard from any of them. I didn't notice their absence until Ty and I were speeding across town in Frank's car. I thought it would be best to proceed as if they had escaped with me, and I hadn't committed seven counts of manslaughter. I forced myself to imagine that the fire would have also forced the ghosts of Olivia and Mrs. Lee to move on, once and for all.

While Ty was cast off to sort out his life, Frank brought me back to his place, and the big comfortable bed. He carried in what was left of my belongings. While I napped, he went out again and returned with a new phone, and computer, and a suitcase of brand new clothes in my size that were all soft, beautiful, and much more fashion forward than I could have picked for myself.

"You don't have to do this. This is too much. I didn't mean to drag you into this drama. You're being very kind. I just kind of instinctively called you." My hands were shaking. The words came out in a garble, affected by my overwhelming and conflicting desires to not cry, and also to start crying and never stop.

"The phone and the computer are from Dave," he said, softly. "Plus, I'm honored. I know that this is painful, but it's so metaphorically amazing, that I'm actually kind of thrilled to be a part of it. To witness the dramatic end of one chapter, knowing that a new one will start any second, but nobody knows what that will look like. It's kind of the best, most interesting thing that's happened to me in a while."

"Um, well, I'm glad.

"I am sure this is traumatic, and I don't mean to be insensitive. But you are nothing if not resilient and creative. You will use this to grow and you will flourish. You should call your family. Are you hungry? How about some chips and dip? I know a place."

I called home. I refused to fly to Chicago, insistent I was in good hands with a nice place to stay, and every important hard copy of anything I had was in the safe that Dad had so wisely required me to purchase. I mustered all of my rationality and calm to explain that it would overcomplicate things if I had family visit. I didn't want my dad here to see me in such disarray. My mother was better equipped to handle such a situation, but I couldn't involve her either. They needed to stay put, and so, somehow, I convinced them that I was adult enough to handle my life. I hung up the phone and let Frank make me a cornmeal waffle and a chocolate milk.

My landlord, an unseen corporate entity who wordlessly collected my rent every month, informed me that in addition to the fire department's investigation, their insurance company would be investigating as well. Just as I hadn't inquired about the fate of his IFs, I also hadn't asked Ty about how the fire had started, nor had he brought it up to me.

Ty showed up the same afternoon I heard from the insurance company. He directed me to take a seat on the edge of Frank's expansive European couch so he could enthusiastically deliver the news that the alert sent through the IF community about the "devastating loss suffered by two of our own" had resulted in an incredible response from Friendlies near and far. He sat down next to me, but before he could settle in to read the letters of support he held in his hand, I asked him, "What happened? How did the fire start, Ty?"

He swallowed hard, and looked at me for only a second before looking back to his letters. "I was asleep. I don't know, the professionals are figuring that out."

"I heard you yelling."

"What?" He turned to me, with wide eyes.

"You were yelling that night, loud and a lot. And then . . . fire."

"You heard that? That was nothing. Did you tell anybody?"

"Was it Iggy? Trey?"

"I was angry with Mabel. But it was nothing. She's kind of unstable, and I was frustrated, and yes, I was upset. It happens. I know you know it happens."

I was the one who wrote those letters from Olivia. I addressed them and sent one to my mother, one to Etta, one to Henry, and one to Ty. I could have stopped. I knew what I was doing. But really, it's what Olivia was doing. I knew Olivia intimately, and I knew that she would have sent those terrible letters, but I had to do it for her.

Mabel burned down our apartment building.

Olivia needed my help to live out her truth. And Mabel needed Ty's help to live out hers.

I knew it. And Ty knew I knew it.

He held the letters up like a trophy. "I've gotten some of the kindest letters from our Friendlies. They're doing some fundraising for us."

I didn't say anything. I just looked at him.

"You, uh," he gulped, "you should take the money, though. Take all of it."

Ty

I only have a vague memory of that night. Yes, I had been drinking, but just a little. It wasn't one of those nights where Trey, Ig, Mabel and I start out with a full bottle of whiskey, and I wake up naked on the rug, the empty bottle two inches from my face, and what tastes like every germ and stray hair in the universe residing in my mouth. It wasn't one of those nights.

I'm not sure how the fighting started that night; probably how it always starts. Mabel says something insulting, usually about my weight, followed by the general pathetic nature of my life. Trey tells her to be cool. Iggy goes to the other room to read.

I tell Mabel to stop. I tell her to calm down, which makes her really mad. I tell her not to be so emotional. She hates that even more and throws something, and screams something like "loser!" Sometimes she calls me a mental patient. Or if she really wants to just stab me directly in the heart, she'll call me irrelevant. I look to Trey to step in, but he just says "be cool" again and doesn't do anything. It makes me feel like everyone in the room knows she's right. Trey knows what Mabel says is true, so why would he argue? I don't like having crazy fights with Mabel, but we're passionate beings. Her passion and my passion just happen to cause friction and fire instead of love and magic.

The night of the fire, Mabel wasn't just mad at me. She was furious and accused Iggy of only working to better humanity to make herself look good. She was mad at Trey for sitting back and letting the world go by, and for wasting all of his potential by associating with me. She was so angry, she burned down the building. I kind of always knew she would. I saw hints of it early on, and she had to live in to her destiny. She knocked over a candle.

As the flames licked up the trail of alcohol that led to my ratty, unevenly hung curtains, I was filled with regret for allowing it to happen; one could argue, for making it happen. I'd told myself Mabel was her own person, who just happened to need physical assistance to be who she was meant to be. Of course, as I watched my apartment burn down, I freaked out, understanding finally that it was happening in real life and not just isolated to a demented corner of my imagination. I cried out like an animal in distress the moment I realized our neighbor's buildings were just on the other sides of my walls. I cried out when I thought about Flossie—Flossie, who I had treated terribly, and who I now wholly understood—was minding her own business in her beautiful apartment. But it was too late, the best I could do was to make sure she got out. Trey and Iggy fled the apartment as I ran to get Flossie. Sadly, it was too late for Mabel. I believe she stayed behind on purpose, in a final act of defiance. That is so Mabel.

I knew I could go to jail, but also, I knew nobody would have a hard time believing I was a bumbling idiot who started a fire in his apartment by accident. It happens.

Frank

I only took work calls while Flossie napped. I'd step outside, or lock myself in my room and whisper into my phone just so she wouldn't have to worry about what she was missing at work, or be unnecessarily reminded of the world beyond the fortress I'd created for her. I read and journaled, and thought about what she might like for dinner. I talked Dave into giving her some time to heal and get back on her feet. I told her she should take her time in finding a new place to live. Rushing would be terrible for her healing, and for her decision making. She asked me to watch *Eleanor* with her, and even though I hated that show, I said of course, and as I watched her watch it, I realized I didn't entirely hate it after all. She wandered around, tidying up my already perfectly tidy space, calling her insurance company, and repeatedly trying to convince whoever was on the other end of the phone in Chicago that she was fine.

Night and day, she wore the Northwestern sweatshirt that she'd hugged and cried over when it came out of the box of her salvaged belongings. She kept her hair in the same messy bun I've seen other girls wear when they are trying hard not to look like they are trying hard. But I really believed Flossie wasn't trying, she was just being. I remember from when we first met, her nervous energy that manifested in small fidgets as well as her her almost palpable desire to simultaneously disappear and be noticed. I think because I am such a skilled field observer, she sometimes forgot I was there in the loft with her. I tried not to stare too much, but she was fascinating, and I'm a trend scientist, and I all I wanted to do was understand how that brain of hers works, and you can tell just by looking at her that it's always working. Her mouth twitches, like she's in the middle of a conversation that never stops. Her eye twitches like she's seeing something I'm not seeing. No wonder she's an analyst. I see things that will be. She sees what is, and more importantly, what isn't.

I've dated eighteen-year-old models, forty-five-year-old executives, a novelist, and a woman who owns half of Napa. I've dated two actresses, one while she was famous, and I broke up with the other immediately before she became famous. I was seeing a beautiful performance artist as I started working closely with Flossie. When I bailed on meeting up with Rian for the fifth time, I explained to her there was another relationship I needed to explore; not yet a romantic one, but my brain and my curiosity were so besotted, I absolutely had to honor that. She understood, and asked that I keep her posted because it sounded so thrilling.

I asked Flossie about her new IFs, and all she said was they weren't around. She wouldn't take Ty's calls, which I totally get. My guess was that he'd started the fire after forgetting about the chili cheese fries he was re-heating on the stove.

Henry

I'd heard about the fire from Mary, who'd started crowdfunding for Ty and Flossie. I tried calling Flossie, but she had changed her number, and my emails to her went unanswered. I wrote a letter to Ty, but I didn't have the time to wait for whatever garbled reply he would send, if any. When I called Cerulean looking for Flossie, the person on the other end said something about privacy, and hung up. I tracked down Flossie's Chicago house though. She had said her dad's name was Tom, and though there were about 1000 Tom O'Briens in the greater Chicago area, I remembered her mentioning something about a restaurant Casa de Lugo, expanded my search to the immediate neighborhood, and boom, there he was.

"Is this Tom O'Brien? Flossie's father?"

"It is, and who's calling me? Is she okay?"

"Yes, sir. My name is Henry, sir, and I'm a friend of Flossie's in San Francisco."

"She's not here."

"I wasn't sure. I heard about the fire, and I haven't been able to reach her, and I was wondering if maybe she'd mentioned me?

And if so, would you be comfortable passing along her new info to me, so I can reach her?"

"Henry? I've never heard of Henry. I've heard about a Frank."

"How about your wife sir? I know she and Flossie are close. Perhaps Flossie mentioned me to her?"

"My wife? Who are you again? You must not know Flossie. I'm hanging up."

"I'm sorry, sir, what?"

"My wife's been dead for almost ten years."

"Maybe I'm mistaken, is it a stepmother?"

"No stepmother."

"But Flossie mentioned her mother so often."

"Of course she did, they were inseparable. Listen. I don't know you, I'm not telling you anything about my daughter. Or any more about me."

Everything was instantly clear to me when I hung up the phone. I was the terrible human being, not Flossie. I had no right to feel betrayed by her. She was more of an original, creative, deep-souled human being than I could have imagined. She was independent, and strong. She was perfect, in so much as a real person can be.

Those parts of her that were lacking—the lonely and sad parts—she filled them how she needed to. She survived, and thrived. She added what she needed to her life, rid herself of things that were bad for her. She shed a skin and grew a new one. Her mother was gone, so she brought her back exactly as she needed to. Her friends were gone, so she made herself a new

one. And when that friendship turned toxic . . . became unnec-
essary, she ended it as best as she could. It was one of my more
productive epiphanies. I was an arrogant idiot. Abe was so right.
I was weak.

Murderer or not, I wanted Flossie in my life. I wanted to meet
her mother. I wanted to take them both to brunch, and drive
them down the coast. I wanted to learn to cook ratatouille, so her
mother could say, "I love it," even though it would definitely
be mushy, and we would all laugh, and Flossie would sweetly
suggest we supplement the meal with vegan pizza. I wanted
her mother to tell Flossie I'm a keeper, so I could look at Flossie
and say, "No. I'm the lucky one."

From the Diary of Jennifer Martin O'Brien
May 13, 2016

*Flossie turns sixteen next month and I am determined to see it.
If I can get her to sixteen, I know she will be fine. There are
lessons we probably won't get to before then like first love, and
managing heartbreak. How to have the best time in college while
also studying. How to get yourself noticed at work. Navigating the
world as a woman.*

*Of course I didn't want it to come to this. There were days
when I didn't think it would, that I would wake up one morning,
and the cancer would be gone, and I would be fine, and everybody
could relax and stop fussing over me. I haven't wasted too much
time feeling sorry for myself . . . only when I couldn't imagine
that I'd done anything to deserve such a crappy outcome.*

Tommy doesn't deserve this, and God knows Flossie doesn't deserve this. But other days, I'm fine, and I even forget for a few minutes, that the clock is ticking and I am out of options. It happens to everybody eventually. It's not like death is known for its graciously impeccable timing. I have peace. Flossie's old enough . . . she won't forget me. Her brain and her body are still growing, but she is already a great human, and me trying to shape her anymore at this point would just be meddling.

That saint of a woman Valeria Lugo has promised to be there for the mom stuff that will come up, and just to keep a gentle eye out from afar, but not too afar. Tommy's a great man and dad and loves Flossie with a depth I can't even imagine. He will always do what he can to protect her. And lucky for them both, Flossie is a force, and she won't need protecting.

CHAPTER EIGHTEEN

Frank was reading aloud from a letter sent from France by his professor friend. Of course he was reading in what I could only assume was perfect French, stopping occasionally to translate for me. The letter, written in beautiful script on translucent delicate paper, was about the professor's travels and his delight in watching from afar as the United States continued to grapple with a centuries-long adolescence. He wrote that by virtue of being French, though he himself was not yet fifty, he could sit back with the wisdom of a grandparent looking at a child with delight, and worry, and sadness that he will not live long enough to see the child grow into her full potential. At some point during the letter, Frank's head ended up in my lap, and I was running my fingers through his hair. His thick hair stayed in position no matter which direction I twirled it. I thought about how much I wasn't thinking about having a handsome, successful man's head in my lap with my fingers in his hair.

"Olivia spoke Italian," I said when he finished reading. His eyes were closed, like he was getting a massage, or getting his hair washed in a stylist's sink. Looking at his features upside down, unnatural and distorted, made me look away.

"Is that right?" he asked, his upside down lips barely moving.

"At first I wanted her to speak Japanese, but it ended up being Italian. Who knows, she probably spoke French too. It seems like she would. I wouldn't have been able to speak with her in French anyway, so it didn't really come up. I did for a moment, consider taking her to France on a girls' trip."

"Hmm."

I twirled his hair a little longer concentrating on the odd angles of his face.

"What's next for you Flossie?" His eyes were open, and I wondered what I looked like upside down.

"I'm getting a place, I promise. I'm checking out a couple of furnished studio apartments next week."

"No. That's not what I mean. What's next for YOU? After this IFs thing."

"I don't follow."

"Obviously, you don't need an IF anymore. Evelyn told me she's taking you to a concert next month. I'm here. Your IFs are in the wind. One's dead."

"They're not all gone."

"Is one here?"

"No, not really. Listen, I'm going back to work in two weeks. I'm getting it together, I promise."

"Seriously Flossie, I'm not kicking you out, I just . . . I mean . . . you're obviously a creative, down there under all the analytical veneer, so there will be something next for you after the IFs. There's always a next, new, different thing."

I wasn't sure what he meant. What kind of *next* was I supposed to have? New IFs? I didn't know where Jack and Amanda were. They were alive, but I couldn't force them on Frank. They were all independent. None of them would have thought to call me let alone attempt to move back in with me while I was staying with Frank, nor would they want to share a studio apartment with me. Someone had surely scooped up Chester by now.

My IFs were all better off out there, without me. My mom however, was worried about me, and I hated for her to worry. Well, at least I was no longer living the charmed life she'd imagined for herself, and she couldn't be jealous of me . . . motherless, homeless, accidentally alone, on-purpose alone, totally weird, and thusly, a magnet for weirdos. My time with Frank had temporarily pulled me from the shadows. He was sunlight. Not like the noontime sun that hurts your eyes, but that first morning sun where the sky turns pink, or that hazy sun right at the end of the day that provides the most flattering light for every skin tone, and for a split second every day, everybody looks their very best. He was that light.

Frank had made me feel as comfortable as much as a human, or a non-human, could. I experienced moments of pure, authentic calm while staying with him. I was able to sit on his couch in my Northwestern sweatshirt that still smelled of smoke after a dozen washes, and feel deep down that things were going to be okay. I could think back to my pretty little living room where I'd spent so much time, and not be quite so sad.

With Frank, I ate warm naan, artisan ice cream, small batch kimchi, and pot roast that had simmered in a thousand-dollar pot. I wore the cashmere socks he'd ordered for me. I poured my thoughts and noticings and rantings into my own leather journal that was embossed with the logo of the paperie in my old neighborhood. I'd woken to find the journal wrapped in a bow and left on the operating-table island, along with a pen of the finest indigo ink.

Half of the time I spent with Frank in his home—whether we were interacting, or he was not-so-subtly observing me wander around his place like a curious toddler—I was Near-Flawless Flossie. I found it was best for Frank and myself, if I thought and acted as though I was a character in a movie, the type of woman whose attentive lover rests his head in her lap while he reads letters in French. The character of Flossie was confident, independent, and infinitely interesting. She knew just how to act in all situations; she was comfortable in her own skin to the point where otherworldly, confident people accepted her as one of their own. If I couldn't create someone else to be there with me, I would just create someone else for me to be.

I felt a twinge of heartbreak knowing that Olivia would have been perfect for Frank. They would have fallen madly in love, and respected the crap out of each other. They would have read books to each other and lose track of time discussing movies and essays and art. As a frequent guest at their legendary holiday and solstice celebration dinners, I would have listened intently to their animated re-telling of their adventures in locales that had never interested me in the least. At those same dinners, I would cheerfully fulfill my role as their kooky friend whose ornately printed place card would always end up next to whatever kooky boy version of me they thought might even mildly interest me. The boy and I would immediately catch on to what Frank and Olivia were trying to do—"That's soooo Frank & Olivia, right?" The boy and I would go out once, maybe twice, and decide that it just wasn't meant to be. I was too distant, he was too needy, there was no chemistry, he would move away . . . whatever. But I would put on a nice dress for the next dinner party and wonder who my dinner set-up might be. Bob and Fiona would bicker after the parties because Olivia's coolness would intimidate Fiona and make her uncomfortable. Fiona would argue that Olivia was mean on purpose, and Bob would tell her she was being ridiculous, and of course, Fiona would be right.

But Frank and Olivia were not meant to be, nor were Frank and Flossie.

I was twirling Frank's hair, looking at his distorted, upside down features, and I knew that's how he would always look to me, the opposite of me, and not in a sexy way, but in a way that made no sense to me at all. I liked feeling his head on my lap, but it wouldn't feel good forever. His head would eventually become too heavy and I would grow to think of it as oversized and potato-shaped. My legs would fall asleep, and I would eventually resent his potato head, and he would resent my weak legs. I sensed that Frank appreciated my weirdness, more than he liked it. He could not possibly know to what depth my weirdness extended, because even I didn't yet know. He could not have known that my eccentricities had grown to be the bigger part of me, and weren't just the outgrowth of curiosity and a whimsical social experiment. The character of Flossie I had performed for him, was not sustainable, and the novelty of my me-ness would wear off, and he would be on to the next thing. He would then probably feel bad, and I would feel bad. Nobody wins in that scenario.

Frank sat up finally, his hair pointing toward the ceiling, and his facial features back to their correct orientation. He smiled sheepishly. It felt like a moment when we could have kissed. Instead of leaning in, or coquettishly batting my eyelashes and biting my lip, I asked, "Have you seen the latest budget projection?" He shook his head, and excused himself to load the dishwasher.

I slept well that night, having made a decision that wasn't birthed from desperation. I didn't cry, or freak out, or yell, or murder anyone. I'd decided for myself what I wanted and what I didn't want, and the best things in my life had come from me deciding for myself.

The next morning, I asked Frank if, when I moved, I should leave behind the new clothes he had given me.

"Of course not," he said.

I asked if I should get a different job.

"Of course not."

That's also the morning that Henry found me.

Ty called me from his new apartment across the bay in Oakland, to spit out in one breath that Henry was downstairs from Frank's building looking for me, but couldn't get in and couldn't call me, and nobody at Cerulean would help him and Frank's neighborhood is sketchy and there's a group of guys circling Henry like he's their prey which was making Henry very nervous, and could I please go downstairs and get him?

After running down to open the door so a sweaty Henry could scurry through with a basket over his arm, I saw the guys Henry was trying to get away from. I waved at Jason, Frank's nineteen-year old "prodigy and vehicular visionary/mechanic" neighbor who was standing outside with his buddies. "Are you okay, Flossie?" Jason called, "I saw this creepy guy outside who was asking around for you. He fits the description of every stalker and serial killer from the movies. We thought he might have a head in that basket."

"He's harmless, but thanks!" I called back.

"They're harmless," I said to Henry once I shut the door. "What's with the basket?"

"Apology tamales, not a head."

"Apology tamales?" We were standing in the concrete and steel covered lobby. I'd been in such a rush to save Henry from his demise, I hadn't even processed that he had come looking for me.

"I guess you heard about the fire. You never got to see my place, it was cute."

"I'm sorry to hear what you went through, Flossie. But the tamales aren't because of that. You are the most wonderful human or non-human, I've met, and I was terrible. I realized

I'm out of practice on real things with real humans, hard things, awkward things, easy things, sad things. I can be better. I want to be better. I am already better, thanks to you."

"Really? I mean . . . really?"

"Yes, really, Flossie. Truly."

"Thank you." I accepted his apology tamales. Olivia would have said I should have required more groveling and expensive non-edible peace offerings. Abe would have said nothing.

Out of respect for Frank, I did not kiss Henry in the lobby of his building, nor did I store another man's tamales in his fridge. Henry, though he departed that day with the basket across his arm, did depart as my boyfriend.

Henry didn't say anything about my mother, nor my persistent omission of her IF status for a long while, and then when he did, he said, "I understand about your mother. I do. I'm sorry. I should have known." And then he pulled me into his long arms for a tight hug.

There was nothing to know about my mom. The new relationship paradigm I'd created with her, had been only for my benefit. I hadn't lied to anybody about her, really. She was real. She had occupied space on Earth, and in my life. I needed her, and there she was.

My mom, the first version of her, died after a short battle with cancer, three days after my sixteenth birthday. It was that summer I tried to distract myself by refereeing games with rules I didn't understand. It was that summer I went for an expensive haircut without my mom to communicate for me what kind of hair cut I wanted, and she wasn't there to fight for me when it turned out to be a disaster. She died before I went from middling student to unfortunately coifed academic standout. Before I could graduate from Northwestern. Before she could see me succeed at anything. Before she could really worry about me or miss me.

I had known my mother well enough—sixteen years was short, but enough time—to know that she would have been so excited me for me to graduate from Northwestern. She would have championed my move to San Francisco, and celebrated my fancy new job. She would have sent me flowers on my birthday, so I wouldn't have to send myself flowers twice in the same day. She would have sent me letters, and she would have saved all the letters I sent, instead of me saving the letters I wrote to her, and she would have complimented my penmanship. She would have been a little envious of me getting to live in California, and a little worried that I was eating well and getting enough sleep.

Bringing back my mother by imagining what she might be feeling and doing and saying was the only way to experience life with her. She wouldn't have loved that I was an adult who relied on imaginary friends; she would have blamed herself for getting sick and dying. She would have tolerated Ty, been suspicious of Frank, and Charlie before him. I'm sure she would have loved Henry, though, and maybe would have looked forward to reading his mother's memoir.

For how sure I was that my mother would have celebrated most parts of my life, I know she would have insisted I be a better friend to Camila after her brother died. She would not have let me disappear into my own awkwardness, or allow the possibility that Robby's killer would stumble on me next as an excuse for keeping my distance. She would have been at the Lugos', delivering her very best casseroles, or a the very least, her very best take out. She would have made sure everybody was hydrating and sleeping as best they could. She would have been at the police station with Mrs. Lugo, demanding answers. She would have wept, and cradled Camila like a baby. The Lugos did that for me when my mother died.

The Lugo family—every one of them—fed my father and me and checked on us every day for weeks. They took care of the details for Mom's memorial. Camila was at my house around the clock, talking, not talking, bringing in the mail and brushing my hair when I could not. She was not offended that my Dad and I were a mess and had not bathed or washed the dishes. My pain did not make Camila uncomfortable, or if it did, she did not let that stop her from experiencing it with me, even though there were a million other things she could have been doing. The Lugos made sure we had a Christmas tree, and that my Dad and I always had home cooked food in the freezer. I stayed over at their house whenever I wanted—school night or not. Robby took me to my senior prom.

But I could not do the same for Camila. She and her family had shown me exactly how to take care of someone whose world has imploded, but even their shining example hadn't been enough to help me. Had I not murdered Olivia, maybe she could have spent more time mentoring me in how to be a better friend. Maybe I would get better at it someday, and I could figure out a way to repay Camila and show the Lugos that they had not wasted their love on me. I'd handwritten all those letters to Camila in mediocre calligraphy, but not one had included an apology. Maybe I could write one more, with improved handwriting and an honest to goodness admission that I had been a terrible friend all those years ago.

I was an adult now, and still practicing basic, introductory-level friendship skills on real humans. My mother would be happy I no longer stared into my phone while people talked. I'd cooked for Ty. If I lived closer to Etta, I would eat chili with her. If Evelyn ever asked, I would be happy to pick her up from the airport. I would like to think that if Frank's house ever burned down, I would be right there for him and find a way to buy him an expensive cardigan in the middle of the night. When I blurted out,

"If your place burns down, I'll get you a new notebook, underwear wrapped in tissue, and small batch kimchi," he looked only mildly surprised.

"That would be nice, Flossie, thank you."

My meetings with Frank had become far more professional since I moved out of his loft and into the high-rise studio apartment south of Market; he'd stopped mentioning my eyes and my skin. We both started repeating outfits.

Frank's name stopped coming up in conversations with my father, and instead was replaced with Henry's. I assured my dad that Henry was not a stalker or a creep, and that maybe Henry might come with me on my next trip to Chicago, which was enough to distract my dad from mentioning Henry's gaffe in asking about my mother. I really could not think of a scenario where my father would benefit from knowing the truth about my "San Francisco lifestyle," let alone my mother's involvement in it. He also didn't need to know that I was preparing to be unemployed.

I arrived unannounced to Cerulean's shipping container, and asked Dave if we could talk at the firing tables outside. He said he had eight minutes. I used my first three minutes to thank him profusely for his support after the fire. During the next three minutes, I explained how I'd gained my expertise in the Imaginary Friend market segment. I gave myself one minute to apologize and ask if I was going to be fired. I left him one minute for his reply.

He paused, using many of his precious sixty seconds to keep me in suspense. I gulped, and I sat on my hands to steady their shaking.

"Well," he said, "I'm not terribly surprised. No offense."

"None taken," I said nodding, agreeing with his assessment of me as someone who might have an imaginary friend.

"I certainly had questions about what might be going on in that mind of yours, but had I asked those particular questions, I would have opened myself to multiple lawsuits. I am disappointed, though."

"Of course. I understand."

"Let me finish Flossie. You were sitting on something that

would have been hugely beneficial to our firm had you talked to me earlier. If you want to advance and thrive here, I need bigger ideas, bolder imagination, and I need you to be proactive, not reactive."

"Of course. Thank you. But I also must say, that I'm not entirely comfortable with how dramatically we manipulate people's lives and relationships for the sake of profit."

"Fair enough. I appreciate that. That's similar to the topic I've been thinking about for my next book. I can see it as a mea culpa of sorts, and a guide for corporate responsibility. Perhaps you'd like to help me with the outline."

The Friendly Fete, became Friendly Fest SF, one of many San Francisco events that earned an instant reputation as a judgment free zone. More than five thousand people and countless IFs of all shapes, sizes, breeds, and persuasions strolled through the Fort Mason venue throughout the weekend. The eclectic crowd of Friendlies was dotted with lookie-loos, as well as the IF-curious. Henry climbed the rock wall with Abe which made me nervous, because Abe had threatened to hatchet Henry's rope "on the off chance he made it all the way up the wall." Etta, having gone through an ugly and painful break-up with Emma (the engagement ring was flung dramatically from a mountaintop) flew out to help work the event upon special request from Cerulean. Bob, Frank, Dave, and Ty gave media interviews all weekend long, and hosted a documentary crew. Ty sent me peonies. Frank introduced me as his colleague and "a revered and proven tastemaker." Friendlies lined up for hours to describe their

IFs to sketch artists, only to be reduced to tears upon seeing faces that had previously only existed in their imaginations take up two dimensions rather than none. Bands played, people danced, lavender beer flowed, and Friendlies celebrated their aloneness together. Salt and Pepper performed for an enthusiastic audience of imaginary art patrons. Mary's life coach IF volunteered at the "What IF" self-help table for reluctant Friendlies, and insecure IFs.

After much coercion by Ty, Henry and Etta, I took my place on stage for the "First Friendly Q&A," where I revealed myself as Nancy, and carefully responded to Ty's questions with the scripted answers that I'd spent hours rehearsing. I made eye contact only with Ty, and I could feel my skin turn crimson as our chat concluded, and the applause started. I raced down the steps and out of the building with Henry in tow.

CHAPTER NINETEEN

Henry kissed me outside at sunset, in front of a spectacular view of the Golden Gate Bridge and in the middle of a swarm of IFs and Friendlies who were also taking in the view. It was our 307th kiss since our first in front of Coit Tower. It took thirty-four total kisses for me to realize I was in real, true, non-imaginary love with him. He said it only took sixteen kisses for him. That evening, right after #308, he led me over to a bench, and sat me down.

"I would kneel," he said, "but I'm allergic to grass, and who knows what's on the cement, so I hope both of us sitting on this bench conveys the same idea."

"Henry? What are you talking about?"

"Sorry. Flossie, I would be incredibly honored if you were to spend a lifetime with me creating and laughing and living in wonder and freedom. I respect and honor your womanhood and your personhood. I love you and I would be the happiest person, real or imagined, if you would agree to be equal partners with me in life going forward."

"Henry?"

"What I'm trying to ask is, will you marry me? Maybe it's

better if I say, will you allow me to marry you?"

Exactly 2,686 kisses later, Henry and I were married in a restaurant that had been a defunct Gold Rush museum, and before that, one of San Francisco's branch libraries. The building had been refurbished to the point where it was more new construction than old, but the second I stepped inside, I could smell the ghosts of the books that had once lined the walls. It was perfect. Henry loved it, as did Ali from Event-u-Ali. My mother gave the final nod of approval.

Jennifer Martin O'Brien looked beautiful in the front row of my wedding ceremony where she dabbed at her happy tears with the lace family heirloom handkerchief that, had it existed, would have been stored carefully in a trunk with other family heirlooms intended for me. To my dad, the chair next to his was an empty seat saved to honor her memory. He didn't ask about the other empty seats saved throughout the small gathering for Abe, Trey, Iggy, Amanda, Jack, Yadiel, Salt and Pepper. Mary, and her boyfriend brought their IFs. Ty brought a girl with skin, Kennedy, who was intrigued with the IFs, but still wary.

The *Hills + Water + Sky + Fog* magazine article never made it to my dad, or to Shannon, or to any of my dad's friends or neighbors who would have brought it up in casual conversation and giving my father any additional reason to be concerned about me living in California. I was marrying a human man which felt like reasonable cover for what I had been up to. Tom O'Brien was stoic through the whole affair. He chatted with Shannon, my Chicago hairdresser about the Cubs and how everything in San Francisco was so damned expensive. They were blissfully ignorant of just how much bigger our wedding celebration was than how it looked at first glance. My dad might have appreciated the idea of imaginary guests as a cost-saving measure.

Henry's parents were kind and very welcoming to me. They were also unaware of our invisible wedding guests. Henry's father, John, was tall like his son, but in a barrel chested lumberjack sort of way. I could picture Abe joining John and my father as they drank their whiskey in comfortable silence at our rehearsal dinner and wedding reception. Henry's mother, Ann, appeared to be primarily responsible for Henry's physique. She was willowy, and the most active and encouraging listener I had ever encountered. Her thin body bent nimbly in the direction of whoever was talking, or whoever Ann thought might not be talking enough. Her embrace was reminiscent of Henry's; it felt as though her arms could easily have wrapped around my frame multiple times. "Oh, Flossie, you are so lovely," she said over and over, as she held my face in her long fingers, and smoothed my hair, and zipped the back of my dress when I could not do it myself. She asked me repeatedly if I'd been hydrating, and sleeping, and if I was in need of a nut-free snack. She snapped pictures for her blog, and made notes about our menu to delight her blog readers for a "Where are they now?" post about Henry and how he had made it through his treacherous childhood and was now trusting his health and well-being to an allergy-sensitive life partner. Henry balked when I encouraged him to talk freely with his mother about our IFs. I wanted to tell her everything about myself, and let her make me tea, and buy me socks. She invited me to fly out and stay in their bed and breakfast so she could show me every photograph of Henry as a child and as an even thinner teen. She promised to show me her log of every funny thing he'd ever said and the dates on which he'd said them, and how to cook vegan nut-free meals that would not kill him.

Etta and Evelyn agreed to be my bridesmaids. With Emma out of the picture, they were free to flirt and blush and giggle. For my bachelorette party, Etta, Mary and I sat in Evelyn's tastefully sparse apartment sipping tarragon-infused gin cocktails in our pajamas and binge watched every episode of *Eleanor*. I said goodbye to my single-girl, carnivore days with overflowing platters of meats from my favorite charcuterie bros. Camila couldn't make it, but she sent regards from Barcelona. The Lugos sent me a silver-framed photo of my mother and I, and a card that simply said, *Felicidades*, La Familia Lugo.

Henry's compromise with Abe and Ty for the bachelor party was a gentleman's club featuring only IF dancers, which to the untrained, unFriendly eye would look like two dudes without much to talk about sharing vegan Indian food in the barely furnished living room of the new Golden Gate Park— adjacent condo Henry and I had just purchased.

Dave came to the wedding, kissed me on the cheek, shook Henry's hand and quietly left before dinner was served. Frank's date was a six-foot tall model named Yve while Bob had replaced Fiona with a model slightly taller than Yve. At no point during our joyous festivities did I see either woman crack a smile. It was quite clear that very tall, serious girls were the next . . . whatever. I expected Frank to follow Dave's lead and disappear into the night, but instead, he asked me to dance. While he moved me slowly around the dance floor, I thanked him for coming, and he told me I was a beautiful bride, and Henry was an unusual and lucky man. He complimented me on the wedding and our interesting venue, and only then did he disappear from the party. Had he and Bob and their tall dates stayed a little while longer they would have missed a liquor-fueled almost-brawl between Ty and Abe.

Henry spent weeks researching the best honeymoon destinations for severe allergy sufferers, and we found ourselves packing our bags for an IF-free trip to Albuquerque, just in time for the hot air balloon festival. We never once considered climbing into one of those death baskets, but we loved having a balloon-dotted sky as the backdrop for our first days as real-life married people.

When we returned from our near allergen-free honeymoon, I had an office to report to, with people waiting for me to occupy my permanently assigned desk. Dave, with his carte blanche power awarded him by Gamboge, made me a Vice President of Creative Analysis Services and Ethical Practices. I bought a new pair of oxblood pumps with higher heels.

That was almost three years ago.

Henry and I are thrilled to find out we are expecting . . . again. Jen is two and a dream child. Our experience with her has helped us to prepare for this baby. After baby Jen was born, my mom stayed and helped for quite a while so I could return to work, and Henry could concentrate on the string of new projects he was tackling from his home office. Mom told us not to worry, there's never a perfect time to have a baby. She doted on her grandbaby, rocking her at night and singing lullabies and reading her the same stories that she'd read to me when I was a baby.

I have so much to do to prepare for a new little one; my mother won't be able to help as much this time.

Henry and I quickly decided to find out what our second baby would be so our imaginations didn't get the best of us.

Just as we hoped, we'll have one of each. This one's a boy . . . with skin.